LETHAL EXPOSURE

A GRANT MARKEY SUSPENSE/THRILLER

JG ROBBINS

Copyrighted Material
LETHAL EXPOSURE

A Novel
by JG Robbins

WEXFORD HOUSE PUBLISHING

This is a work of fiction. Names, characters, organizations, places, events, and incidents are either products of the author's imagination or are used fictitiously. Any resemblance to actual persons, living or dead, businesses, companies, locales, or actual events is purely coincidental.

Text copyright © 2023 by JG Robbins
All rights reserved.

No part of this book may be reproduced, or stored in a retrieval system, or transmitted in any form or by any means, electronic, mechanical, photocopying, recording, or otherwise, without the express written consent of the publisher, except for brief quotations in a book review.

Published by:
Wexford House Publishing
4800 Cox-Smith Road
Mason, OH 45040

ISBN 978-1-7348529-3-6 (paperback)
ISBN 978-1-7348529-2-9 (ebook)

Editor: Parisa Zolfaghari
Cover by: Damonza

Dedicated to my brother

David Mark Robbins

We lost you too early, and miss you every day

LETHAL EXPOSURE

PREFACE

PLOTS OF NOVELS used to be local affairs, taking place within a city or town or maybe even within one city block. But now, with modern technology, stories can occur over a vast geography. A character can hop on a plane and be in another city in a few hours or overseas in less than a day.

When a character has psychic abilities, a story can occur across thousands of miles in real-time. This opens endless possibilities for an author. And, who knows, there actually may be a few people who have the psychic powers ascribed to Grant Markey in this book. They may work for the CIA, an allied country, or an adversary — or themselves, and we would never know.

Things happen in the real world that are hard to explain, so maybe we have found one possible explanation.

JG Robbins
May, 2023

LIST OF MAIN CHARACTERS

Grant Markey IV – The main character with psychic powers.

Angie Reynolds Markey – Grant's wife, and FBI Special Agent.

Craig Clayton – CIA Agent-in-Charge, and Grant's primary security agent.

Karen Spencer – CEO of Russell & Associates.

Tony Russell — Director, CIA.

Guardian Major-General Farzad Ghorbani – Commander of the Islamic Revolutionary Guard Corp-Quds Force (IRGC-QF).

Colonel Amir Hashemi – The General's adjutant.

Admiral Ahmad Mousavi – Secretary of the Supreme National Security Council (SNSC).

Dr. Hossein Yazdani – Director of the Research Division of the Atomic Energy Organization of Iran (AEOI-RD). Doctorate in Physics from the University of Tehran.

Leroy Allen McDaniel – A deck hand.

Navid Sadeghi – Leader of the terrorist group, Hurras Ansar al-Haqq.

Farzin Sadeghi – Son of Navid and boss of the Hurras Ansar al-Haqq smuggling network.

Miss Doris Webb – Grant's housekeeper, friend, and family employee for many years.

Roya Deghani Sadeghi – Wife of Navid Sadeghi.

Alex King – Former Marine, assistant to Ross Taylor.

Ross Taylor – Billionaire entrepreneur, former Marine, and current owner of Russell & Associates.

Sharon Honderich – CIA disguise artist.

Levi Weiss – Director of Mossad, the national intelligence agency of Israel.

Moshe Kadosh – Commander of the Caesarea Department of Mossad.

The Warthog – American-based terrorist.

Baraz Sadeghi – Son of Navid and leader of the Hurras Ansar al-Haqq terrorist operations.

Zubin Deghani – Hawaladar and cousin of Navid's wife, Roya Deghani Sadeghi.

Javad Azimi – Member of Hurras Ansar al-Haqq, childhood friend of Baraz, and a demolition expert.

Mikhail Belyaev – Director of the SVR (Russian equivalent of the CIA).

Maaike van Leersum – Undercover foreign agent.

TRANSLATION OF FARSI AND ARABIC EXPRESSIONS USED IN THIS BOOK

Farsi

Salaam alaykum	Peace be upon you (Used as hello, formal)
Khoda hafez/Khodafez	God be with you (used as goodbye, formal/informal)
Agha	Sir, Mister
(Name)-*joon*	A term of endearment

Arabic

Sabah al-khayr	Good morning
Assalamu alaikum	Peace be with you
Wa alaikum assalam	And peace unto you
Ma'a salama	Goodbye
Shukran Jazeelan	Thank you
Ahlan wa sahlan	Hello, welcome
Ahlan bik	Hello
Allah yusallmak	May God protect you
Alhamdulillah	Praise be to God

Lebanese Arabic

Mar Habā	Hello
Mar Habtén	Double Hello
Sār waĀit nrūH	It's time for us to go
Ma'e Ssalēmet	Goodbye

PROLOGUE

IT TOOK ME months to get my mind around everything that had happened. The Iranians made an unthinkably poor decision and lost control of radioactive material, which led to a plan for the worst terrorist attack on America since 9/11.

The seemingly unrelated threads — which eventually all came together into one explosive conclusion — started long before I became involved. I'm talking about myself — Grant Markey, CIA analyst, consultant, or contractor — take your pick.

I knew what I knew, including what I had learned from exploring the memories of some key players in this saga. But there was a lot that I didn't know — but wanted to find out.

My associates agreed for me to explore their memories to review some of the critical events. That was helpful but incomplete.

Among the unknown elements was the role of the Iran, Israel, and Russian governments, none of which knew exactly what the others were doing until the end. And there were also the covert actions of the terrorists who brought the radioactive devices from Iran to America but didn't live to tell about it.

In the course of my search for the facts, I discovered a new skill. Previously, using my extrasensory skills, I could access any moment in the memory of any living person I had ever met or seen.

But now, I found that a memory was not a discrete piece of information — it was part of a larger narrative that connected multiple people. I discovered that, like finding a loose thread on a sweater, I could keep pulling and following the thread. I could keep pulling even if it was connected to other people I had never met. So now I can access a narrative, not just a discrete point-in-time memory. That's the best description I can give of what I can now do.

Just as a sweater will unravel if you keep pulling the thread, so did the tangle of events I was trying to understand.

And during all this time, someone was trying to take me out.

I decided to write this account as a story so that you can understand the emotions and motivations of those involved. People, not governments, were the primary cause of this near catastrophe, and we need to learn from it.

The best place to start is the meeting between my boss, Karen Spencer, and Tony Russell — the CIA Director. Their meeting, which started the chain of events resulting in Alex King joining our team, was — as you will see — a signal event.

CHAPTER 1

IT WAS A short drive over to CIA Headquarters in Langley for a meeting with her former boss, Tony Russell, the CIA Director.

Karen Spencer checked in at the reception desk after passing through several layers of security. She had decided to wear an expensive dark suit, with the objective of looking, as well as acting, like the executive she was. She carried an expensive leather briefcase. It was sometimes hard for her in a man's world, especially being a petite woman. But she had an aura of authority, and she knew it. Her expertly cut short brown hair and her pale blue eyes weren't enough to do it. Neither was her square jaw or her cleft chin, both of which gave her face an interesting look. She thought it was a combination of everything and not just her appearance. She carried herself with confidence. She wanted to subliminally remind Tony that she was now the CEO of Russell & Associates.

She was escorted quickly to Tony's office overlooking the courtyard in the original headquarters building. She was handed off by the security person to Tony's administrative assistant, who escorted her into Tony's office.

He smiled, stood, and walked around his desk to shake hands with her. She already had her hand extended. She thought that Tony hadn't changed much since she's known him. He was still slightly overweight, with thick black hair flecked with gray and piercing blue eyes. And she knew he was always full of surprises.

"Thanks for coming over today. How are things going?"

"Business is good," Karen said. She had succeeded Tony as CEO of Russell & Associates after he had been required to divest the private contract security firm upon being confirmed as CIA Director. "Thanks for sending work our way. We're still building our private client business, and things are going well."

"How is Ross Taylor treating you?"

Ross Taylor, a Texas billionaire and former Marine Raider — their special operations unit — had purchased Russell & Associates from Tony in the divestiture.

"He leaves us alone. He's happy as long as the money keeps rolling in."

"Don't forget that he doesn't know Grant's capability. All he knows is that Grant's our very best threat analyst, and important to the financial success of Russell & Associates. He may be the new owner, but he doesn't have a high enough security clearance to know anything more than that."

"Yes, I know." She thought, *Tony always has to think he's in charge.*

"How are Craig, Angie, and the rest of the crew?"

"They're all fine."

"How about Grant?"

"He's okay, but bored, I think."

"That's what I want to talk about. We're paying Grant a huge retainer and not getting much in return. I believe it's over forty thousand per month now."

Karen nodded. "Yes, that's right. And keeping him under wraps was as much your idea as mine. We agreed only to use him for the most important cases. Otherwise, it was increasing his risk to involve him when not absolutely necessary."

"I know, and that was the right decision, but there's got to be something he can do to get himself better prepared when the time comes," responded Tony.

"Well, he could use more self-defense training. He was almost kidnapped once and nearly assassinated a couple of times."

"There's nothing stopping you from doing the training."

"We'd have to hire someone locally or send him to the FBI or the CIA training school," she said.

"We'll arrange for him to attend 'The Farm' if you like."

The CIA training facility, called "The Farm," had long been located at Camp Peary near Williamsburg, VA.

"Okay, but Angie and Craig will need to go with him," she said.

"I'll arrange it and give you the information on who to contact, but I was thinking of something else that might be more worthwhile," said Tony.

"What's that?"

"The United Nations is going to hold a special session in a couple of weeks. If we can obtain a pass for Grant, then he'll have a chance to be in the same chamber as a number of world leaders. That may come in handy in the future if we need to get information from any of them," said Tony.

Karen shook her head. "That's going to give Grant more exposure than we like. Every country will have its security service there, and we don't want them to know anything about Grant. But if you insist, it might work if you assign one of your disguise artists to work with us. Then we can change his appearance whenever we like to whatever we want."

"Good idea. How about Sharon Honderich? You know her, don't you?" asked Tony.

"She'll be perfect, thanks."

"Okay, I'll have her get in touch with you."

"Tony, is there any serious national threat underway right now that might eventually involve Grant?"

"No, but there is more chatter than usual between terrorists in the Middle East. They say they're tired of US meddling — and that something needs to be done — especially in the wake of the Israel-UAE agreement, which they blame on the US. But no specific threats that we have identified — not yet anyway."

"And you know Grant doesn't want to be involved until there's a threat."

"Yes, I know, and I'm not asking for that. I'm just tired of him doing nothing."

Karen pasted a smile on her face and nodded. "Okay, we'll be in touch. You can have someone fill me in later with the target list for the UN special session and all the arrangements. And don't forget about 'The Farm.'"

"I'll do that. Take care, Karen."

She stood, picked up her briefcase, and walked out of his office to the waiting security escort. *That damn Tony — never satisfied and always meddling*, she thought.

CHAPTER 2

I'D BEEN WORKING in my office on the third floor of the First Mississippi bank building when I heard Craig Clayton and my wife, Angie, talking on the speakerphone. Craig, the CIA Agent-in-Charge of our team, had taken the office next door to coordinate security for me under cover of a fictitious company called Canal Street Investments, Inc., and he'd left the door between our two offices slightly ajar.

It wasn't long before Angie stuck her head in and said, "Karen's on the speaker, and she wants to talk to us. Why don't you come over?"

I put down the auction catalog I was perusing and went over to join them.

Craig said, "We're all here now. What is it?"

"I met with Tony yesterday. He agreed for Grant to get some self-defense training at 'The Farm.' And that will include refreshers for you two. And he wants Grant to attend a special session of the UN to get exposure to a number of world leaders, which might be useful later. He's finally given me a preliminary list. It includes the presidents of Russia, China, Iran, Israel, and France. Also, the British Prime Minister and the German Chancellor," said Karen.

"That sounds interesting, but I thought Tony wanted to keep me out of sight?"

"Yes, but he wants to better prepare you for whatever's coming next. I think it's a good idea. By the way, Craig, I want you to keep a list of those persons whose memories Grant can access. We need to keep up with that and take opportunities to add to the list. And to keep you safe, Grant, Tony agreed to add a CIA disguise artist to our team," said Karen.

"What? You've got to be kidding! You mean fake beards and wigs?" I asked.

"Yes, but just enough to make you blend in and not be noticed. She'll also be able to supply fake IDs and that sort of thing, too. It's Sharon Honderich. Craig knows her. She's good, really good."

"Will she move here?"

"No, but she'll be available wherever and whenever we need her. I imagine New York will be the first place. I'll have to get back to you on the timing of all this."

"Okay, well, this should make life interesting," I said.

But actually, I wondered, *Is Tony losing it?*

CHAPTER 3

GENERAL FARZAD GHORBANI, a large swarthy man with coal black hair, sat at his desk with a scowl on his face. He was angry, very angry. The international news services had just reported that the UAE signed a treaty to normalize diplomatic relations with Israel.

The General, in his role as the head of the Islamic Revolutionary Guard Corp-Quds Force (IRGC-QF), had been working behind the scenes with representatives of the UAE to reduce the tensions created by several unfortunate incidents between Iran and the UAE. But this — an agreement between the UAE and Israel — was unthinkable.

In the convoluted world of Iranian politics, while the Ministry of Foreign Affairs was the public face of Iran, the real power was exercised in the realm of the IRGC and the clerics, led by the Ayatollah.

"Colonel, come in here immediately," he shouted to his

adjutant, Colonel Amir Hashemi, sitting at his desk in the outer office.

"Yes, General, what is it?" said the Colonel as he rushed into the General's office.

"Did you see the report about the UAE and Israel?"

"Unfortunately, I did, General," Hashemi said.

"They must be punished."

"Yes, but how? They now have protection from Israel as well as from Saudi Arabia."

"I don't know, but I'm sure the Supreme National Security Council (SNSC) will want options."

"Yes, General. The list of Arab nations aligning against us with Israel will grow unless we make an example of those Sunni traitors."

"I want you to draft a letter to the SNSC asking for strategic direction. We cannot make plans if we don't know the objectives or the target, and that will be a policy decision."

"Yes, sir, I'll work on it now."

He added, "And please call Dr. Yazdani and tell him I want to see him here in my office today — as soon as possible. Tell him he doesn't need to prepare anything in advance. That's all."

As soon as Hashemi left, the General fantasized about visions of rockets and missiles crashing into Abu Dhabi and Dubai. *Those proud Emiratis — and their gleaming cities built with oil money — will be cut down to size!* He would not hesitate to give the launch order.

The worst thing was his failure to repair relations with the UAE had given ammunition to his nemesis, Admiral Mousavi. The General had reached the pinnacle of his career as head of the IRGC, and he wanted to stay there until he retired — on his own timing. He knew the Admiral wanted his job, and it appeared they would fight each other until one of them was totally defeated. And he was determined that it wouldn't be him.

He was still angry at his failure. Yes, he was angry with the Emiratis, but also at himself. He had been given the job of repairing relations with them and had obviously failed. They had misled him. He believed them when they said relations could be improved. And he had been naive. He hated himself for that mistake, but they would pay.

He would see to it.

CHAPTER 4

THE BUZZER SOUNDED at the door to Canal Street Investments, Inc., startling Craig. They never had unexpected visitors come to the office. Craig grabbed his Glock 19M from the desk drawer and motioned Karen and Angie to shield themselves behind their desks. Then he went through the connecting door into Grant's office, put his finger to his lips, and motioned for Grant to get his gun and take cover in his bathroom.

The buzzer sounded again. Craig looked through the peephole and was startled to see a short Indian lady wearing an elaborately embroidered purple sari with a matching headscarf covering her black hair. She had a red dot on her forehead between her eyebrows, called a bindi, indicating that she was married. Her complexion was dark, and Craig estimated her age at about sixty. She was carrying a large purse.

Craig cracked open the door. "Can I help you, ma'am?"

"Yes, I am here to discuss investments," she said with a thick accent. "This is Canal Street Investments, is it not?"

"Yes, but we aren't taking new clients at the moment," Craig said.

She patted her purse. "I have a letter of introduction. If you will permit me, I will show you."

Their purpose in opening the office was to provide a cover and to keep a low profile. Craig didn't want to do anything that would cause her to complain to local authorities, so he made a quick decision to let her come in and then brush her off as quickly, and as gently, as possible. And she looked harmless enough.

He said, "Please wait just a moment."

Craig went over to Karen and Angie and whispered, "Wait with Grant while I get rid of her."

They nodded, went through the connecting door to Grant's office, and closed it quietly.

Craig concealed the gun in his waistband, stepped to the door, and looked through the peephole to see the lady waiting patiently. He unchained and then opened the office door.

The lady walked in, waving her hands, muttering something in a low tone that he couldn't understand.

She walked right over to the chair next to the desk and plopped down. Craig followed her and, exasperated, said, "What did you say about a letter of introduction?"

She handed him the letter. It was addressed to Canal Street Investments, Inc. and said, "Please help my friend, Mrs. Neesha Dhawan." It was signed, "Tony Russell."

He was taken aback.

She started laughing as she removed the headscarf and the black wig. It was Sharon Honderich in disguise.

Craig started laughing, too. He had known Sharon for many years.

He said quietly, "Put it back on. Let's have some fun."

When he saw she was ready, he went to the connecting door, opened it, and motioned to Karen, Angie, and Grant to join them.

"This is Mrs. Neesha Dhawan. She was advised to visit us by Tony Russell."

Karen and Angie looked confused. "Tony Russell?" Karen asked.

"Yes, Tony Russell," Sharon said in her normal voice. Then she removed her headscarf and wig.

Karen's eyes widened, then she started laughing too. Angie and Grant were still confused.

"This is Sharon Honderich, the CIA disguise artist sent by Tony," Karen said. "Sharon, let me introduce you to Angie and Grant Markey."

"We didn't expect you to show up in disguise," said Grant.

"I wanted you to see an example of my work and what makes a good disguise. Sometimes, you want a disguise that just lets you blend in. But, at the other extreme, you can also have a good disguise if you stand out in a crowd. If people are staring at your clothing or listening to your accent or wondering why you're here and who you are — they're distracted. Then they don't really study your face, and the chances of recognizing you are small," said Sharon.

Craig asked, "Sharon, why did you come to Natchez instead of meeting us in New York?"

"I want to work on disguises for Grant and the rest of the team. And I can't produce fake IDs until I can get photos of you in disguise. We'll start on this tomorrow. May I change clothes now?"

"Yes, you can use the bathroom in my office," said Grant as he pointed the way.

Sharon opened her large purse and pulled out a folded cloth shopping bag and a makeup kit. After a few minutes, she returned from the bathroom with the Indian garb in the shopping bag and all of her makeup removed. She definitely looked and acted like a different person — blonde, slim, and perky.

CHAPTER 5

COLONEL HASHEMI BURST into the General's office, opening the door at the same time as he knocked.

"It's here! SNSC's answer to your request! A military messenger just delivered it."

The General swiveled in his chair and looked annoyingly at Hashemi, as if to say, "Well?"

He handed the General a large brown envelope.

The General carefully sliced open the envelope with a letter opener. Inside was another envelope marked "Top Secret." Inside the envelope was a single sheet of paper.

It was addressed to Guardian Major-General Farzad Ghorbani, Commander, Islamic Revolutionary Guard Corp-Quds Force, and it read:

*In response to your letter to the Supreme National
Security Council, dated September 3, your directions are
as follows:*

1. *The SNSC, with the approval of the Ayatollah, desires to take action against the Israeli alliance in order to warn other Arab nations against making the same mistake.*

2. *The target nation will be the UAE.*

3. *The tactical objective will be to damage the Bu Hasa oil field of ADNOC (The Abu Dhabi National Oil Company) in western Abu Dhabi, putting it out of operation for a lengthy period of time and causing significant damage to the UAE's finances.*

4. *The intention of such an operation is to cause the minimum loss of life, to the extent possible, while achieving the desired objective.*

5. *Carry out the mission, as usual, with trusted proxies. We want to maintain plausible deniability, even if our involvement is obvious.*

6. *The intended timing, while ordered to occur as soon as possible, should not be scheduled for later than November 15.*

7. *Please schedule a review of your operational plan with the Secretary of the Supreme National Security Council for final approval no later than four weeks ahead of the intended attack date.*

/signed/

Respectfully, Admiral Ahmad Mousavi, Secretary
Supreme National Security Council

The General shook his head and handed the letter to Colonel Hashemi, who read it, then asked, "General, what do you have in mind?"

"I've been thinking about a different approach than we've

used before. And that will be to explode a 'dirty bomb' in the complex. If it contains enough radioactive material, it will shut down the complex for a long time because clean up would be very slow or impossible."

"But, General, would the SNSC and the Ayatollah approve such a plan?"

"They are very upset with the UAE and Israel, so they might — if it's carried out by a proxy, as they stated. It could be explained as an independent terrorist act. And several terrorist groups hate the Emiratis and the Israelis enough to do it. And if it turns out to be a suicide mission, they won't be around to talk, and we can cover any tracks that might lead directly back to Iran.

He hesitated as several thoughts ran through his mind.

Then the General said, "Let me think more about it. And, Colonel, please gather as much information as you can about the Bu Hasa complex."

The Colonel said, "Yes, sir, I will begin gathering information on Bu Hasa immediately," and hurriedly left the office.

The General was already thinking of proxies he could trust enough to use for the mission.

CHAPTER 6

NAVID SADEGHI SAT in the back of his rug shop, eating his lunch of jujeh kabab and rice. It wasn't easy with only one hand. He was an Iran-Iraq war veteran, and he lost his right arm in a rocket attack at the First Battle of al-Faw.

His childhood friend from Qom and fellow soldier, Farzad Ghorbani — now General Ghorbani — saved his life after the rocket explosion blew off his arm. Farzad was awarded a medal for bravery for pulling Navid from the fiery wreckage of the bunker, and they still stayed in touch, even working together on several "projects" on behalf of Iran.

If it was not for Farzad, he would not have survived to marry Roya Deghani and fathered four sons — Kaveh, Baraz, Javed, and Farzin. Unfortunately, Kaveh and Javed were killed in an American drone attack in Iraq in 2014. There was not even enough left of them to bury.

Navid's hatred of Iraq, and now the Americans, too — kept him going. He founded and secretly led the terrorist group,

Hurras Ansar al-Haqq, for the past fifteen years. Al-Haqq originally targeted the Sunni government in Iraq and the American forces supporting them.

Kaveh and Javed were loading IEDs onto their truck near Salah Ad Din when the American drone struck. Roya had never been the same, and neither had Navid, only more bitter and determined for revenge.

Baraz and Farzin were now in charge of al-Haqq operations, and Navid was now more in the background. Baraz ran the terrorist side. And al-Haqq has recently been more active in Syria and in the border regions of Iraq in support of Bashar al-Assad. But there was another dimension to the operations — al-Haqq needed funds to operate, and the funding from the Iranian government through their clandestine channels was not sufficient. Even private funding by sympathizers located in other countries didn't close the gap. So Navid began a smuggling operation, which naturally began with Persian carpets. Farzin had taken over the smuggling operation from his father.

Imports from Iran were barred in most countries — one of the sanctions against them for supporting terrorism and for refusal to give up their nuclear program and their development of ballistic missiles.

Navid's hometown, the holy city of Qom, was a producer of high quality hand-woven carpets, though perhaps not as renowned as Isfahan or Kashan. A typical high-end Qom carpet might contain four million knots, or more at five hundred or six hundred knots per square inch, and take over three years to weave. These rugs were valued by collectors all over the world for their classic designs, colors, and quality — and sold for many thousands of dollars.

In addition to Qom, Navid had sources for collector carpets from Isfahan, Kashan, Tabriz, Nain, and Kerman. He smuggled them to cities all over the world where the demand was strong.

Bribing a customs official to look the other way or a ship's captain to take illegal cargo, was not that difficult.

But getting the payments from the purchasers in foreign countries back to Qom could be difficult and was done "off the grid." Navid found that using a private network of hawaladars was the most reliable, least expensive, and safest method; everything was done in cash with no official records.

Navid finished his lunch and decided to call Farzin.

"Yes, Father?" answered Farzin.

"Where are you, son?"

"I am just now leaving the Bandar Lengeh Port, Father."

"Did you get the carpet shipment loaded, son?"

"Yes, the ship's captain sent a truck to meet me about an hour ago. The cargo should be on board by now. The ship sails for Dubai tonight."

"Okay, then, I will see you tomorrow. Drive safely, Farzin."

"I will, Father."

Navid smiled. By the end of the day tomorrow, the carpets would be in the shop of an exclusive interior designer located near the entrance to the Palm Jumeirah. There were always customers in Dubai eager to pay inflated prices for rare top quality carpets to decorate their luxurious homes, and the more expensive the carpet, the better. He didn't mind taking money from these oil-rich Sunnis, knowing that the profits would be used by al-Haqq to fight and kill them and their brethren.

But he still had to accept that his al-Haqq operation was considered a minor terrorist organization. It couldn't compare to Hezbollah, the Islamic Front, ISIS, Al-Qaida, Al-Shabbab, Taliban, Abu Sayyaf, and many others. He hated that. He wanted to be known and respected within the shadowy world of terrorists. But for now, he had to operate in the shadows with whatever money he could raise.

CHAPTER 7

KAREN WAS IN Natchez for the first time in months. She'd shown up this morning with no warning — at least, no warning that I knew of. I wondered what was so important that we couldn't deal with it over the phone.

We all settled around the conference table in my office, looking expectantly at Karen.

"Grant, I talked to Ross this week," she said. "He's concerned about Tony's plan to send you to the United Nations, especially since he doesn't understand why it's necessary. He knows you're important to the operation, but he's never been told exactly why. He thinks you're a highly skilled intelligence analyst. Tony told him he wants you to study these top leaders in person for signs of health issues, stress, or any other problems, and to establish a baseline for future evaluations. Ross thinks increasing any agent's visibility is a bad idea, so he wants to beef up security.

"He has an assistant who was in the Marines with him in

the Middle East. He describes him as a 'very tough guy,' and he trusts him. Ross talked to Tony, and he appointed the guy as a CIA special agent, which he has the authority to do. His name is Alex King.

"Tony and FBI Director Lambert checked him out, and they say he's okay. Alex'll be here next week."

"So, what exactly is Alex going to do?" Craig asked.

Yeah, I want to hear this. I didn't know how I felt about a stranger coming onto our team. I wondered if working with Tony — and having the threat of discovery constantly hanging over my head — had made me less trusting, and whether that was a good thing or not.

"He's going to be with you and Angie full time, at least for a while," Karen said, "and I know you're not going to like it — at least initially. But actually, Grant, I agree. We felt you were well protected when Angie and I were both with you full time, so having two bodyguards again seems like a good idea."

"So, what's his cover?" I asked.

"Ross has been using Alex to manage some of his European investments, which doesn't take a lot of time. Ross set him up a few years ago as a collectibles dealer in Nice, France. The south of France is a good source for such items, and it gave him a side-line to earn a little money on his own efforts. He has an office in the antiques district near the port, and he's set up a website. So he's been learning the collectibles business. The business is called Antiquités de Collection.

"His cover in Natchez will be that he'll be here to work with you in a partnership, specializing in collectibles such as music boxes, porcelain objects, vases, figurines, etc. He will ostensibly supply you with French and European collectibles from his contacts in Europe, and you will supply him primarily with Asian collectibles, which are hot in Europe right now.

"The good thing is that he actually knows something about

collectibles, which is why Ross thought he would be a natural fit. We want him to stay with you and Angie at Wexford House while he's here, unless you really don't like him," she said. "And he'll be part of the team, taking direction from Craig, but I imagine he'll be talking to Ross unofficially on a regular basis, so be careful how much you tell him or he overhears."

"At least let us meet him first before we decide where he's going to stay," I said angrily. Angie nodded.

"Okay, you're right. It's your home, and you should make the final decision on any guests," Karen said, "but can you at least make arrangements — assuming it works out?"

"Yes, we can let Miss Doris know we might be having a house guest. We might even let her meet him first to see what she thinks of him. She's a good judge of people. And if we decide not to invite him to stay with us, there are several empty apartments nearby in converted carriage houses. I know the owners, so that won't be a problem."

Doris Webb is our housekeeper and cook. She arrives at Wexford House early in the morning and leaves after dinner.

"Craig, what do you think?" Karen asked.

"Yes, I think we all ought to check him out to see if he's going to fit in. Just because he's a friend of Ross doesn't mean a thing to me. And, by the way, if Tony thought Grant needed more security, why couldn't he arrange to assign another CIA or FBI agent?"

"Tony thinks some added muscle is all that's needed, not necessarily agency experience. And any new agent that they might have assigned would have an adjustment period to fit in with the team, too. Tony will arrange for Alex to go to 'The Farm' when you all go for training. And remember, Ross owns Russell & Associates, so he can't just be ignored.

"Let's meet Alex, and if there's a problem, we'll deal with it. I'll stick around here in Natchez until he arrives. And since I'm staying at Wexford House, there'll be no rush to move him in for extra security," Karen said.

We all nodded.

"The United Nations session starts on September 18. We'll talk more about it when Alex arrives. Unfortunately, there's not enough time to first go to 'The Farm.' I'd suggest you go ahead and make arrangements to go to New York on the 16th or 17th.

"Okay, folks, it sounds like we've got a plan," said Karen as she pushed away from the table and headed for the door.

I wasn't happy, but I knew the additional security wouldn't hurt.

CHAPTER 8

IN A NONDESCRIPT building complex located in north Tel Aviv, not far from Tel Aviv University, Levi Weiss, Director of Mossad, the feared and hated Israeli state security organization, was meeting with Moshe Kadosh, commander of the Caesarea Department.

Director Weiss was frowning, this time much more intensely than usual. His deeply wrinkled, leathery face made him look like a genuine Dogue de Bordeaux. And his dark, almost black, hair made an interesting contrast to his ruddy complexion. His black eyes seemed able to look right through anyone who tried to hide the truth from him. At age fifty-five, he had already been at the top of Mossad for ten years and was responsible for more than his share of killings and violence in defense of Israel. His facial appearance, plus his short, stocky physique, made him look more like a taxi driver than one of the top spymasters in the world. As the saying goes, "You can't judge a book by its cover."

Moshe Kadosh was just the opposite. He was tall, blonde, athletic, and almost always had a smile. But he was ten years younger than the Director and didn't have the baggage that Director Weiss had accumulated over the years. Moshe had returned from being a field agent only two years ago. He had been a member of Kidon, the elite group of Mossad assassins, and before that, a member of the IDF special forces. He was a rising star in Mossad and a candidate to someday replace Director Weiss.

"Why do they do these things, Moshe?"

"Who and what, Director?"

"Things that motivate our enemies to take action against us. I'm talking about our own government."

"Such as?" asked Moshe.

"Making that stupid agreement with the UAE."

"They do it because they are politicians. And politicians want to be in the news. They want to create the illusion they are doing something magnificent, at least for a moment," said Moshe.

"But they have infuriated Iran, and Israel will bear the brunt of their anger if we don't take action," Levi said.

"But then why wouldn't Iran take action against the UAE or Saudi Arabia?" replied Moshe.

"Why alienate Arab countries when you have a common enemy like Israel?" said Levi.

"Perhaps the UAE double-crossed Iran. We don't know the exact state of their relationship before the UAE signed the treaty with us."

"Maybe so, but we need to protect ourselves."

"How?"

"By sending them a strong warning, Moshe."

"I assume you mean the type of warning we have given before."

"Yes, when someone important suffers an unfortunate 'accident,' it gets their attention. I think now is the time for a reminder that they are not untouchable before they do something really stupid.

"We have an approved list of potential targets in Iran, as we do in many other countries. I've been studying the list. I suggest that we eliminate Dr. Rodin Soltani, the head of Iranian cyber warfare," said Levi.

"Yes, he would be a good choice. He's a snake, and it'll be difficult to replace his expertise."

"I'll talk to the Prime Minister and get his sign-off. Who will carry out the assassination?" asked Levi.

"Uri Davidoff's team — the best in Kidon. They have an assassination plan for everyone on their list. They'll make sure the plan is still viable, and then they'll be ready to strike. It will only take a day or two once I send the order," Moshe said.

"Go ahead and tell Uri to validate their plan for Dr. Soltani and then await further instructions."

"Yes, Director!" Moshe pushed back his chair to stand, then left Levi's office.

Director Weiss turned in his chair, looking out his window at Country Club Tel Aviv and the Mediterranean in the distance.

He wondered what his predecessors were thinking when they located Mossad headquarters in this vulnerable location. He could only assume that their reasoning was that in protecting themselves, they protected every Israeli citizen, and the Mossad was intentionally made no safer than anyone else.

CHAPTER 9

EVERYTHING WAS CAREFULLY rehearsed. The plan to eliminate Dr. Rodin Soltani was dusted off, and surveillance was briefly reinstated to make sure he was following his established routine. He was.

The upscale neighborhood of Elahiyeh, in northern Tehran, was very quiet in the early morning. Individual properties were protected by high brick and concrete walls topped by iron spikes, and automobile entry was controlled by tall, heavy, wheeled iron gates manually opened and closed by at least one security guard. Dr. Soltani lived in one of the villas on Sarveston Street, undoubtedly owned by the government of Iran, and provided to him as a perk.

At exactly 6:58 a.m., a black Mercedes sedan approached Sarveston St., where it would turn right, as it did every morning. The car was driven by a uniformed member of the IRGC-QF, and a uniformed bodyguard was in the passenger seat. They were on their way to pick up Dr. Soltani and take him to his office.

But when they were almost to the intersection of Chenaran St. and Sarveston St., a white panel truck turned into the path of a car crossing the intersection. There was a crash, and the two vehicles blocked the intersection. The driver of the black Mercedes opened his door and shouted to the drivers to move their damaged vehicles out of the way. The drivers of the two vehicles shouted back, cursing, and saying they were going to wait until the police arrived.

The two Quds soldiers got out of their car and approached the drivers. The bodyguard told them they were going to move the car out of the way, or else. The driver of the car pointed to the radiator fluid that was running out from under the car. The driver of the panel truck pointed to the left front wheel that was bent at an unnatural angle, indicating something underneath was obviously broken, and to the tire, which was flat.

"All right, then, we'll push them," the bodyguard said.

And so they did, but it took time, and the vehicles were still partially blocking traffic. Meanwhile, traffic was backing up in all directions. And it didn't help when the two drivers, part of Uri Davidoff's team, suddenly melted away into the crowd.

It was clear the soldiers in the black Mercedes were going to be late picking up the doctor this morning, and he would not be happy.

At 7:00 a.m. sharp, an identical black Mercedes sedan with uniformed passengers pulled into the entrance to Dr. Soltani's residence, as expected. The guard rolled open the gate and waved the car through, leaving the gate open because he knew they would be leaving as soon as the doctor was in the car. Once it had stopped at the front of the villa, he walked toward the driver's side of the Mercedes to exchange pleasantries, as was his custom, when the heavily tinted window came down and a hand holding a Sig Sauer P226 with a SRD9 suppressor came out and fired two shots into the guard's chest from about ten feet away. The guard made a gurgling sound, fell to the ground, and didn't move. The body was not visible from the street, shielded by shrubbery surrounding the paved turnaround, and the car blocked the view of anyone looking out from the house. But no one was looking out, anyway.

Just after the guard fell, the door to the villa opened, and Dr. Soltani stepped out. He was carrying a briefcase and a computer bag. As he approached the car, the passenger side window came down, and the doctor was momentarily confused by seeing a face he didn't expect. He started to say something, but before he could, Uri Davidoff fired two rounds from his suppressed Sig P226 into the doctor's chest. After the doctor fell, Uri fired two more rounds into Soltani's head, and a pool of blood started to collect on the stone driveway. It was fortunate that Uri was left-handed. It made shooting through the passenger window so much easier. But that's why they planned it that way.

The black Mercedes sedan eased back out onto Sarveston St. and headed toward Sharifi Manesh St. and then turned south toward central Tehran.

The IRGC-QF's black Mercedes finally arrived at Dr. Soltani's villa about five minutes later. The driver and the bodyguard would have a lot of trouble explaining the two dead bodies and why they had been late.

All that was visible on the security cameras that could possibly be of any use was the license plate number, but naturally the plates were stolen. The IRGC-QF didn't have a hint of a viable clue, but they suspected, of course, that the Kidon had pulled off another high profile assassination right under their noses.

CHAPTER 10

CRAIG CLAYTON WAITED outside security at the Jackson-Evers International Airport for Alex King's arrival. He didn't have a photo of Alex, but he was told by Tony that he would know him when he saw him. Based on that, and the description of Alex as a "very tough guy," Craig was looking for a big man, fairly young, in good physical shape.

Finally, a stream of people started exiting the secure area and headed toward the escalator to the baggage claim. Craig didn't see anyone fitting the description, so he headed down to baggage claim. He checked the screen and saw that the luggage for Alex's flight was coming up on carousel #2.

Craig went to the carousel and watched as passengers retrieved their luggage and left the area. Eventually, the crowd around the carousel dwindled. Then he saw a youngish man wearing a USMC T-shirt in Marine Corps green waiting patiently. He had a backpack slung over his shoulder.

But Craig was confused. The younger man was much

smaller than he expected. He also thought that maybe he wasn't as young as he looked. He was about Grant's six-foot height, but a little heavier, around two hundred pounds. However, his appearance was nothing that made him look like a "very tough guy."

But with no one else coming close to matching his expectations, Craig walked over to the man.

"Alex King?" asked Craig.

"Yes. That's me! Craig Clayton?"

Craig stuck out his hand, and Alex shook it firmly, looking him straight in the eyes. Craig noticed his dark brown eyes, almost black, his short dark hair, and his olive complexion.

The wheeled bag came up the conveyor onto the carousel, and Alex grabbed it. He put his arms through the straps in his backpack and grabbed the handle on the bag.

Craig said, "I'm parked across from the terminal."

They walked through the automatic door and crossed the street to the parking lot. After Alex put his wheeled bag into the trunk and his backpack in the back seat, they took off for Natchez.

"So, what did Ross tell you about our operation?" asked Craig.

"He told me you would be my boss; is that what you wanted to hear?"

Craig was taken aback. Alex said it matter-of-factly, but what did he mean by it?

"No, I wondered what he told you about what we do, and why he sent you."

"Well, he said that Grant was the most valuable asset the company has, and he wants him to have more protection. He knows me, trusts me, and has seen what I can do in dangerous situations. Plus I already work for him, so he can assign me to whatever part of his empire he wants."

"Did he say what Grant does?"

"No, I assumed that I would find out when I got here. I figure he's a spy of some sort. Maybe he's a hacker or something."

"I guess that might be one way to describe it," laughed Craig. "He's an intelligence analyst. That's all you need to know."

Alex had a puzzled look on his face, but Craig didn't want to give any more information than absolutely necessary until they knew if Alex King was someone they could trust.

Changing the subject, Craig asked, "How are you with a gun?"

"I'm pretty good, but I haven't used one in a while."

"We have a CIA issue Glock 19M for you; you'll need to practice. So, what does Ross think is your number one qualification?"

"I imagine it's hand-to-hand combat. I'm good at that, and it saved us more than once." He smiled.

"You mean you and Ross?"

"Yes," answered Alex.

"That's good. We can use that skill. And you might even be able to teach Grant some basics of self-defense."

Alex nodded. "Yes, I can do that."

"Did Ross tell you how long you would be with us?"

"No, just that it would be as long as needed. He didn't ask me to get rid of my place in Nice, so I doubt it will be too long. To tell the truth, I like it in France, so I hope I can get back soon."

If that was the case, Craig thought their decision to keep Alex in the dark wise, though he worried about how seriously Alex would take the job if he was so keen to get back home. "So, how do you know Ross?"

"We were in the Marines together, but before that, we were friends in college."

"And where was that?"

"Cal Poly-San Luis Obispo. We both majored in business. But Ross was a lot smarter than me, which he's proven since he got into business."

"I meant, where were you together in the Marines?"

"Well, first at Camp Pendleton, then Kosovo, Okinawa, and Iraq, though we were sent on a few special ops into Afghanistan."

"Why did you enlist together in the Marines?"

"As soon as we graduated in 1999, we enlisted. Ross wanted me to join up with him, and I decided 'What the hell'! And we've been partners ever since."

"Partners?"

"Well, he's the boss, but you know what I mean. Maybe close friends would be a better description."

"I assume you're not married, right?"

"Yeah, I never had the time or inclination for that. And I'm having too much fun, I guess, being single."

"Well, you probably aren't going to have much fun in Natchez — not like on the French Riviera, anyway."

"That's okay. I'm not expecting to be here that long."

Craig really didn't quite know what to think about Alex. He seemed to be willing to do whatever Ross wanted him to do without needing to know any details. He wondered what kind of commitment Alex would have when he found himself in real danger, which could be very soon.

CHAPTER 11

After arriving back in Natchez and grabbing a bite to eat at the Natchez Tavern, Craig took Alex over to the office to meet the crew.

When Craig opened the door to Suite 302, Karen, Sharon, and Angie were all sitting there patiently waiting. Alex looked them over, then looked back at Craig.

Craig said, "Everybody, this is Alex King. Alex, this is Karen Spencer, Angie Reynolds — or should I say, Angie Markey, and Sharon Honderich. Karen is our boss, Angie is Grant's boss, and Sharon is here to help us keep our low profile by helping us change our appearance and identities, usually only when we're traveling."

As he smiled and shook hands, Alex said, "Hi, everyone, I look forward to working with you. I don't know much about what you do, I just know from Ross that Grant needs some extra protection for a while. Speaking of which, where's Grant?"

Angie said, "Oh, he's in his office next door talking to a client on the phone. He'll be off in a minute."

Alex grabbed a chair, sat down, and looked around the office. He noticed a white screen set up against the wall behind

Sharon. And he saw she was fiddling with a device on her desk that looked like a printer but was smaller, narrower, and deeper, and connected to the laptop. She noticed he was staring at her and the equipment, obviously trying to figure out what she was doing.

Sharon looked at him and said, "This is an ID printer. It's not enough for me to come up with disguises — IDs are required, too. This little machine can produce ID cards with photos, holograms, signatures, and even with embedded smart chips.

"The printing is easy; it's the software that's the secret sauce. And that's been supplied by another department in the CIA. They can also hack into security databases and plant false information so that card readers at a target company or organization will accept these cards. I can also make driver's licenses; we have agreements with several states. And I can provide the images and data files necessary to make passports, but those have to be printed at headquarters.

"The hard part, really, is coming up with the disguises, but that's my specialty."

Alex said, "Impressive. When do I get a new identity?"

"I need to assess you to decide what's going to work for your physical characteristics and what will be compatible with Grant's disguise. He's the primary client, you'll just be in a supporting role. I've got all the costumes and accessories next door. I've got a makeup table over there, too, with the proper lighting and everything else I need."

The connecting door opened, and a taller than average man, about Alex's age, entered the suite. Alex stood, extended his hand, and said, "I assume you're Grant. I'm Alex."

Grant smiled, shook his hand, and said, "Glad to meet you — glad you're here. We need all the protection we can get."

"I'll do my best."

Grant smiled, but it didn't show in his eyes. There was an awkward moment as they stood there quietly.

Alex wondered what Grant was thinking, but rather than dwell on it, he turned to Karen and broke the silence. "Well, when are you going to tell me what this operation is all about and what Grant does? I need to know so I can protect him."

Karen said, "No, actually, you don't. You're here temporarily, and we are a highly secure operation; the less you know, the more secure we are. Imagine yourself as more of a bodyguard. They typically don't know the details of what their client does. Grant has excellent skills of observation and analysis. That's all you need to know. And there are people that Grant's skills threaten.

"He's been the target of several assassination and kidnapping attempts, once for sure by the Russians. We don't know who made the other attempts, probably the Chinese and perhaps Iran, but it could be others.

"No need to bother you with more, until and unless you're going to be with us permanently. We'll tell you everything you need to know, when you need to know it."

"Okay, then that's how I'll play it, just like in the Marines — operational details only. Thanks for explaining," Alex said easily. There was no hint of a frown on his face, though he knew it would be tough for him to do his job protecting Grant without knowing what the team was up against.

"For now, all you need to know is we're going to the UN session in New York in a few days."

Alex said, "New York? Great!"

CHAPTER 12

SEPTEMBER 15
TEHRAN, IRAN

DR. HOSSEIN YAZDANI ARRIVED at the General's office at 3:00 p.m. He was a tall man with curly white hair, about sixty-five years old, dressed in a dark blue suit with a white shirt and no tie. His face was weathered, and his eyes — dark, with bags underneath — were lively, as if he knew something and couldn't wait to tell you.

The doctor was apprehensive about this meeting with the General. He didn't have any idea what the General wanted, but he knew the General had a reputation of being demanding, and even cruel, to other government officials.

"Please sit down, Doctor," the General said as he motioned to the couch on the other side of the office.

"How can I help you, General?"

"Do you remember when I assumed command of the Quds, I visited your laboratory and asked you to give me the background on all your current and previous development projects?"

"Yes, General, it was my pleasure."

But it was not a pleasure. The General was only interested in when he would have new weapons available to use. And he encouraged the doctor to take unimaginable risks to speed up his research.

"Dr. Yazdani, please refresh my memory on the research and development of a so-called 'dirty bomb.'"

So, this is what he wants, the doctor thought. *Is it because Iran might be threatened by a dirty bomb or because the General wants to use one for an operation? He'll probably check what I tell him with other scientists, so I can't withhold anything.*

"Yes, General, before we decided to concentrate our efforts on enriching uranium, we spent most of our resources experimenting with nuclear fission and perfecting the handling and separation of the resulting fission products. In the absence of having the ability to construct atomic weapons, we looked into using radioactive materials to make RDDs — radiological dispersion devices — the so-called 'dirty bombs.' We determined they could be used for the intended purpose, but there were difficulties."

"And remind me, what were these difficulties, Doctor?"

"The problems were primarily logistical. A dirty bomb is comprised of radioactive material, explosive material, and a detonator. Because of the radiation, there is thick lead shielding to protect those handling the device, making the RDD bulky and heavy and relatively easy to detect. This is not desirable because the RDD would need to travel a significant distance and cross at least one border, undetected, to be delivered into foreign territory.

"However, now that we have ballistic missiles, it is possible to deliver an RDD on a missile. And we can always fire it in an artillery shell if we are close enough. But it will be obvious who fired it, so retaliation is guaranteed.

"For all these reasons, we shelved the project."

"Do we still have an inventory of radioactive material?" asked the General.

"Yes, we do."

"How much radioactive material would be required to contaminate an area of, let's say, ten square miles?"

"It depends on the material, but even accounting for the age of our material — if it was fairly evenly dispersed . . . a quarter of a pound, maybe less. Radioactive material like Cesium-137 is unbelievably active, long-lasting, and powerful. Do you have a piece of paper I can write on?"

"Yes, of course." The General went to his desk, picked up a notepad and a pen, and placed it on the coffee table in front of the doctor before sitting down.

The doctor continued, "Cesium-137 is constantly decaying — radiating beta particles and gamma rays as it decays, making it extremely dangerous. Here is the number of decays and, therefore, the releases of beta and gamma rays per second, from only ONE GRAM of Cesium-137."

He wrote the figure on the notepad — 3,215,000,000,000 decays per second. "Scientists refer to this decay rate as 3.215 Terabecquerels, which we write as 3.215 TBq. Each time there is a decay, a gamma ray and a beta particle are released. Gamma rays can travel a hundred feet and can penetrate the human body. The energy in these rays can cause damage to the tissue in vital organs, causing cancer or outright organ failure, in addition to radiation burns on the skin. Beta particles are not as dangerous, but they can cause radiation burns. If even a very small amount of Cesium-137 is dispersed over a large area, there is enough continuous emission of radiation to be deadly for a long time. The half life of Cesium-137 is thirty years."

Yazdani could see the wheels in the General's head turning as the man stared at the gigantic number written on the notepad.

"The level of contamination in the Chernobyl permanent

exclusion zone was about 1500 kBq per square meter — theoretically only about half an ounce per ten square miles."

He waited for the General to ask more questions about the health effects of the radiation, but the General just stared at him.

"To get to your question as to how much material would be required to contaminate ten square miles — as I have said, I would advise using four ounces of Cesium-137 because it would be physically impossible to evenly distribute a half ounce of material over such a wide area. A larger quantity will have a better chance of achieving the desired result. In addition, our inventory of Cesium-137 has aged and is only about half as strong now as when produced in the reactor."

The General made some notes and nodded his head. "And, Doctor, what explosive would you use for such a device?"

"Our experiments showed that military grade C-4 would be a good choice, as it is readily available and can be safely handled. One of the difficult problems, though, is how to direct the force of the blast in such a way as to get maximum airborne dispersion. Personally, I think it would be advisable to detonate an RDD atop a building or a similarly tall structure, or from a drone, assuming the target is in an urban area. Otherwise, buildings surrounding the blast would tend to contain it and reduce the dispersion."

"Doctor, how likely would it be for the radioactive material to be detected prior to the device being exploded — in the normal course of security monitoring in urban areas?"

"Unless it's a primary urban center such as New York, London, Paris, Berlin, or Rome, I wouldn't consider it likely, except, of course, anywhere in Israel where they have monitoring equipment everywhere. However, it would likely be detected in all major ports where they routinely screen containers and freight for radioactive devices. But that also depends on the amount of lead shielding."

Yazdani shifted uncomfortably, hesitant to continue. He did not like that the General hadn't asked about potential health issues yet. The man seemed to have no concern whatsoever about the harmful effects of radiation on anyone who might be exposed. Feeling he was not able to withhold any information without dire consequences, he decided to go ahead.

"There is one other thing I need to mention, General. For as much material as you are requiring, you probably need to consider multiple RDD devices to better manage the logistical issues and ensure wide dispersion. I would like to also point out that with exposure to high doses of Cesium-137, an individual will get radiation sickness and die within a short period of time. In smaller exposures, cancers will develop in a significant portion of the population over many years. Therefore, a land area contaminated with high radiation levels would have to be evacuated, and it would take a very long time to remediate — years, if ever."

Again, the General nodded. "How long could someone be in contact with the shielded lead container and not become ill from radiation poisoning?"

"I would say days or maybe even weeks, as long as it wasn't constant exposure, so long as the container was thick enough and remained tightly closed."

"And what would be involved with the cleanup effort?" asked the General.

"It would take years and billions of dollars, not to mention the economic impact of shutting down the area for a considerable time. The exclusion zone around Chernobyl, because it is so large, will never be remediated. I have read scientific reports that the worst parts of the exclusion zone, if left to gradually and naturally lose its radioactivity, will not be safe for several thousand years."

The doctor made the last statement with some emphasis, hoping that it would shock the General, but the General seemed unaffected. This frightened the doctor.

"Thank you, Doctor. I will make note of that. I believe I have enough information for now. You have refreshed my memory and added some new information. I will be in touch if I need anything more."

The doctor stood, nodded, and left the General's office.

The doctor had difficulty imagining that the government of Iran would allow a "dirty bomb" to be used as a weapon of foreign policy. However, the political fanatics were now in charge, so who knew what might happen next?

He needed time to think about how he could prevent such a disaster without being considered a traitor himself.

CHAPTER 13

SEPTEMBER 16
QOM, IRAN

THE NEXT DAY, the General arrived at the Qom International Hotel precisely at noon, dressed in civilian clothes. If he arrived in uniform, he thought it would create too much attention. His driver, as well as the security detail in the car following behind, were also in civilian clothes. The Iranians had learned the hard way that they were never safe from the Israelis, even within their own country, so high ranking officers of the IRGC always had armed security with them.

The General entered the hotel and saw Navid already waiting for him, sitting across the lobby on a couch, reading a newspaper.

As he approached, Navid looked up and stood. "*Salaam alaykum.*"

The General repeated the greeting as they kissed each other on both cheeks.

"Let's have lunch, Navid *agha*. I'm buying," said the General, leading the way to the Toranj Restaurant across the lobby.

Navid said, "No, it's my turn," but the General insisted, and Navid bowed his head in appreciation.

There were only a few people in the restaurant, and the General, after looking around the space, asked if they could be seated by the window. The host guided them to their table.

"Navid, how is your family?"

"The boys are fine, and so is Roya, but sometimes I worry about her. She's always thinking about Kaveh and Javed."

"I am so sorry to hear that, but maybe with enough time?"

"I doubt it, but only Allah knows," he said with a sad look on his face.

When the waiter came over to take their orders, they both ordered koobideh kabab, made with ground lamb and beef, and tea.

As soon as the waiter walked away, Navid asked, "Why did you want to see me today?"

"I have a project for you, if you are interested, *agha*." He watched carefully for Navid's reaction.

"If it hurts the enemies of Iran, I am always interested," Navid said, smiling.

"I assume you have heard of the recent treaty between Israel and the UAE?"

"Yes, the Sunnis are traitors to Islam to make such an agreement," Navid said with an edge to his voice.

"The SNSC wants to take action against the UAE to punish them and warn others. And I have been assigned the task."

"And how do you propose to do that?"

"The SNSC has decided to order an attack on their largest oil field, Bu Hasa, and I have to figure out the best method."

"Well, the last oil field attack was by missiles fired into Saudi Arabia, right?"

"Yes, and it was effective, but only for a short time. We want to do something that will be longer lasting."

"And what have you identified that can do that?"

"I'm going to propose using a radiological dispersion device — a 'dirty bomb.' It may put the oil field out of commission for years. But I need a means to deliver it. We cannot use our own troops, and we don't want to be directly connected to the attack."

"So, you want Harras Ansar al-Haqq to do the job, is that it?"

The General waited for a moment before answering. Navid did not sound as excited as he had hoped. The General got a serious look on his face and said, "You've done dangerous projects for us in the past."

"Yes, but this would make us pariahs if we were ever found out."

"But you would be heroes to many people, Navid."

He watched Navid closely for a reaction. He knew that most Arabs and Iranians had felt betrayed by the UAE's treaty with Israel, but Navid was hard to read.

"*Agha,* it sounds extremely dangerous, so we must be very well compensated."

"Yes, of course, billions of rial."

"Our operation extends across many countries, so we must be paid in euros and dollars."

"Okay, then, how about one million euros?"

Navid momentarily considered, then replied, "Tell me what's required, then we can discuss the price."

The General wondered if Navid knew the options for a trusted proxy were limited for an operation like this because it was clear with that comment that the upper hand had shifted to Navid.

Just at that moment, the waiter brought their tea and the food, and they sat patiently as he set up everything for them.

They ate their kababs and rice and drank tea. The waiter

brought them an extra order of sangak flatbread to eat with their kababs.

The General said, "I'll give you an overview of the operation. The oil field is about fifty miles inland, in the desert. There is a main operating area that contains collection equipment and tanks to store crude oil that comes from the wells, and equipment to separate the gas from the oil. And then there are pumps, compressors, and transmission lines to move the oil and the gas to the petrochemical and liquified natural gas production complex, Ruwais, on the coast. The operating area of about six square miles is the main target. It's surrounded by undulating desert."

Navid said, "Do you know anything about their security?"

"No, not yet, but I'll be getting information from our intelligence sources."

Navid frowned, then said, "Well, then it might not be possible to get closer than a few miles from the center of the complex. But if a drone can be used, then it might be possible to deliver the bomb right to the heart of it. If not, then detonating it at the perimeter, if the wind is blowing in the right direction, will be the best that can be done."

Then he added, "Unless it is possible to burst through the security gate with a truck and get to the center of the complex before being stopped. But that would be a suicide mission." Again, Navid frowned.

"Yes, drones are a possibility," said Navid. "Everything you described is extremely risky. I'm willing to take it on, but we would want to do some reconnaissance of our own before agreeing. And if we do, I will only commit to exploding the device at the perimeter of the compound. If we can get closer, we will, but we can't promise that. Also, I can't be responsible for the result. I can only be responsible for exploding the device. And we may be exposed to radiation ourselves, so that's another risk beyond being killed outright or jailed. In other words, we are going to require a substantial fee, say three million, half in euros and half in dollars."

"Okay, I'll let you know if my plan is approved by the SNSC. If so, then you can do your reconnaissance. Oh, the attack must occur before November 15." He stared at Navid, waiting for a reaction.

"All right, let me know if your plan is approved. I'll be thinking about how many men to use on our end, and also devising options to get the materials into the UAE," said Navid.

The General paid the bill. They walked into the hotel lobby and stopped just before walking out the front door.

Navid said, "Thank you, Farzad *agha*. It was nice to see you again."

They said their goodbyes, walked out the door, and turned in opposite directions.

He wondered what Navid was really thinking. Navid had always been receptive to jobs in the past, but it was clear he was not fully on board yet.

The General was worried. He didn't have a backup plan.

CHAPTER 14

ROYA SAT IN the kitchen, waiting for Navid to return home. His meeting with the General had her worried. Farzad had gotten Navid into terrorist activities in the aftermath of the US invasion of Iraq. The Shi'ite militias needed men to fight against the Americans and against the hated Sunni traitors who had sided with the Americans.

It seemed so long ago, but it was only a little more than fifteen years. So much had happened since then that had almost destroyed her family. She had lost two of her sons, and, as far as she was concerned, her husband had lost his conscience.

She had once been pretty, and happy, too. That was when she first met Navid, and they had married. He was kind and cheerful, in spite of losing his arm. He was just content to be with her. But then, he got caught up in the ultra-religious movement, and he began making hateful statements against the Sunnis. His dislike gradually turned to hatred.

Navid had a lot of friends who hated the Sunnis, and Farzad

had convinced Navid to take on a terrorist mission in Iraq with those friends. Farzad, or rather the IRGC, paid Navid a lot of money to blow up a government building in Najaf. He couldn't do a lot with one arm, but he could plan and lead his group. And he could still shoot a pistol.

Roya knew that although Navid said he undertook the terrorist operations for religious reasons, he liked the money, but his real motivation was revenge. He should have been protecting his family, but his desire for revenge caused him to put his sons in danger and to recruit them into his terrorist operation. She still loved him, but she hated him for that.

She ran her hand over her long hair, now streaked with gray. At least she didn't have to wear a hijab inside her own house. She sighed and looked out the window as she waited.

It wasn't long before she saw Navid's car stop beside the house. He got out and, in less than a minute, came through the back door.

"I was worried about you," she said.

"Why?"

"The General always brings trouble."

"Not always," he scoffed.

He sat down. She looked at him expectantly, waiting to hear what happened.

"He wants us to take on another operation, and he's willing to pay big money. The best part is that it's not in Iraq or Syria," he said.

"Where is it?"

"I can't tell you yet. It's not approved. The SNSC has to hear his plan."

"I hope you won't involve the boys in it."

"They are the only ones I can completely trust. But I will keep them safe. I may have to go myself."

"What can a one-armed man do?"

"Not much, but I can direct the operation."

"Navid, please give this up before you all get killed!"

"Do we have to talk about this again? The answer is no."

He stood up quickly and stormed out of the room. She sat there and cried, as usual.

CHAPTER 15

SEPTEMBER 18
NEW YORK, NEW YORK

THE SURREY HOTEL on East 76th Street was once again the headquarters for a Russell & Associates team visit to New York. It was not as close to the United Nations' headquarters along the East River as we might like — about twenty minutes by taxi on most days — but it was perfect in every other way, and we were thoroughly familiar with it.

After Sharon did her magic with makeup and disguises, Angie and I left the hotel at 9:30 a.m. to meet Alex, who'd gone ahead of us, at the UN. Karen and Craig had debriefed everyone on what was expected of them the night before after they'd arrived. The UN meeting began at 10 a.m., and Karen said Tony had finally decided he wanted me to check out the Prime Minister of Israel, David Baruch; the Russian President, Taras Drozdov; the Iranian President, Amir Rostami, and the UK Prime Minister, Garrett Ainsworth. Luckily, they were all scheduled to speak on the same day.

We exited our taxi to find Alex, wearing a wig of fairly

long, tousled light brown hair and semi-rimless glasses, waiting for us. He wore a pair of dress jeans, a yellow button-down shirt, and a dark blue sport coat. I knew his cover was as Henry Goertemiller, journalist for the *Journal of Foreign Affairs,* and I thought Sharon did a great job of making Alex look just different enough to fit the bill.

When we approached, Alex eyed us up and down and raised an eyebrow. "Sharon does good work."

She did. Our covers were also for the *Journal of Foreign Affairs.* I was posing as Mark Wexford, editor. I had on a wig of salt and pepper gray hair of medium length, as well as a mustache and matching gray goatee. Large black-framed glasses, a black suit with charcoal pinstripes, and a blue tie with tiny white polka dots completed the look.

But it was Angie, posing as Jeanne Schellman, also a journalist, with whom Sharon outdid herself.

Angie's black hair was gone, replaced by a golden-blond wig of the same length. Sharon had lightened Angie's eyebrows and used lighter makeup and lipstick. To finish the look, she wore a dark blue pantsuit. The result left me in awe. I loved Angie's usual look, but I didn't mind the blond at all, either. I joked that she should keep the wig just to spice things up sometimes.

We walked to the UN's media entrance on 46th St and 1st Ave. The guards looked over our credentials and IDs closely, running them through a device of some kind to authenticate them, and our headshots popped up on the monitor. Then we passed our belongings through the X-ray machine, and we were each put through a full body scanner before we were finally let through. The guard directed us toward the main entrance of the General Assembly Hall.

Once inside the main lobby, we found the escalators and made our way to the media gallery on the third floor, where we were given a printed copy of the daily program.

We had a private box that looked out into the great hall. It contained three seats behind a writing surface, which ran the width of the box right along the window opening.

The box was set up somewhat like a broadcast booth at a baseball stadium. The box was darkened when the General Assembly was in session, with only enough light coming in from the hall to see your own handwriting. And the media were not visible to the delegates, which eliminated any distractions caused by our presence.

At precisely 10:00 a.m., the session was called to order by the Secretary-General of the UN, who introduced the first speaker, the UK Prime Minister, Garrett Ainsworth. He was a polished speaker who droned on about the necessity of the UN and the importance of its various missions and activities.

Angie reached in her bag and handed me a black case containing a Leica Monovid, an 8x20 monocular lens. I used the monocular to closely study Ainsworth's face as I listened. I had never tried to make a connection with a subject under these conditions. As the speech continued, I figured I'd see if I could penetrate Ainsworth's memory. I took the monocular away from my eye and laid it on the table. I decided to try a point in time fifteen minutes before the speech began. I concentrated intensely, and images began to appear.

Ainsworth was talking to someone who I didn't recognize. He said, "No, I'm not going to mention the UN's failure in Syria. This is not the time or place for that. We need to show our support, not say that we were right and our allies were wrong." The other person nodded and walked away as Ainsworth studied the draft of his speech and mentally rehearsed. I was satisfied.

After the UK Prime Minister finished speaking, the Secretary-General introduced the Iranian President, Amir Rostami. He was dressed in a dark blue suit, with a white shirt and a banded collar. The Iranians never wore a tie as it was banned as a "Western" symbol during the 1979 revolution. Therefore, a collar was unnecessary, and in some ways the banded shirt was a sign of protest against the Western democracies, especially the United States.

Rostami was medium height and weight, with heavy black eyebrows, and sporting a stubbly beard and medium-length graying hair. He spoke through a translator, reviling the enemies of Iran and asking for fairness, saying Iran had done nothing to deserve financial sanctions and other mistreatment. He warned other countries against ganging up against Iran and asked for peaceful negotiations to resolve all disputes.

I studied Rostami closely, using the Monovid, for most of his speech, but then lost interest and decided to try to connect with Rostami's recent memory. It only took a few moments to make the connection.

"Are the Israelis here?" asked Rostami. Another man, likely the Iranian Ambassador, said, "No, they will not enter the hall until after you leave."

Of course, I had no problem understanding Rostami even though he was speaking in Farsi. That was one of the unique features of my psychic powers. I could understand any language I encountered mentally with my targets.

"And what about the UAE?"

"No, they are not here, either, sir."

"That's good. I want to leave immediately after my speech," said Rostami.

"Yes, sir, we will go back to the hotel to freshen up before going to the airport."

Rostami nodded.

I came back to the moment, looked over at Angie, and nodded. She understood and smiled.

After Rostami finished his speech, the Secretary-General adjourned the meeting until 2:00 p.m.

Alex said, "Let's go to lunch!"

We left the media box and made our way to the fourth floor of the UN Conference Building and the Delegates Dining Room. We were seated by the window overlooking the East River.

Alex asked me, "Well, what did you observe?"

I told him, "I could tell the speakers appeared to be in good health and believed what they were saying. I look for little things that could mean all is not as it appears, and I did not see anything of that sort." I was happy that Alex had apparently swallowed the story about me being an intelligence officer.

"For example, if they had stumbled over their words, or were sweating, or their complexion was not normal, or they had trouble walking to the podium, or appeared to have stage fright — those are the kinds of things I look for," I said.

Alex said, "Oh, okay," but he had a slightly skeptical look on his face. I imagine because he wondered how anyone could come to definite conclusions just by watching someone from a hundred feet away.

CHAPTER 16

After lunch, we went back to the General Assembly Building, took our seats, and waited for the afternoon session to begin.

The Secretary-General introduced the Russian President, Taras Drozdov. He was a veteran Russian bureaucrat and former KGB officer. Drozdov looked old, but he was big and strong and had a powerful voice. He spoke of the history of terrorist attacks in Russia, all the way back to the assassination of Tsar Alexander II in 1881. He said Russia was committed to working with the rest of the United Nations to fight terrorists anywhere in the world.

I watched him closely through the monocular. Drozdov had droopy eyelids and bags under his eyes, which made him look both sleepy and ill. Finally, I decided it was just genetics, but I was certain medical specialists from many countries were also making the same type of evaluation.

I decided to try to connect with Drozdov. I picked yesterday at 12 noon as a place to start. Drozdov was sitting at a table with two other men eating lunch. One companion was apparently the Russian Ambassador to the UN.

"And what should I say to the Secretary-General tomorrow?" asked Drozdov.

"Tell him you'll protect the UN peacekeepers in Syria. But in return, you don't want any criticism of Russia over Crimea."

"Yes, of course."

Drozdov took a drink of wine and wiped his mouth with a white napkin.

"I will be very diplomatic," he said as he laughed loudly.

"Taras, sometimes that is easier to say than to do," said the other man with a smile.

"That is why I am President and you are only the SVR Director, Mikhail. I will handle it just fine," said Drozdov.

I rubbed my forehead. Alex asked, "Are you okay?"

"Yes, I was just thinking. I was wondering how the Iranians avoid the Israelis and the British. And how the Russians avoid the Americans. I wonder if they have multiple hallways and green rooms behind the stage?"

Alex nodded. "I was wondering where their security is while they're speaking. Their security details probably don't like each other, either."

President Drozdov finished his speech and was given polite applause. The Secretary-General thanked him, and he left the podium.

The Secretary-General then introduced the Prime Minister of Israel, David Baruch. I watched Baruch closely. He had a reputation as a wily politician, a veteran of the rough and tumble Israeli Knesset. He was a short man, medium build, with thinning dark hair. He had a nice smile and was known to be very friendly in every public interaction.

Baruch talked about the difficulty of being a small country, threatened by every neighboring country and their powerful friends. He spoke of Israel's genuine desire for peace but their need to protect themselves from terrorists.

I finally decided to put down the monocular and try to make a connection with David Baruch.

The images came quickly from lunchtime, just a few hours ago. Baruch was eating in an ornate room with a man I recognized as the Israeli Ambassador, Eliya Zohar.

"When will we leave for the UN?" Baruch asked.

"We'll get in the car at 2:00 p.m. in the alley behind the consulate. It's only two blocks over to the UN," said Zohar.

"Okay, I don't want to cross paths with the Iranians."

"They'll be gone by then. Rostami spoke this morning."

Baruch nodded.

I came back to the moment. I'd made connections with everyone Tony asked. I said to Alex, "I've seen all I need to see. We can leave any time."

I handed Angie the Leica Monovid, which she put in her bag.

Alex said, "Okay, follow me."

We gathered our things and followed Alex out of the box.

CHAPTER 17

Once they arrived at the security gate, Alex said, "Wait here until I check things out. I'll call you. Stay here until I do."

Alex looked across 1st Avenue at the 46th Street intersection. That was where they needed to go to catch a taxi, but he saw something that looked out of place.

A Consolidated Edison panel truck was pulled partway onto the sidewalk facing 1st Avenue. There was a portable orange safety railing around a manhole in the sidewalk, and the manhole was open. As Alex walked across 1st Avenue, he noticed a man in a ConEd uniform wearing a yellow vest and a blue hard hat standing next to the manhole and looking in his direction. He also saw that the man seemed to be working alone, which was unusual.

Wanting to check out the situation, Alex moved closer. When he approached the man, he noticed he was not wearing boots or work shoes; he was wearing dress shoes. Alex's eyes narrowed. Something was very wrong. The man was holding a phone to his ear, listening but not talking. As Alex got closer, he thought he should try to remember as much about the guy as possible. The man looked like he might be Southern European

— maybe Italian, Albanian, Croatian, or Greek. It was hard to tell — the bushy dark mustache and long black hair dominated his appearance.

He approached the man and took the folded UN program from his coat pocket with his left hand. When he got within speaking distance, he said, "Can you give me directions?" and extended the program toward the man.

The man stuck out his hand to take the program.

When he reluctantly took the program, Alex wound up and landed a vicious punch with his right fist to the man's left temple, which sent the helmet flying. The man was unconscious before he hit the ground. As he began to slump down, Alex landed another savage punch with his left fist to the right side of the man's face to make sure he stayed down. The man's phone dropped to the pavement and clattered into the manhole. Alex instantly thought, *Damn!*

Alex caught him just before he hit the ground, dragged him to the back of the open ConEd truck, and dumped him inside. He quickly searched the man and found a Glock 17 in a waistband holster. Alex stuck the weapon into his own waistband.

Then he shut the doors to the van and called Angie on her phone.

"Get over here — now!"

Then he reopened the van and checked the man's pockets but didn't find any ID. But he did have the presence of mind to take a photo of him before reclosing the door.

Alex met Angie and Grant at the corner. "Let's grab a taxi at the hotel." He pointed down 1st Avenue toward the Millennium Hilton at the intersection of 44th Street. He only shook his head at their questioning looks and said, "Walk as fast as possible, but don't run."

When they reached the Hilton, Alex told the doorman, "We need a taxi over to Times Square."

The doorman nodded, flagged a taxi, and they piled in. The taxi passed by 46th Street and the ConEd truck; there was no activity. Once they reached Times Square, Alex asked the driver to let them out at the corner of 47th Street and 7th Avenue. They crossed the street and hailed a taxi to return to the Surrey Hotel.

When they finally got back to Craig's suite at the hotel, Grant said, "Alex, are you finally going to tell us what happened?"

Craig, Karen, and Sharon all turned concerned looks at Alex.

"There was a guy dressed in a ConEd uniform next to a ConEd truck, loitering around an open manhole, obviously watching for someone to cross the street from the UN. But he wasn't wearing work shoes and was by himself, which is not how ConEd operates. So I decided to put him out of commission, at least temporarily, with a few solid blows to the head. After I knocked him out, I put him in the back of the truck, and guess what?" he asked.

"Okay, what?" asked Karen.

"I found a gun on him," Alex said, pulling the Glock from his waistband. "No ConEd worker is going to be carrying a gun."

"I'm not so sure of that in New York," said Craig.

Karen said, "Let's get the FBI to check the serial number on the gun, if it has one, and see if there are any prints — besides yours, Alex."

Alex said, "I took the guy's photo after I put him in the truck."

Karen said, "Okay, we can give that to the FBI, too."

"But how would the ConEd guy, or anyone else, know you were going to the UN? And how would they know what you looked like with your disguises?" said Craig.

"True, but we can't take any chances," said Karen. "We all

should pack up and get back to Natchez as quickly as possible. Grant got to observe the four political leaders, so he accomplished his objective, right?"

Grant said, "Yes, I saw what I needed to see."

"Okay, then, let's get out of here. Craig, will you make the arrangements?"

Craig nodded.

CHAPTER 18

OUR TEAM ARRIVED back in Natchez late in the evening. We decided that, at least for now, it would make sense for Alex to stay at Wexford House as extra protection. Karen and Sharon stayed together at the Natchez Grand Hotel overlooking the river, about a block from the office. And Craig stayed in the renovated carriage house out back of Wexford House with CIA Agent Lloyd Hart, who was part of the security team stationed there.

Early the next morning, I knocked on Alex's door. When Alex answered, I told him, "Miss Doris will be here soon. When she arrives, I'll tell her you're here and part of our team now, just like Karen has been in the past. That's all she needs to know. Don't tell her any more than that. If she asks questions, tell her she needs to talk to me. After you get dressed, come downstairs, and I'll introduce you to her."

I had explained my relationship with Miss Doris to Alex on the trip back to Natchez. Now in her mid-sixties, Miss Doris was a tall, thin black lady with silver hair, a quick wit, and a just-as-quick smile. She had worked for my family for over forty years, as far back as when my grandfather lived here.

It would have been simpler to keep Alex away from Miss Doris for now, but I wanted her impressions of him. I was getting more comfortable with Alex, especially after the way he had handled the potential threat in NYC, but I thought having Miss Doris check him out would be smart. She was a good judge of character.

When Miss Doris let herself in the back door at 7:30 a.m., I was waiting for her in the kitchen. She was startled to see me sitting at the table.

"Mister Grant, you scared me to death! I thought you weren't coming back until at least tomorrow."

"We finished our business early, Miss Doris. And we have a house guest, Alex King. I told you about him before we left on the trip. I want you to talk with him this morning and tell me what you think. He might be with us for a while. just like Karen was. I'll go bring him down now. Angie and I will be down for breakfast in about a half hour."

"That'll be fine, Mister Grant."

Later that morning, Angie and I came to the kitchen as Alex finished his bacon, eggs, and toast. Miss Doris poured our coffee and started cooking bacon, eggs, and grits. Alex excused himself while we were still waiting for our food.

After Miss Doris set our plates in front of us, I looked up at her. "Well, Miss Doris, what do you think of Alex?"

"I think he's okay, Mister Grant. He has some issues because of how he was raised, losing his family so young. But I think he'll find his way. It just takes some people longer than others."

We wondered what she was talking about, but Alex returned to the kitchen table and sat down before we could ask.

"What's the agenda for today, folks?" asked Alex.

"We're going to go to the office and figure it out," I said.

CHAPTER 19

SEPTEMBER 18
TEHRAN, IRAN

It took the General about an hour to drive across the city to the Tehran Nuclear Research Center at Amirabad. When he arrived at Dr. Yazdani's office, the doctor was anxiously waiting. The General had called to say he was on the way.

"General, I've seen you more in the last week than in the last five years."

"Yes, Doctor, but these are troubled times," the General said, handing Dr. Yazdani the letter from the SNSC, showing Bu Hasa as the intended target.

The doctor read Admiral Mousavi's letter and frowned.

"What's the matter, Doctor?"

Looking up, Yazdani said, "Now I know what you want from me."

"And why is that a problem?"

The doctor sighed. "When you release radioactive material from your control, there can be unintended consequences."

"How is that, Doctor?"

"Well, for one thing, there can be accidents. Who will be given this material to carry out such a mission?"

"I will recommend that it be a trusted proxy that we've used before. We cannot use our own military, as that would constitute an act of war."

"And this would not?" asked the doctor. He could not believe what he was hearing from the General.

"No, it would be considered a terrorist act carried out by persons unknown and never traced back to Iran."

"But they could be captured entering or leaving the country, or get exposed to radiation, and go to a hospital for medical treatment and then be reported. And then the truth would eventually come out," said the doctor.

"No, they are committed to never be taken alive."

"But if these are terrorist mercenaries, how do you know they won't get a better offer once the material is in their hands?"

"I know their leader very well, and he won't double-cross us."

Dr. Yazdani sat quietly for a moment and then said, "It's possible that the SNSC will not approve such a risky plan."

He certainly expected SNSC to realize how dangerous such a plan could be.

"Of course, that is always a possibility," the General said. "However, they will consider all sides of the question and make the correct decision, don't you agree, Doctor?"

"Yes, of course," Dr. Yazdani said, not very enthusiastically. "But to protect the Nuclear Research Center, I will require a signed release by the Admiral before I turn over any material."

The General said, "Yes, of course," rather unhappily. "Assuming that the plan is approved, let's talk about what must be done over the next month or so to prepare."

"Yes, we can do that. Would you like some tea while we talk?"

"I think that would be very nice, thank you," said the General.

The doctor wondered if there was anything he could do to derail the General's plans. He sighed internally, knowing there was no good outcome no matter what he tried. With that thought, he put a kettle on for tea.

CHAPTER 20

THE GENERAL WAS sitting at his desk reading messages on his computer when there was a knock on his door. He looked up with a scowl on his face as Colonel Hashemi entered.

"Have you heard from the Admiral, sir?"

"Yes, and the SNSC is not happy about the assassination of Dr. Soltani. They, of course, are concerned for their own personal safety. They want to know what extra precautions we will take to ensure their security. And I don't know."

The Colonel shrugged his shoulders. "And what do they say about the Bu Hasa operation, sir?"

"They think it's more important now that we press ahead. Israel is sending us a message with the Soltani assassination, warning us not to attack them, but it is a matter of national pride that we do something, and taking action against the UAE is the best option we have."

"Is there anything you wish me to do, General?"

"No, not at the moment."

The Colonel saluted, turned, and left the General's office, closing the door softly.

The General shut the lid on his laptop computer and sat quietly at his desk, still scowling, thinking about the Bu Hasa reconnaissance. Then he called Dr. Yazdani.

Two days later, General Ghorbani met with the SNSC and presented his operational plan. He was not sure, but he suspected that Admiral Mousavi had talked with Dr. Yazdani before the meeting. Actually, that made the SNSC approval much easier because the council had the utmost respect for the physicist. It also meant that Mousavi's trust in the General would be bolstered since the General told them accurately everything he and Yazdani had discussed regarding drone capability and tactics.

There was a lot of discussion about using Hurras Ansar al-Haqq as the proxy to carry out the plan. But after considering all viewpoints, it was unanimously agreed the terrorist group was the best option, and all agreed that the risk was acceptable.

Dr. Yazdani received a call from the General on his secure phone and was advised the plan was approved. The doctor did not tell him of his discussion with the Admiral, but he thought to himself that he was now as responsible as the General if something went wrong.

"Doctor, I need you to complete your testing of the final design as soon as possible."

He obviously was talking about the new detonator, which must work across a greater distance as needed in the Bu Hasa complex, but was careful what he said, even over the secure line.

"General, we actually tested it successfully yesterday."

"Doctor, when can we do the training?"

"How about tomorrow?" replied the doctor.

"I'll be there at 10:00 a.m."

"What about the others?" asked the doctor.

"I will train them myself. We need to preserve security and the anonymity of our 'people.'"

"Then you are responsible for ensuring that they follow the instructions exactly."

"Yes, of course."

"See you tomorrow, General."

CHAPTER 21

THE GENERAL ARRIVED with Colonel Hashemi at Dr. Yazdani's office in the Nuclear Research Center at 10:00 a.m., just as scheduled. They were escorted to one of the laboratories, where they were met by the doctor and his assistant, Dr. Firuz Usmani, who, tall and gaunt, looked more like an undertaker than a scientist. Both doctors wore plain white lab coats, which made an interesting contrast to the General's dark green uniform, dripping with insignias and braids.

"Doctor, will you give me written instructions, or should I take notes?" asked the General.

"You will have digital instructions available on a tablet device we will give you," said the doctor. The General was impressed.

"We cannot train you to fly a drone here in the lab, but an army drone pilot will do that separately at the army's drone training station. Follow me, please," said the doctor.

Dr. Yazdani walked from his office down the hall to a set

of double doors, swiped an ID card, then entered a code into a keypad, releasing the doors, which opened automatically. They followed him inside and walked down a long hallway until they reached a door with a sign that read, "Packaging and Assembly." Again, he swiped his card, entered a code, and the door opened.

They walked to an open area in the center of the lab, with long work benches surrounding the open space on three sides. In the center was a low, stainless steel cart with a long handle like on a child's wagon.

On the cart was a stainless steel cylinder, about twelve inches in diameter and about the same height. On the top of the cylinder was mounted a black steel box with the number "1" stenciled in yellow paint.

Dr. Usmani explained as he showed the General a drawing, "We've ensured the RDD weight is a maximum of fifty pounds, per the drones' capability across the launch distance you provided. Each cylinder contains a small lead tube containing 22 grams of Cs-137, packed in two pounds of C-4 explosive. The lead shell encloses the tube, and the explosive weighs over forty pounds. More C-4 is packed around the lead shell, using shaped charges, and a stainless steel shell with an inner lead lining surrounding the outer layer of C-4. And there is the detonator, a blasting cap, embedded in the outer layer of C-4. The detonator control explodes the blasting cap, and the shock wave from the blasting cap causes the C-4 to explode. Any questions so far?"

"Is there only one device?" asked the General, looking around the lab.

"No, but we only need to show you one of them. We have four more just like this one," said Dr. Yazdani.

On one of the lab benches was another box about the size of an iPad but thicker. It had a touch screen, which Dr. Usmani turned on.

"This is the detonator activator module. You can detonate

all five devices from here. We can also set a permissible time range, meaning the detonator will only work during a certain time period, or set it to work only after a certain date and time. This also means that it can be set to act as a time bomb."

"That may give us some interesting options," mused the General.

"We can also set a minimum altitude if we don't want it to detonate at ground level. And we can set it to automatic mode on this screen, which means it will detonate automatically if all conditions are met."

"Who can set the detonation parameters?" asked the General.

"Dr. Yazdani is the only person who can set them. He will work with you to decide the individual parameters, but he is the only person who can set or change them."

"That is a wise precaution," said the General halfheartedly.

Dr. Yazdani smiled. But the General wondered what other security precautions, back doors, and/or trap doors the clever, and perhaps devious, Dr. Yazdani had built into the control device?

Most of these parameters and security protocols seemed to limit the use of the RDDs to their intended targets and not allow them to be used elsewhere. Dr. Yazdani was trying to provide some discipline once the devices were out of his control, but the General didn't like interference; he wanted to be solely in control.

"Can the parameters be changed from anywhere or only from the detonation activator device?" asked the General.

"Only from the detonation activator device," said Dr. Usmani.

"We will also set the agreed target geographical coordinates into the drone controllers to make them easier to fly accurately to the target. Each RDD will be matched to its own drone."

"Now there is one more screen — the battery screen. It shows the battery's charge status on the detonation activator and for each controller. If a battery runs down as low as fifty percent, we recommend recharging it. We suggest using a battery pack. You can charge the battery pack anywhere and then bring it to the RDD devices or to the controller to charge them in place. We'll give you several battery packs."

The General nodded and asked, "Are there any considerations in packing it for shipment?"

"It would be best to handle it carefully to prevent damage to the detonation control module. Otherwise, the only thing is that the radioactive material will generate heat that needs to be dissipated — not much. Still, you would want to ventilate the shipping container. There is information in the training material," said Dr. Usmani. "Any other questions?"

"No."

"Okay, then. Let's go look at the drone," said Dr. Usmani.

Once Dr. Usmani showed them how the drone worked and how the RDD would attach to it, he said, "I want to remind you, General, that it is essential to consider the wind conditions. We advise only detonating these devices when the wind is calm. Otherwise, the radioactivity might blow back into your face," said Dr. Yazdani.

The General thought wryly, *No, not into my face.* He nodded without commenting.

Dr. Usmani said, "You can arrange flight training with Colonel Keshavarz at the Army Drone Center. It should only take a day or two to gain the proficiency needed. Do you have any further questions, General?"

"How will you arrange the transfer of the devices and the drones to me?"

"We are ready as soon as you tell us where you would like delivery, assuming we have the authorization in writing from Admiral Mousavi," replied Dr. Yazdani. The General nodded.

"Any other questions, General?"

"Did you tell me you would give me the training information on an electronic device, Doctor?"

"Yes. It is all here," said Dr. Usmani, handing the General a device that looked like an iPad.

"And is there a passcode?"

"Yes, the code is 'Destruct.'"

"How appropriate. Thank you so much — both of you," said the General.

The two doctors escorted the General and the Colonel out of the laboratory to the entrance. They said their goodbyes and hurried to his waiting car. He was anxious to begin the training of Navid and his people.

∽

Dr. Usmani watched the General and the Colonel climb into the car's back seat with the driver and bodyguard in front, the escort car following right behind.

He turned and asked Dr. Yazdani, "Do you think they bought it?"

"Yes, I'm sure of it. Unfortunately, we don't have the technology on such short notice to put all the constraints we described on these RDDs. But, if they believe they are in place and thus train the proxies, that is enough.

"Yes, but do you think they had any idea the RDD didn't contain the actual Cs-137 capsule or the C-4?"

"No, of course not. But in case the General asked us to show him the radiation level with a Geiger counter, we did have enough radiation encapsulated to give a minimal reading. In the meantime, we'll need to decide how much Cs-137 and C-4 we'll actually provide in each RDD."

That was all true, but otherwise, Dr. Yazdani was lying through his teeth to his assistant. He actually had installed every one of those constraints with the help of Iranian engineering genius Dr. Rahim Ghanbarzadeh. Dr. G., as he was called, was a genius, all right, but had questionable ethics and morals, as Dr. Yazdani knew well. Therefore, they had reached an accommodation years ago.

Dr. Yazdani would allow Dr. G. to do what he wanted in his private life, though he should have reported him as a security risk. Dr. G. would, in turn, do whatever Dr. Yazdani wanted, encouraged by under-the-table payments from unaccounted slush funds provided by the Iranian government to Dr. Yazdani for secretive nuclear program development. And Dr. G would keep his mouth shut.

The most crucial feature Dr. G provided for this operation was the ability to change the detonator settings via the Iranian satellite network. In other words, they had lied to the General. They could change the settings at any time, if necessary, and there would be nothing the General could do.

CHAPTER 22

UPON ARRIVING AT the bank, the entire crew gathered in my office around the large conference table.

"Sharon's going to store all the disguises plus her equipment in Suite 303," Karen said, "then she'll head back to D.C. She'll come back as soon we need her. And thanks, Sharon, your disguises were great!" We all nodded and gave Sharon a little round of applause.

Karen continued, "The FBI has gotten back with information on the ConEd guy. He's a Russian mafia soldier named Oleg Volkov. ConEd reported that none of their people were working near the UN that day. So, the question is — who was Volkov waiting for? It might not have been for any of us, because how would he know we would be there? And the Russians would have never recognized any of you, so they couldn't have followed you. It doesn't make any sense. The most likely scenario is that Alex busted up an unrelated operation — and probably saved someone's life.

"The gun was stolen in Los Angeles several years ago. There were no other identifiable fingerprints on it, except for Alex's. Volkov was identified by facial recognition as a ninety-eight percent match using the photo Alex took.

"But we can't take chances, so we have to assume the Russians were looking for us until we know otherwise. After all, they attacked us before. For now, we'll stick around Natchez and stay vigilant. I've arranged for a few more resources to be added to the backup team. FBI agents Sterling Brown and Russ Chandler will arrive this week and will bunk with Agent Hart out in the carriage house.

"And I've talked with Tony. He admits he was wrong in exposing Grant to potential danger by sending him to New York. So he wants you, Grant, to lay low here until there's an active case."

So, Tony was really worried about me?

I had no problem hanging around Natchez tending to my business, enjoying life with Angie, and collecting my retainer. We'll see how long that lasts. Knowing Tony, not long.

Karen added, "Alex can practice at the gun range and teach Grant some self-defense moves. If you don't object, Grant, I'd like Alex to move in permanently with you and Angie."

I looked at Angie. She nodded and said, "That's okay with me. The more protection, the better."

Alex smiled weakly and said, "It's okay with me if it's okay with them."

Karen said, "Okay, that settles it then. I'll stay a few days, then I'm going back to D.C, and Craig will be in charge, as usual."

CHAPTER 23

GENERAL GHORBANI PRESENTED his plan for the Bu Hasa attack to the SNSC. It was approved — but with conditions. Admiral Mousavi provided the General with a confirming letter.

> *This is to confirm the approval of the Supreme National Security Council for your plan of attacking the Bu Hasa oil field of ADNOC in western Abu Dhabi with the following conditions:*

1. *The findings of your reconnaissance operation will be shared with the SNSC before final approval.*

2. *The route of the RDD devices to Abu Dhabi will avoid Saudi Arabia and Qatar.*

3. *The three million payment in euros and dollars will be made as follows: 50% in advance and 50% upon completion.*

4. *Final payment will be made only after the oil field is out of operation for two months.*

5. *General Farzad Ghorbani is responsible for successfully completing the attack and has full operational authority.*

6. *The SNSC will provide the necessary authorizations to Dr. Hossein Yazdani to prepare and release the working RDD devices to General Ghorbani and the proxy organization.*

7. *Due to the complexity of the operation, the deadline has been delayed to January 1.*

/signed/

Respectfully, Admiral Ahmad Mousavi, Secretary
Supreme National Security Council

The General was not happy that the Admiral and the other members of the SNSC had made him personally responsible if the mission failed.

And he didn't like their meddling in the operation by asking for reconnaissance details and placing restrictions on the movement of the RDD devices. However, he understood this was politics as usual — everyone covering their ass. And his rear end was hanging out there, especially since he was the one who failed to smooth over the Iranian relationship with the UAE.

CHAPTER 24

SEPTEMBER 21
NATCHEZ, MISSISSIPPI

I SAT AT my desk, staring out the window and thinking. I finally decided now was as good a time as any to talk with Alex.

"Alex, can you come over for a minute?" I shouted through the connecting door where Alex was talking with Craig.

"Yes, sure." Alex came through the door, and I gestured for him to sit in the chair next to my desk. Alex was dressed casually, with muscles filling the sleeves of his dark blue Polo shirt. He wore khaki pants with a skinny black belt, accentuating his slim waist. He was as fit as anyone you would ever hope to see.

"I want to thank you for your action to protect me — actually, all of us outside the UN. I'm impressed that you didn't hesitate when you saw a possible threat. We don't know if he was, but he could have been, which his Glock 17 proved."

"Well, I was just doing my job, right?" said Alex.

"Yes, but some people would have been more hesitant. But you were exactly right. You sized up the situation perfectly. I liked that, and I wanted to tell you personally."

"Thanks, Grant. I understand you have important work to do, and you might be a target, and that's why Ross sent me here — to protect you."

I had the impression that Alex was being sincere. He had been given a job and was just trying to do it.

"I think you're off to a good start fitting in with our team. If things keep going this way, we may ask that you stay longer than planned. What would you think about that?"

"Well, I'll do whatever Ross wants me to do. But, yes, I like everyone on the team. I'm not sure I would like this as a permanent assignment, but I'm all in as long as I'm here."

"I'm glad to hear that, Alex," I said. "You'll be living here for a while, so I want you to know that you can ask me anything about how people act around here — the social norms, the culture, the language they use, what they mean, or anything else. I think you know Natchez is my hometown. I've never lived in other parts of the world like you have. I'm kind of envious. But I know this place like the back of my hand. I'll be able to explain to you much better than anyone else on the team how it operates, so don't hesitate."

"Okay, that's fair. Thanks for the offer."

"We haven't had much of a chance to get to know each other. What's your background? I mean your family, where you grew up, what you want to do, what you like and don't like — that sort of thing," I said.

Alex settled back into his chair. "Well, I grew up in California, but I lost my parents when I was young — my father to an accident and my mother to a long illness. My grandmother raised me. She passed away a few years ago, so I don't have any family left."

"I'm just wondering . . . you appear to be a very eligible bachelor; I can't see why you're not married. I'd think most men who had lost their entire family would be anxious to start their own family."

"Well, if I had to explain myself, I'd say that I'm afraid if I do get married, I'll eventually lose her, and I can't go through the loss of family again."

"Yes, I can understand that. I lost my first wife to cancer," I explained, "but sometimes you have to take a risk in life to find happiness."

"Maybe you're right. I'll think about that."

"So what do you like and don't like?"

"I like people who are honest and straightforward. And I hate cucumbers."

I laughed.

"I suggest you tell Miss Doris about the cucumbers, otherwise, she'll think you don't like her cooking."

"I like Miss Doris," Alex said with a grin. "She seems straightforward and honest."

"Yes, she definitely is."

"Alex, what do you want to do a few years down the road?" I asked, my tone turning serious. "We won't be young forever. Have you thought about that?"

"Yes, but honestly, I haven't found the answer yet. But I envy those that have." Alex ran a hand through his hair, contemplating. "I figure the more life experiences I get in the here-and-now, then one day the answer will come to me."

"Fair enough. There's one more thing I want to talk with you about. You already know we deal with national security issues. You can never repeat what happens here to anyone, even Ross. I know he's your friend and our boss, but he lacks the security clearance to know what we're working on. Neither do you, but you might see and hear things."

"Yes, I understand that."

"Also, I need to keep a low profile here in Natchez. It's my home, and everyone around here knows me. So, unless it's absolutely necessary, don't use your gun or start an altercation.

We don't want to do anything that will draw attention to me. I don't want people to know that I work on national security or anything like that. They just need to think I'm a collectibles dealer, that I inherited the family money, and that I live quietly with Angie at Wexford House."

"I understand. I think Ross will respect that. He's pretty good at keeping his mouth shut, based on my experience with him in the military."

"Then I think everything will go smoothly," I said. "Thanks for taking a second to chat with me. Now I need to call a client and try to sell her something."

Alex smiled, got up from his chair, and went back next door.

I watched him leave, thinking that I liked what I knew of Alex so far. We would get along just fine working together.

CHAPTER 25

THE OVERNIGHT VOYAGE from Bandar Lengeh across the Persian Gulf to Dubai, less than one hundred miles, was uneventful.

Navid had sent Farzin to check out Bu Hasa's security. The General wanted to evaluate the security of the oil field and needed first-hand intelligence, but didn't trust the IRGC agent he employed in the UAE, Yousef Nair. Navid wanted to do his own intelligence, but he was both happy and wary to pair Farzin with the IRGC agent, as he explained to Farzin. That put Farzin on edge, because the agent would be his contact in Dubai, and he preferred to work alone.

Yousef Nair was a short, swarthy man in his fifties. Farzin had the distinct feeling that his father's warning should be heeded. Navid told Farzin to be very careful in his dealings with Yousef. According to the General, Yousef was an undercover UAE intelligence officer, but Yousef decided years ago that if he was clever enough, he could double his earnings by also being an agent for the IRGC.

The man had the uncanny ability to blend into his surroundings and never be noticed. Yousef's family was politically well-connected and of Iranian descent, but had lived in Dubai for many generations and became Emirati citizens when the UAE was formed in 1971. The fact that Yousef was a Shi'ite Muslim, while the Emirates was overwhelmingly Sunni, suited the UAE State Security agency. They wanted to have a window into the Emirati Shi'ite community as that was where they thought security threats were most likely to arise.

Farzin definitely did not have a good initial impression of Yousef. He did not seem trustworthy. Maybe it was his forced smile. Maybe it was because he was overly friendly. Maybe it was because he was a double agent. But if Yousef made a wrong move, Farzin had his knife ready and would use it.

They had made contact the day before, soon after Farzin, to be known as Abdullah while with Yousef, had arrived in Dubai, and now were on their way to Bu Hasa, under the guise of Yousef's cover as a food service delivery driver.

He made regular deliveries to many businesses and government installations around Abu Dhabi, including the Bu Hasa oil field operation. This allowed him access to many secure places on a regular basis and allowed regular interactions with many different people. He had a network of informants that he had cultivated over the years, most of them in the non-Emirati population that kept the UAE economy humming along.

Farzin was dressed appropriately in the clothes that Yousef had given him: a uniform with the logo of Al Sayyad Food Service Distributors on the pocket. The shirt was dark blue, the pants khaki, with a dark blue baseball cap decorated with the Al Sayyad logo.

The landscape they passed through was limited to monotonous, undulating sand as far as the eye could see. Then suddenly they cleared a rise and approached a security checkpoint, which was a structure that covered the entire road for a length of about 150 feet with one lane in each direction. On each side of the checkpoint, Farzin could see a ten foot high chain-link fence with razor wire at the top extending far into the distance. He wondered what type of vehicle could actually navigate the terrain. He suspected that even a four-wheel drive vehicle would just sink down into the sand.

"What type of truck can drive across the sand, Yousef?"

"Only tracked vehicles, but sometimes, only camels can do it, my friend."

As they got closer, they saw that the road widened to two lanes in their direction, and there were three alternating rows of thick stainless security bollards across one lane and then the other. Every vehicle had to slow down to weave around the rows of bollards. Farzin thought, *So much for ramming through the barrier.*

They entered the enclosure, and an armed guard closed the heavy gate behind them. The double rows of exit gates in front of them were also closed. One of the guards had a mirror on the end of a long pole, which he used to look under the truck for a bomb or hidden cargo.

Meanwhile, the guard who seemed to be in charge approached the driver's window. Yousef lowered the window.

"*Sabah al-khayr*, Yousef!"

"*Sabah al-khayr*, Ali!"

"Who is with you today?" asked the guard.

"This is Abdullah," Yousef replied.

Farzin sat quietly and listened to the conversation.

"But why is he with you, Yousef?"

"He's training to be my backup when I'm off work for illness or vacation, my friend."

"You know we are supposed to have prior notification of visitors, Yousef."

"You weren't notified?" asked Yousef.

"No, there is no record of it."

"I can't take responsibility for my boss's error, Ali. Abdullah is supposed to help me make deliveries today in the Camp, so he will know what to do when he is on his own. You want your fresh fish delivered on time, right?"

"Yes, of course, but he's going to have to come back another day."

"Ali, we've known each other a long time. I'll vouch for Abdullah. We have a long history, right?" Yousef put an emphasis on the words "long history," Farzin noticed. "And I don't want to take this fish all the way back to Abu Dhabi City."

"Well, let me check your identity card. Step out of the truck, Abdullah."

Farzin climbed down from the truck. He had the forged identity card in his hand. He was fortunate that he spoke Arabic almost as well as he spoke Farsi. Though they basically used the same alphabet, they sounded very different and were from different language families. In any case, Navid made sure his sons were prepared to travel and do business throughout the Middle East. They even understood and could speak English, though not as well as Arabic, but they could get by.

Ali looked at the photo on the card, then at Farzin to see if he matched the photo. He was satisfied.

"I'll have to run your ID card to make sure. Please step over here with me."

The guard went over to a card reader device and inserted the card. The device read the chip on the card. He pointed to the fingerprint scanner. Farzin hesitated for a moment but knew that he had no choice. And he knew this was a critical moment. He put the tip of his right index finger on the scanner. A green light lit on the card reader, and "Valid" showed on the display. His knees went weak with relief.

"Okay, you may pass, but stay with Yousef — don't wander around." Farzin nodded.

Yousef said, "I almost forgot, Ali. I have something for you in the back."

He went to the back of the truck, unlocked and raised the door, and pulled out a small bag that contained two cartons of Marlboro cigarettes and handed the bag to Ali.

Ali smiled and said, "Thank you, my friend," then peered around inside the cold truck stacked to the roof with boxes, without really making any effort to see what was buried further inside.

"Okay, you may proceed."

"*Ma'a salama!*" said Yousef.

"*Ma'a salama!*" replied Ali.

"*Shukran Jazeelan!*" said Farzin.

When they were on their way again, Farzin said, "How close was I to being arrested?"

"Never, Abdullah. Those are the games we play. He wants me to know that he did me a favor by letting you through, and I want him to know that the bribes he has accepted in the past make him vulnerable, so he needs to cooperate. And I knew the Emirates ID card would not be a problem. The IRGC, with help from their friends, have a reliable way to create fake cards and also to enter data into the Emirati's 'foolproof' system." Yousef laughed, but Farzin was not amused. They drove for several miles through the desert on the two-lane highway toward the Bu Hasa Camp.

"If this is a huge oil field, why don't we see any oil rigs, Yousef?"

"I've heard that much of the oil well infrastructure is underground to protect it from the corrosive effects of the sand, but I don't really know. The oil field collection lines all come together at the Camp for initial processing and separation of the oil from the gas. Then the gas and oil are sent through separate pipelines to Ruwais for further processing. It's my understanding that the crude oil pipelines to Ruwais are underground and the gas pipelines are above ground, but I have no understanding of the reason. You will see a lot of large and impressive equipment at the Camp. It's less than five miles ahead."

A few minutes later, the truck topped a large rise in the dunes, and Camp Bu Hasa was laid out in front of them.

"Well, there it is," said Yousef.

"Explain to me what I'm seeing."

"There are three main sections to the Camp. The first, on the main road, is a residential development that includes apartments, a cafeteria, a school, a grocery store, and a mosque. Actually, the cafeteria and grocery store share a commissary/ warehouse. Then there is a road leading off to the left, which is the older part of the Camp. It has more housing, another cafeteria, a grocery store, and a commissary/warehouse. It also has a mosque. There is also row after row of equipment storage buildings and other buildings used for repair and maintenance operations. Then straight ahead, another three miles in the distance, are the actual oil and gas processing and transmission operations."

As they got closer, Farzin could see a large tank farm, each tank as large as an office building. He could also see several towers of some sort, perhaps telecommunications, but it was too far away to make out any details.

Farzin checked his phone again; the signal was still strong.

"We'll deliver to the residential commissary first," Yousef said.

As they made their deliveries, Farzin took everything in. He had not seen a place to detonate a bomb that would affect the oil field operation — at least not yet. He had also decided that he definitely didn't like Yousef; he didn't believe he could be trusted. Farzin thought Yousef was too confident. He wondered if the man had already betrayed him. He would be happy to see the last of him, and the sooner, the better.

They'd made two deliveries, and more bribes, before arriving at a security checkpoint of the same design as the earlier one, about a mile from the operational complex. They pulled into the covered structure and this time was greeted by a man named Mahmood. Another armed security guard was already checking under the truck with the mirror on the pole.

"*Ahlan wa sahlan, Mahmood,*" said Yousef.

"*Ahlan bik, Yousef,*" replied Mahmood.

"I brought a trainee today, Mahmood. This is Abdullah."

"Yes, I know. I heard from Ali. That's fine, but I'll need to check his ID again — standard procedure."

Farzin produced his Emirates ID and again had his fingerprint checked on the scanner. He passed.

Meanwhile, Yousef had opened the back of the truck for Mahmood to look inside. He quickly scanned the contents, which now was only about one third full, but still held an impressive wall of boxes.

Yousef said, "Mahmood, I brought something for you, my friend."

He handed him a bag with two cartons of Marlboros, the same as he had given Ali and the other guards.

"Thank you for your kindness."

Farzin scanned the security enclosure for cameras and other equipment. He saw several cameras but nothing else, such as radiation detectors. He was surprised that they didn't randomly check for explosive residue on the vehicle, contents, or the visitors. Apparently, Yousef was such a frequent and well-known visitor, he was not considered a threat and was taken for granted.

Yousef and Farzin climbed back into the truck, said goodbye to Mahmood and, as soon as the exit gates were opened, headed for the operations section of the Camp.

As they got closer, Farzin began to realize the immense scale of the operation. The tanks, which seemed large from a distance, now looked huge. Fortunately, Farzin had done some research so that he would recognize the processing equipment. This was the part of the Camp they would need to put out of operation.

Just to the left of the huge tanks was a row of more than a dozen large diameter stainless steel flash separation columns glittering in the hot sun, at least a hundred feet tall, each set almost a hundred feet apart from the next, amid all sorts of pipes, pumps, and other equipment. These flash columns, under high pressure, split the mixture collected from the wells into individual gas and crude oil streams for storage and subsequent transmission. To the right of the tanks was a maze of electrical power equipment, pipes, compressors, and pumps — working together to send the gas and crude oil through the large transmission lines to the Ruwais petrochemical complex, about seventy miles away.

It was an enormous processing, storage, and distribution operation, and the entirety of it would need to be the primary target of the radiological dispersal device. The crude oil and gas processed through Bu Hasa was equal to almost one million barrels a day and billions of dollars a year for the UAE treasury.

CHAPTER 26

NAVID HADN'T GOTTEN much sleep since Farzin had come back and given him the news that Bu Hasa would likely be a suicide mission. He'd seen no place to explode a bomb that would be effective, except deep in the complex. Farzin had mentioned the cell signal was excellent throughout Bu Hasa. He was hoping that one large drone might be an alternative, but the distances, coupled with the weight, seemed too great. And there would be no way to plant a bomb, escape the area, and detonate it remotely. Whoever detonated it had to be on site.

Now that he had an established cover, Farzin was the only person who could get a truck into the Bu Hasa site with the "dirty bomb." But Navid couldn't think of a way to explode the bomb and get Farzin out safely.

Navid sighed. He wanted the money offered by the General, and he knew that rumors would spread through the terrorist underworld that al-Haqq had pulled off the Bu Hasa attack. It would allow Hurras Ansar al-Haqq to become one of the most important and feared terrorist organizations in the Middle East. And it would be a step toward realizing his ultimate dream of unleashing such devastating attacks on Iraq and the US troops supporting them, that the Shi'ite could establish rule over Iraq. But he couldn't ask Farzin to sacrifice himself.

Finally, an alternate plan came to him. Why not take the fifty percent advance payment, one and a half million, and then sell the "dirty bomb" to the highest bidder? Surely, if he chose a sympathetic terrorist organization, he could ensure the target for the radioactive material would be one of his enemies. He felt sure he could get much more than the 1.5 million final payment. More likely, he could get five or ten million, maybe even more. But he would have to disappear from Iran, and his family, too — forever. He thought, *That wouldn't actually be so bad.*

But first, he needed to decide what to tell the General.

The bookstore was a small shop with a few couches and chairs amid the many tall shelves of books. A clerk sat at a desk near the front door, looking at his phone and glancing up occasionally at the few customers who were perusing the shelves or sitting on the couches reading.

Navid walked into the store, stepped up to the desk, and said, "I'm here to see Mr. Ahmadi. He's expecting me."

The clerk led Navid through a curtain into the back room. The General was waiting on a couch in the small space.

Farzad stood and said, "*Salaam alaykum,*" and grabbed Navid's left arm, shook his left hand, and kissed him on both cheeks.

Navid responded, "*Salaam alaykum*" and kissed Farzad on both cheeks.

The General said, "What did you learn at Bu Hasa?"

Navid told him what Farzin had seen, then said, "We believe

we can get an RDD all the way to the operational compound in the truck and then detonate it. But it'll be a suicide mission for the driver. And with only one large device, the entire mission will likely fail if anything goes wrong. I would propose delivering one device by truck, setting it off at the operational compound, primarily as a diversion, though it will cause some contamination by itself. Then a few minutes after the diversion, send in multiple drones from outside the furthest perimeter fence to detonate above the operational site and contaminate everything. All these actions will need to be closely coordinated, but luckily we found that Bu Hasa has excellent cell phone service.

"The drones will be carried by a second truck, which will be unloaded at least a half mile outside the first security checkpoint. The drones will disperse over the operational complex and detonate the RDDs. It would take about ten minutes for the drones to reach their targets. We probably won't be able to handle more than four drones with one truck, though.

"It will make sense to use the smallest drones possible. Dr. Yazdani will have to tell us if a drone with a fifty-pound maximum payload can handle the weight of the radioactive material, the lead shielding, the C-4, and the detonator. You said the IRGC has drones of that capacity, right?"

"Yes, but why not just send in the drones and forget about the suicide mission?" asked the General.

"Because we need to get as close to the first checkpoint as possible before deploying the drones, and a diversionary explosion will make it less likely the unloading and deployment of the drones will be noticed. Also, if the drones are seen flying toward the operations area, they will be assumed to be part of the emergency response effort," replied Navid.

"But won't the diversionary explosion draw more people and cause more deaths?"

"No, not really. Anyone close enough to respond to the initial blast would have been exposed to radiation by the drone explosions, anyway."

"How will you get the RDDs and drones to the UAE?"

"We'll ship them in the same style wooden crates we use to smuggle rugs. The ship's captain won't ask any questions, and neither will the people we regularly bribe in the port. And we'll add our team to the ship's crew, with all the proper credentials. The Captain might object, but a little more money will ease his concerns."

"Okay, then, I'll ask Dr. Yazdani about the fifty-pound drone payload. If he says it's feasible, then we have an operational plan to recommend. If not, then a single truck bomb seems like the only other option," said the General.

"Yes, that's right. Let me know."

Navid noted that Farzad didn't ask anything about the suicide bomber or show any concern about the welfare of the other team members. His only concern was the mission — the sacrifice of dedicated and loyal people didn't bother him at all — or, sadly, even enter his mind.

CHAPTER 27

I LOOKED UP from the gems I was examining when Craig walked into my office. "Karen wants to talk with us privately." Alex took the hint and went over to Craig's office. I called Karen's mobile phone.

"Grant, I have some bad news," Karen said. "Tony can't stand the fact that you're here doing nothing and he's paying you a big fat retainer. Since you were 'introduced' to four world leaders at the UN, he wants you to probe their minds to see if you can find anything interesting."

I frowned, not liking that idea at all. "He knows that's not what I signed up to do."

"Yes, but you know Tony."

"Then I'll call him."

"Okay, that's what I thought you'd say. Good luck, and let me know what you work out."

I wasn't happy with Tony. He's always trying to push the

boundaries, trying to get a little extra in every situation. I decided to put him in his place this time.

After a few minutes to compose myself, I dialed Tony's phone number. Tony answered, while Craig listened.

"Yes, Grant. I suppose you talked with Karen, am I correct?"

"You're damn right. When we agreed to my personal services contract, it was on the basis that I would use my abilities to help defeat identified security threats against the United States. I didn't agree to go out and try to find threats. No, you would identify the threats, and I would do my best to help defeat them. That was what I agreed to do. Don't you respect anyone's privacy? What if I searched your mind? How would you like that? You remember that I can quit at any time, right?"

"All right, calm down," said Tony.

"There's no reason to think that Israel, Iran, Russia, or the UK have any threats underway against us — is there?"

"No, but they might, we just don't know it yet. And maybe the Russian that Alex flattened is an indication. He was waiting for you to leave the UN, right?"

"We don't know why he was there."

"Well, okay."

"If you want me to do something useful, why can't I go to 'The Farm' for training? You promised."

"Because I talked to the superintendent and he said that it would be disruptive. They now train classes of agents together in teams for the entire curriculum, and you don't need to know most of what they're teaching. Just work with Alex on self-defense techniques. That's what you need."

"Okay, I'll do that. So, you're not expecting any more from me on the four world leaders, right?"

"No, you made a good point, so forget it — for now. If we have reason to suspect a threat from any of them, I'll get back to you."

"All right, Tony."

"I'll talk to you soon. Bye," and Tony hung up.

I just shook my head. *Same old Tony.*

Craig said, "Well done, Grant. I'll talk to Alex. I think we can set up Suite 304 as a training room."

"That sounds like a good plan. Let's do it."

If I couldn't train at 'The Farm,' I'd do what I could in Natchez. And self-defense seemed like a useful thing to learn. I didn't want to be a field agent. I wanted to just stay right here in Natchez, under the radar, and be involved only when necessary. But I knew that I could be in danger at any time, so I needed to be ready. I wished I had never agreed to work with Tony, but here we are until I can find a way out. In the meantime, I need to be able to live safely, and as normally as possible.

CHAPTER 28

SVR HEADQUARTERS WAS located in a large secure compound just outside the Moskovskaya Kol'tsevaya Avtomobile'naya Doroga — better known as the MKAD — the outermost Moscow Ring Road, about sixteen miles south of the Kremlin in the Yasenevo District.

The SVR was the foreign intelligence service of the Russian Federation, comparable to the CIA, and reported directly to the Russian President, unlike the better-known GRU, which was part of the Russian military. Importantly, the SVR was responsible for providing personal security for Russian government officials and their families. And they also handled foreign intelligence operations, including assassinations.

Mikhail Belyaev, Director of the SVR, awaited a visit from General Alexei Galkin, Deputy Director and Chief of Directorate S, famously responsible for planting and handling "illegals" in America and other countries.

Director Belyaev had been a KGB field agent, and he

thought of himself as old school, very old school. He had a commanding presence. He was exceptionally tall, with a head full of curly hair, and built like a bear — but his most prominent feature was his bushy black eyebrows. He was sixty-five years old.

There was a knock on the door. "Come in."

Deputy Director Galkin walked into the large office, and Belyaev motioned him to take a seat at the conference table.

Alexei Galkin was younger — part of the new generation. He was trim, energetic, and handsome, and he had a distinguished military background.

Belyaev walked over and sat down with his elbows on the long mahogany conference table, his hands clasped in front of him. "What is it, Alexei?"

"I want to report a very odd occurrence in New York and ask your direction."

"Yes, what is it?"

"On the day that President Drozdov spoke to the United Nations, one of our operatives was attacked outside the UN."

"What happened? He wasn't killed, or I would have already heard about it."

"No, a man walked up to him and punched him in the face — knocked him out — then ran away. Our agent was part of the usual security detail we post in the area whenever the President is visiting the UN. It makes no sense for anyone to do something like that, so we investigated."

The Director nodded. "And what did you find?"

"We were able to access security video from the UN, and we saw that the man who attacked our agent had exited the UN just before the attack. Then he was joined by two others, a man and a woman. They ran down the street to the Millennium Hotel and grabbed a taxi. We contacted the taxi company and found out they were dropped off at Times Square and then picked up another cab, which dropped them at the Surrey Hotel. We sent a man posing as a police detective to the hotel. He was able to obtain two days' worth of security video, and after analysis, we found that the three were wearing disguises. We narrowed them down to a group that arrived the day before. Using facial recognition, we found the group included Grant Markey."

"That name is familiar." Belyaev rested his chin in his hands, thinking.

"Yes, he has a connection to CIA Director Tony Russell. We think he's a CIA agent, and we believe he has some special skill we don't quite understand. Because of China's interest in him, we tried and failed to kidnap him several years ago, and our agent, Irina Rachkova, was killed during the operation. The CIA obviously considers him a valuable asset and has assigned him a permanent protective detail."

"Yes, now I remember him. And I remember Agent Rachkova's unfortunate demise. Go ahead — is there more?" Belyaev stared at Galkin. He wondered if this would lead him down a rathole. He knew that Galkin wanted his job, so he was wary.

"Well, Grant Markey was at the UN when President Drozdov addressed the General Assembly. And then our agent was attacked, so there must be some connection. We would like to resume surveillance of Grant Markey. Perhaps we should even develop a new plan to capture him?"

"But there were other world leaders speaking that day, right? Maybe this was a more random event than you think. Maybe our agent threatened him in some way?"

"No, sir, he just walked up and punched him for no reason. We have it on video."

Belyaev was skeptical. "He had a reason; we just don't know what it was. And I would like to see that video." He looked at Galkin for a reaction, but there was none.

But then he said, "Surveillance on Markey is probably a good idea, but not another kidnapping attempt, not yet anyway."

"Yes, sir. We will activate the surveillance."

"Good, keep me informed, Alexei. And make sure I see that video." Belyaev wanted to see for himself if he could determine if it was a setup of some kind by Galkin. One could never be too careful.

Galkin nodded, stood up, turned, and left the Director's office.

Belyaev watched him leave and wondered what this was all about. He thought that Deputy Director Galkin was probably jumping to conclusions. But he was well aware of CIA Director Tony Russell's ability to get the best of Russia in every encounter. He wondered if there was more to this than met the eye, but he didn't know yet what that could be.

CHAPTER 29

I was at my desk studying an auction catalog of Royal Doulton china figurines. One of my regular clients loves these figurines, and is willing to pay exorbitant prices for those she likes. Now she wants me to find her the rare Alexander the Great figurine by Royal Doulton. The one with Alexander riding his famous horse, Bucephalus, mounted on a leopard skin saddle. You don't even want to know what that figurine would cost — if you could find one. This is the kind of work that I really like to do.

There was a loud buzz letting me know someone was at the door.

I got up from my desk, walked over, and checked the security video display on the wall next to the door.

I opened the door. "Hi, honey. I thought you weren't coming to the office until later." I gave Angie a kiss and ushered her in.

"I thought you might want to see this as soon as possible."

She handed me an official-looking envelope. The return

address was "Circuit Clerk, Adams County Circuit Court, 314 State Street, Natchez, MS."

The letter was addressed to Grant Markey, IV. It read,

Dear Sir,

As a registered voter, you have been randomly selected for jury duty, serving in the Adams County Circuit Court, beginning October 5, for up to one month. Please call the number below after 3:00 p.m. on October 4 to determine if you must report at 8:00 a.m. the next day. You will receive more instructions when you call. If you have questions, please contact the Circuit Clerk's office, or read the information for jurors posted on the Circuit Clerk's website.

/signed/ Adams County Circuit Clerk

I handed the letter to Angie. After reading, she frowned — obviously concerned. "You better show Craig and Karen. Tony's not going to like this."

We entered through the connecting door into Craig's office in Suite 302.

Sitting at his desk and looking at his computer screen, Craig glanced up. "What's up?"

"Jury duty, starting in about two weeks." I handed Craig the letter, which he quickly read.

"Oh, that's a problem. Karen's not going to like it, and neither will Tony."

"That's what Angie said, but it's my civic duty."

"Guns aren't allowed in the courtroom or the jury room, so how can we protect you?"

"Well, I guess you'll figure that out. I can't get out of jury duty without a legitimate reason. I think serving will help maintain my cover as an ordinary citizen of Natchez."

Tony and the other top US government officials, including President William Cameron, who were aware of my psychic ability, had concluded after the first successful mission that the more they used me, the bigger the risk that I would be in danger. They were trying to keep me under wraps as much as possible. But as far as I was concerned, jury duty would reinforce the idea that I was just like every other citizen of Natchez.

"All right, we've got less than two weeks to figure it out, but we need to tell Karen now and maybe involve Tony, too."

Craig called Karen at her office in D.C. She quickly answered.

"Hi, Craig, what's up? It's not like you to call instead of text."

"You're on the speaker with me, Grant, and Angie. Grant got summoned for jury duty in about two weeks. He thinks he should report as instructed instead of trying to pull strings to get excused. We won't be able to carry guns in the courtroom or be outside the jury room, so I'm concerned about his security. Also, he won't be available during the month he's on call. And he definitely won't be able to travel."

"The jurors, as well as the deputy sheriffs and bailiffs, are all local residents, right?" Karen asked.

"Yeah, I guess they are."

"Well, then, they won't pose any risk. The only issue will be entering and exiting the building, plus the risk that a foreign agent could smuggle a weapon into the courtroom. And you'll be sitting outside the courtroom watching everyone who enters, correct?"

"Yes, that's right."

"That seems to be an acceptable level of risk to me. I agree with Grant that he needs to preserve his cover. I'll let Tony know and get back to you if he disagrees. He won't like Grant not being available while he's at the courthouse, but I think he'll have to live with it."

Craig hung up the phone. "It looks like you're going to be a juror, Grant."

I smiled but, on second thought, worried just a little. Maybe being a juror wasn't a good idea if Craig couldn't be right there in the courtroom, protecting me as always.

But I wanted to lead a normal life — with Angie. If I could figure a way out of this arrangement with Tony, I would take it, but not at the cost of jeopardizing Angie. I'd be happy if we could live normally and safely in Natchez for the rest of our lives. That's what I really wanted.

CHAPTER 30

THE GENERAL SAT in the back of the bookstore, waiting for Navid. While he waited, he carefully assessed the situation. The technical capability for the attack was now in place. The missing piece was the execution, which depended on the human element. He was convinced he could trust Navid, but how competent was Navid's team?

He was willing to give Navid's sons the benefit of the doubt. But how many others would be involved? And what about other third parties, like the ship captain? There was always risk.

On the other hand, he had to redeem himself for his failure with the UAE. If not, he could not predict what might happen to him. He surely would be replaced, but would that be the only humiliation? Some members of the SNSC, especially the Admiral, were itching to take his place as IRGC-Quds commander.

There was no better option. He would need to take his chances on this operation and with Navid's team.

He had mixed feelings about his friend, Navid. Farzad did

not have a family. He was not married unless you could say he was married to the Army. His whole life had been dedicated to his advancement through the ranks. Now that he was at the top of his profession, he was dedicated to keeping his status and protecting his reputation. He saw that Navid had a family, but it brought him a lot of heartaches. He thought on balance, he preferred his life to Navid's — as long as he could maintain it.

At 3:00 p.m., Navid pushed open the curtain to the back room, and the General got up to exchange hellos.

Once they'd greeted each other, Navid asked, "And why did you want to see me so urgently?"

"The operation has been approved. I have seen one of the devices, and I've been trained on how to detonate it. I also saw one of the drones — large and impressive. Now we're ready to train you and your team."

"I think it's best if you train only me, Baraz, and Farzin. We will train others as needed."

"Yes, that makes sense. When can you be available?"

"I don't know how fast Baraz can get here. He's in western Iraq or maybe Syria. I'll find out and let you know. It will probably be a few days, maybe longer."

The General frowned. "I want to keep things moving along."

Navid spread his arms wide, palms out. "There's nothing I can do. He'll get here as soon as he can."

"All right then, I'll take a chance and give you the training material now. After you, Farzin, and Baraz review it, we can get together to answer any questions you have."

He reached down and picked up a bag with a handle. He took out an iPad from the bag and handed it to Navid.

"The password is 'Destruct,'" he said.

Navid turned on the iPad, entered the password, and waited for the home screen. Once he was satisfied he could navigate through the contents, he turned it off.

"I see that it includes videos, drawings, and written material. The videos should make it much easier for us to understand."

The General nodded.

"And when can we take possession of the devices and the drones?"

"Almost immediately after the training, probably within a few days. Where will you store them?"

"I have a small warehouse for my rugs in Qom. I'll keep them there. But it would be better not to take possession until just before we move. Otherwise, I'll have to post guards, which will draw attention."

"Yes, that's a good point."

"So when will I get the upfront payment? I need money to make my arrangements." Navid sounded demanding, which was not normal.

The General paused and thought about the demand for payment. Navid did not usually worry so intensely about when payments would be made. He wondered why he was so anxious. The arrangements couldn't cost that much. He said, "Not until after the training — maybe not until you take delivery. I need to get approval for the payment from the SNSC."

Then he thought perhaps Navid reasoned that as soon as he got directly involved with the radioactive devices, he accepted personal risk and wanted to be paid upfront for that risk. That made sense to him, so he put it out of his mind. He decided not to confront Navid; he was now too dependent on him.

"I'll push the SNSC to authorize the payment as soon as possible."

The General stood, and they embraced and said their good-byes. The General slipped out the back door.

CHAPTER 31

OCTOBER 8
NATCHEZ, MISSISSIPPI

THE SEATS IN the jury box were not very comfortable. I supposed that's intentional and intended to keep jurors like me awake.

So here I was, seated in the front row of the jury box. I was juror #5 in the case of Leroy Allen McDaniel, being prosecuted in the Adams County Circuit Court on the charge of aggravated assault with a switchblade knife.

I was selected as a juror on my first jury duty three days ago. I was sure Tony was happy because jury duty would end soon, and I'd again be on standby.

The judge, Julia Wickham, was a large and imposing figure in her black robe, with a head full of curly white hair that looked like one of the powdered wigs worn in English courts. She seemed even more formidable when she peered out into the courtroom, and at the jury, over the top of her black-framed reading glasses. This lady wouldn't be taking any crap.

The defendant, Leroy McDaniel, had been sitting at the

defendant's table during *voir dire* — the jury selection process. Today he was in the same seat, looking just as ill at ease.

No defendant could have looked more guilty. He was a tall, wiry man, about fifty years old, with short reddish-blond hair, shifty eyes, and a guilty look on his face, though he had defiantly pled "not guilty." He was dressed in an ill-fitting blue suit and bright yellow tie that looked utterly out of place, no doubt chosen by his attorney, who was dressed just as badly. I guess that's what you get if you have to use a public defender.

Judge Wickham rapped her gavel and said, "Good morning, ladies and gentlemen. I'm now calling the case of the People of the State of Mississippi versus Leroy Allen McDaniel. Are both sides ready?"

"Ready for the People, Your Honor," the prosecutor for the state, Jed Duvall, said.

The defense attorney, Richard Bagwell, a local attorney appointed by the court, said, "Ready for the defense, Your Honor."

Judge Wickham said, "Will the clerk please swear in the jury?"

"Will the jury please stand and raise your right hand?"

We all stood in front of our chairs in the jury box.

"Do each of you swear that you will fairly try the case before this court and that you will return a true verdict according to the evidence and the court's instructions, so help you, God? Please say, 'I do.'"

We all said, "I do."

As soon as the formalities were over and we were seated again, the judge said, "Ladies and gentlemen of the jury, I want to clarify one point of law before the trial begins. It is not illegal in Mississippi to carry a switchblade knife except by a convicted felon, which Mr. McDaniel is not. And remember, the defendant is presumed innocent until proven guilty."

Judge Wickham said, "I want to caution the jury that the

opening statements should not be considered evidence. They are an opportunity for the lawyers to tell you how they will present their case. Mr. Duvall, you may make your opening statement."

Duvall took a final look at his notes, then stood to his full height of well over six feet and buttoned his tailored charcoal pinstriped suit. He had a full head of dark, almost black hair, recently cut and styled. He was well aware of his ability to make a favorable impression on the jurors, and he used it to full advantage.

Duvall stepped into the aisle next to his chair, turned to the jury, and said, "Ladies and gentlemen of the jury, the People will prove through eyewitness testimony that Leroy Allen McDaniel did inflict serious injury on Robert Guthrie with a switchblade knife, a deadly weapon, on the evening of May 20 and is, therefore, guilty of the charge of aggravated assault."

His statement was short and sweet.

He then returned to his seat and sat down, looking extremely confident.

"Mr. Bagwell, you may make your opening statement," said the judge.

Richard Bagwell struggled to stand, probably from being fifty pounds overweight. His thick brown hair stuck out in all directions. He was much older than Duvall and was quite rumpled in his brown suit.

He stood in place and said in a carefully rehearsed but authentic Mississippi vernacular, "Ladies and gentlemen of the jury, we'll show y'all that Mr. McDaniel acted in his own self-defense. The People, therefore, cain't prove their case, and Mr. McDaniel s'not guilty."

He sat down slowly, supporting himself with his hands on the defense table, with a look of pain on his face. It seemed to me that he had connected with many on our jury of ordinary Adams County citizens — among them two farmers, a factory worker, a horse trainer, a housewife, a mechanic, and two shopkeepers — people who felt especially comfortable with Bagwell's folksy demeanor.

Judge Wickham said, "Mr. Prosecutor, call your first witness."

Duvall stood and said, "The People call Officer James Watkins."

Officer Watkins, a large black man in his mid-fifties, wearing the uniform of the Natchez Police, strode to the witness stand very confidently and waited to be administered the witness oath.

Once Watkins had settled on the stand, Duvall walked and asked, "Officer Watkins, did you arrest the defendant, Mr. McDaniel, at the Magnolia Bluffs Casino, 7 Roth Hill Road, Natchez, Mississippi, on the night of Wednesday, May 20?"

"Yes, sir, that's right."

"Please tell us what happened."

"I was called to the casino at 9:15 p.m. after the report of a disturbance. I was only a few blocks away, and I was down there at the river within about three minutes."

"And what did you find when you arrived?"

"The defendant was being held down by a security guard and several customers, and the other security guard, Mr. Guthrie, had been slashed and was bleeding profusely. Two witnesses said the defendant had slashed the guard," replied Officer Watkins.

"Officer, will you point out the man you arrested at the casino?"

"Yes, sir, he's the man sitting at the defendant's table in the blue suit."

McDaniel glared at the officer. Officer Watkins stared back dismissively.

Duvall said, "That's all, Your Honor," and walked back to his seat.

The judge asked, "Cross-examination?"

"No questions, Your Honor, ma'am," Bagwell said.

Judge Wickham said, "Thank you, Officer, you may step down," and Officer Watkins left the witness stand and walked out of the courtroom.

"The People call Mrs. Susie Langis to the stand."

A well-dressed lady in her seventies walked cautiously to the witness stand and was administered the witness oath.

"Mrs. Langis," Duvall began, "please tell us what you saw at the casino on the night of May 20 that led to the arrest of Mr. McDaniel."

"Well, George — that's my husband — and I like to go to the casino once a week to play the slot machines, usually on Wednesday evening. My husband had taken a smoke break outside, and I was at the slot machines by myself when I heard a commotion. The defendant had been playing the slot machines in the same area, and he was smoking cigarettes, which isn't allowed. Actually, I had moved away from him earlier because the smoke was bothering me. But suddenly, I heard him yelling, 'No, you can't tell me to do that, and I'm not going to do it,' and then I turned and saw them."

"And who did you see, Mrs. Langis?"

"I saw Mr. McDaniel and one of the casino employees yelling at each other. The casino employee was telling Mr. McDaniel that he couldn't smoke inside the casino and that he had to go outside."

"Mrs. Langis, will you point out Mr. McDaniel to verify who it was that you saw?"

"Yes, he's that man in the blue suit at the defense table."

"Thank you. And Mrs. Langis, how did you know the person he was shouting at was a casino employee?"

"Because he was wearing one of those employee badges, and I've seen him around the casino before."

"All right, then what happened?"

"Well, maybe ten or fifteen seconds after the shouting started, the security guard who's normally at the front door came running over and tried to calm things down. But Mr. McDaniel kept yelling and was pushing the employee and then he started pushing the security guard."

"And what happened next?"

"The employee backed off and then it became a confrontation between the security guard and Mr. McDaniel. I saw the security guard take a swing at Mr. McDaniel with his baton. But Mr. McDaniel was too quick. He jumped out of the way, pulled out a knife, and slashed the guard.

"The guard dropped to his knees, holding his arm where he'd been cut. The defendant was standing over him when several other employees jumped him from behind, knocked him off his feet, and held him down.

"When they jumped him, the knife slipped out of his hand and fell on the carpet. I think a waitress in the bar had called 9-1-1, and the Natchez police officer arrived within a couple of minutes. I had the impression Mr. McDaniel already had too much to drink when this happened, but I don't know that for sure."

"Objection!"

"Sustained. Jury disregard that last comment," said the judge.

"Thank you, Mrs. Langis. That is all, Your Honor."

"Cross-examination?" asked the judge.

Bagwell hobbled over to the witness stand.

"Mrs. Langis, did the security guard tell Mr. McDaniel to calm down and to back off?"

"No, not that I heard."

"Did the security guard try to shove Mr. McDaniel away with his baton?"

"No, sir."

"Mrs. Langis, did the security guard swing his baton first, or was he threatened with the knife beforehand?"

"I saw him swing, then I saw the knife."

"Thank you. I'm done with this witness, Your Honor, ma'am.

Judge Wickham said, "You are excused, Mrs. Langis. Call your next witness, Mr. Duvall."

"Judge, the People call Mr. Ali Ghaffari."

A man who I judged to be in his mid-thirties approached the witness stand and raised his hand to take the witness oath. He stood rigidly as he took the witness oath.

"Mr. Ghaffari, will you please tell us in your own words what happened during the incident on the evening of May 20?'

"Yes, I was the slot machine floor manager that evening, and several customers complained to me about a man smoking, which is against the casino rules and against the law in Mississippi. So I politely asked him to go outside if he wanted to smoke. There are several areas available, one out by the front door and another along the walkway on the side of the building that overlooks the river. But he refused and started shouting and calling me names and pushing me."

"Mr. Ghaffari, what did Mr. McDaniel call you?"

"A stinkin' Muslim."

"And why did he think you were Muslim?"

"Because of my knit skullcap. It's called a kufi. Many Muslim men wear them."

"Is that the same kufi you are wearing today, sir?"

"No, it's similar but a different color."

"And what else did Mr. McDaniel say?" asked Duvall.

"He said 'no damned Muslim was going to tell him what to do.' That's when the security guard came over and the physical altercation started."

"And Mr. Ghaffari, just for the record, are you an immigrant?"

"No, I was born in New Orleans. My family has been here for three generations."

"Mr. Ghaffari, does wearing a kufi meet the casino dress code?"

"Yes, sir, the casino has a policy against discrimination for race, color, sex, national origin, or religion. So, Muslims can wear a kufi or hijab, Jews can wear a yarmulke, Sikhs can wear a turban, and Christians can wear a cross."

"Thanks for explaining, Mr. Ghaffari. All right, then what happened."

"Mr. McDaniel started yelling and pushing the security guard. The guard swung at him with his baton, and Mr. McDaniel knifed him. Then several other employees subdued Mr. McDaniel until the police arrived."

"Mr. Ghaffari, how bright are the lights in the casino?"

"I don't know, sir, but it's not as bright as outside in the daylight or as in most retail stores."

"Isn't it true that it's impossible to see things clearly inside the casino, such as whether someone is holding a small object like a knife?"

"I don't know, sir, but I'm used to the low lighting."

"That's all, Your Honor," said Duvall as he walked back to the prosecution table.

"Cross-examination?" asked Judge Wickham.

Bagwell rose and stood behind his chair, holding on for support, and said, "Mr. Ghaffari, did the security guard swing his baton at Mr. McDaniel before or after he was cut?"

"Before, sir."

"Did the security guard swing the baton with his right or his left hand?"

"He swung with his left hand."

"And where was the security guard cut?"

"On his left arm."

"Thank you, Mr. Ghaffari. That's all I have, Your Honor, ma'am," said Bagwell.

"You are excused, Mr. Ghaffari," said Judge Wickham.

"The People call the security guard, Robert Guthrie, Your Honor," said Duvall.

A stocky man of medium height, about thirty-five years old, walked slowly to the witness stand and raised his hand and took the witness oath.

"Mr. Guthrie, you were on duty as a security guard at the casino on May 20, is that correct?"

"Yes, sir."

"Mr. Guthrie, please tell us in your own words what happened at the casino on May 20."

"Well, sir, I was on duty at the front when I heard this commotion in the slot machine area. I rushed over there and heard the defendant yellin' and threatenin' the floor manager. I told him to stop, and he turned and started yelling at me and advancin' toward me with a knife, and I saw he was fixin' to use it. I had my baton in my hand, and I took a swing at him. He dodged it, and before I knew it, he had cut me across my left arm with his knife. I was startled, the pain was terrible, and I dropped to my knees. But before he could do anything else, two bartenders grabbed him from behind and took him to the ground. The knife popped loose and was laying on the carpet. Then right after that, the police arrived, and then the paramedics."

"What did he say to you or to the floor manager?"

"He said 'no damned Muslim was going to tell him what to do.' That's what I heard."

"So, Mr. Guthrie, just to be clear, you saw a knife before you swung the baton, is that right?" asked Duvall.

"Yessir, that's right."

"That's all, Your Honor."

"Cross-examination, Mr. Bagwell?"

Attorney Bagwell stood at the defense table, looking even more rumpled, and asked, "Mr. Guthrie, how many altercations have you had since you've been employed at the casino during the six months prior to this situation?"

"Oh, maybe three or four. There are quite a few gamblers who drink too much and then get rowdy when they lose their money. Sometimes things get a little rough."

"Innit true that you struck all of them with your baton during these altercations, sir."

"Well, that's the only weapon I have, sir. They won't let us have guns in the casino."

"So you hit first and ask questions later, ain't that right?"

Prosecutor Duvall said, "Objection, Your Honor."

Judge Wickham said, "Overruled. I want to hear the witness's answer."

"Well, sir, if you don't get the upper hand right away, then things can go bad real fast."

"That's all I have, judge — Your Honor, ma'am," said Bagwell.

"You're excused, Mr. Guthrie," said the judge.

After hearing all this testimony, I wondered if there was more to this case than met the eye. Maybe it wasn't so cut and dried after all.

Judge Wickham said, "This seems like a good time to break for lunch. The jury will be escorted to the jury room for lunch, but you are not to discuss the case. Court is adjourned until 1:00 p.m."

CHAPTER 32

We were ushered into the jury room and given box lunches. We couldn't talk about the case, so a few of the jurors complained to each other about the hot, humid weather, but most just sat quietly.

I was thinking about the crux of the case. And that was whether McDaniel had pulled his switchblade knife before or after the security guard swung at him with the baton.

I had decided against using psychic power while on jury duty, but now, with witnesses giving conflicting testimony, I wanted to be sure. I didn't want McDaniel to be convicted based on his looks instead of the facts. So while the other jurors were talking, I tried to make a connection with McDaniel's memory at the time of the altercation.

I closed my eyes, put my head in my hands, and started getting images from McDaniel's memory.

McDaniel was shouting at Mr. Ghaffari and pushing him backward with both hands. He saw the security guard approaching out of the corner of his eye. Guthrie already had the baton in his left hand. McDaniel reached into his right pants pocket and pulled out his switchblade knife but kept it closed in his fist.

Guthrie started yelling at McDaniel to shut up and calm down. But McDaniel yelled, "No damned Muslim is going to order me around," and stepped threateningly toward Guthrie. However, the knife was not visible and was still closed in his fist.

Guthrie swung the baton, but McDaniel quickly stepped back and leaned away; Guthrie missed. But Guthrie had overswung, and his left side was now exposed. McDaniel didn't want to get hit with the baton and thought the guard would surely take another swing. So to protect himself, he pushed the button on the handle, and the blade popped open instantly as he swung it with his right hand and caught Guthrie across the upper left arm.

Guthrie dropped to his knees. The knife popped out of McDaniel's hand and landed a few feet away. At that instant, two bartenders grabbed McDaniel and took him to the floor.

"Five minutes until time to return to the courtroom," the bailiff said, interrupting my connection. I'd seen what I needed to, though, and I felt better now because I had the answer. McDaniel had acted in self-defense after Guthrie attacked him with the baton. There was no question, but could Attorney Bagwell convince the jury?

CHAPTER 33

NAVID WAITED IMPATIENTLY for Baraz. He'd sent him an encrypted message right after meeting with the General, telling him to come home and bring their entire crew — eight men, all from Iran. Baraz had said he'd be there in five days. That had been almost two weeks ago.

And Navid was also still waiting on Farzad. He was not happy about the foot-dragging by the General — or the SNSC — on the initial payment. And he was not satisfied with the amount of the payment, which he considered inadequate for the amount of risk he was taking.

He revisited his idea of stealing and selling the RDDs to the highest bidder. His other alternative was to drop the whole thing and tell the General he had changed his mind. But he didn't like that option, either.

He was a terrorist, through and through, and he thought that now was his chance to do something big. And that's what he wanted — the prestige and the revenge.

He suddenly had an idea . He got on his phone, opened the Signal messaging app, and typed a message. He addressed it to "Warthog."

The message read, "I have some extraordinary merchandise on offer. It won't last long. Once-in-a-lifetime opportunity! Urgent! Can we meet? /signed/ Scorpion."

He hit send.

Within a minute or two, Navid received a reply.

"Yes, suggest a location."

Navid replied, "Radisson Blu Hotel, Dakar, Senegal, in three days. Confirm, then message me upon arrival."

About an hour later, Warthog replied, "Confirmed." It must have taken him that long to make his travel arrangements.

Senegal was one of the few countries that would allow visitors from Iran. It was perfect for US travelers, too, with no visa requirement. And, importantly, Dakar approximately split the distance.

Navid had never met Warthog in person, but he knew him through his terrorist contacts. Warthog lived in the US and was an occasional financial supporter of Hurras Ansar al-Haqq.

Other terrorists had told Navid that Warthog had access to significant financial backers interested in funding terror attacks in the US. He assumed Warthog was an Arab refugee who had immigrated to the US because Warthog always communicated in Arabic, the only language besides Farsi that Navid was proficient in, due to all the time he had spent in Iraq.

Navid made his airline reservation with Emirates, leaving from Tehran the day after tomorrow and changing planes in Dubai, then to Dakar, and returning two days later. Then he made his hotel reservation at the Radisson Blu.

Next, he sent a message to Baraz. "If I'm not here when you arrive, wait for my return."

Navid explained to Roya that he had to go on a short trip

for the General, but he could not tell her where he was going. He said he would be gone about three days and that Baraz would be coming home soon.

Roya asked, "Will Baraz be staying?"

"Only for a short while."

She crossed her arms and frowned. "Is he also involved in this scheme with the General?"

"Yes, it's important, and we will be paid well," he said.

"But the General always brings trouble," she said. "Baraz will be in danger, won't he?"

"Is that all you think about?" he asked.

The frown on her face deepened, and she stared at him with a mixture of worry and disgust. "Yes, after losing two sons. You should be concerned, too."

He waved his one hand dismissively and walked away, feeling her disappointment enveloping him.

CHAPTER 34

ONCE WE WERE back in the courtroom, and I was in my assigned chair, the judge said, "Mr. Prosecutor, you may call your next witness."

Duvall said, "The People call Detective Paul Pomeroy."

A tall man in gray slacks, a dark blue sport coat, and a red tie walked to the witness stand and took the witness oath. I thought he looked impressive.

Mr. Duvall asked, "Detective, how long have you been doing investigations for the Natchez Police Department?"

"Twenty-one years, sir."

Attorney Bagwell stood and said, "Judge, the defense will stipulate Detective Pomeroy is a qualified and competent detective, ma'am."

Duvall continued, "Detective Pomeroy, please tell us in your own words what you learned when you interviewed Mr. McDaniel on the night of the incident."

"Well, he told me he was an employee of the Orleans Petroleum Products Company and has worked as a deckhand for the last ten years on their boat, which delivers petroleum products from New Orleans to Houston and all the way up to St. Louis. They had stopped at the Port of Natchez to offload and would spend the night before returning to New Orleans the next day. He said he walked to the casino, a little over two miles north of the port, after supper on May 20. He arrived at the casino at about 7:30 p.m. and started playing the slot machines and drinking a little beer. Then, sometime after 9:00 p.m. Mr. Ghaffari started yelling at him about smoking. He said he wouldn't take any crap from a damned Muslim, and that's when the guard, Mr. Guthrie, intervened, and the real trouble started."

"What did you learn about Mr. McDaniel's prior police record?"

"He had been convicted of several misdemeanors for theft and simple assaults."

"Had he ever gotten in trouble for using a knife?"

"Yes, sir, he has threatened people with a knife but has only been charged with menacing. He said he has always used that weapon to defend himself."

"And why did he say he preferred a knife?"

"Well, because he's tall and rangy, with long arms, and his reach is well-suited for using a knife as a weapon."

"And what did he say about Muslims?" asked Duvall.

"He said he knew a lot of no-good Muslims who worked on the ships around New Orleans and in the Gulf of Mexico, especially in the oil industry. Quite a few Muslims immigrated here twenty-five or thirty years ago, before 9/11, because they had experience working on oil ships of various sorts in the Persian Gulf, and better-paying jobs were available here.

"McDaniel said they were all terrorists and couldn't stand them. He said something like, 'The only good Muslim is a dead Muslim.'"

"That's all, Your Honor," said Duvall.

"Cross-examination?" the judge asked.

Bagwell said, "No questions, Your Honor, ma'am."

Judge Wickham said, "The defense may present its case."

"The defense, respectfully, will not call any witnesses, Your Honor, ma'am."

Judge Wickham gave him a stern look and started to say something but then nodded her head.

Then she asked, "Mr. Bagwell, has the accused decided whether he will testify in his own defense?"

"He has decided not to testify, Your Honor."

"Is that correct, Mr. McDaniel?"

McDaniel nodded his head.

"I can't hear you, Mr. McDaniel. Have you decided to testify or not to testify?"

"I have decided not to testify, Your Honor."

"Thank you, Mr. McDaniel."

Judge Wickham said, "Jurors, the prosecutor, and the defense attorney will now make their closing arguments. The prosecutor will go first, followed by the defense attorney. The prosecutor has the opportunity for a final rebuttal since the People have the burden of proving their case."

Duvall walked right up to the jury box, wasting no time. "Mr. Guthrie, the security guard, saw the knife and felt threatened, so he swung the baton at Mr. McDaniel to protect himself, but McDaniel was able to cut him anyway. The facts require that you find him guilty as charged." His closing argument was short and sweet, and he was obviously happy with his statement.

Still moving with apparent difficulty, Attorney Bagwell stood and barely stepped out in front of the defense table.

"Mr. McDaniel din't pull the knife until Mr. Guthrie tried to hit him with the baton, then he used the knife to protect himself. Nobody saw the knife until after Guthrie swung at McDaniel, and that's a fact. Mr. Guthrie had a record of using his baton in such situations and, when asked 'if he hit first and asked questions later,' had actually said, 'Well, sir, if you don't get the upper hand right away, then things can go bad in a hurry.'

"You can't convict my client under that scenario. The victim has impeached his own testimony."

His argument was also concise. He looked in the direction of Duvall and smiled slightly as he limped back to the defense table and sat down.

Duvall again swiftly approached the jury box for his rebuttal. "There was no justification for Mr. McDaniel to slash Mr. Guthrie. It is very possible that none of the other witnesses could see that Mr. McDaniel already had the knife out before Mr. Guthrie swung, due to the poor lighting. So their testimony that they didn't see the knife is not conclusive one way or the other. Therefore, the People believe the accused has been proven guilty." He looked at Bagwell with contempt as he returned to his seat.

Judge Wickham sat up very straight on the bench.

She said, "Members of the jury, I am going to read the jury instructions, and I want you to listen closely." I sat up straight in my chair and gave her my full attention.

"To reach a guilty verdict, you need to unanimously agree. Two tests have to be met for aggravated assault under Mississippi law.

"1. The accused attempts or causes serious bodily injury to another purposely, knowingly, or recklessly, under circumstances manifesting extreme indifference to human life.

"2. The accused attempts or purposely causes bodily injury with a deadly weapon.

"A common defense for aggravated assault is self-defense.

This can be established by showing the defendant believed they faced imminent harm if they did not act." Judge Wickham paused, looking at the jurors and then at the attorneys. "Now I am going to explain 'beyond a reasonable doubt' so you don't have any confusion as you deliberate.

"The Court instructs the jury that you are bound, in deliberating upon this case, to give the defendant the benefit of any reasonable doubt of the defendant's guilt that arises out of the evidence or want of evidence in this case. Mere probability of guilt will never warrant you to convict the defendant. You might be able to say that you believe him to be guilty, and yet if you cannot say on your oaths, beyond a reasonable doubt, that he is guilty, it is your sworn duty to find the defendant Not Guilty.

"Also, I want you to assume no inference of guilt or innocence from Mr. McDaniel's decision not to testify in his own defense. He has the right to testify if he desires, but he is not required to do so.

"The jurors may now proceed to the jury room."

We filed out of the courtroom and headed down the back hallway to the jury room. All the while, I was thinking about how to convince everyone that McDaniel wasn't guilty.

To my surprise, the initial discussion revealed most jurors believed it was self-defense. Therefore, a verdict of 'Guilty' seemed out of the question. I was relieved. A few said they initially thought he was guilty, but they were won over by Attorney Bagwell's arguments. They felt sure that Bagwell was an honest attorney and wouldn't say his client was innocent if it wasn't true. I didn't think that highly of Bagwell, but I thought the facts spoke for themselves. However, based on how the discussion was going, I decided to not say much and just vote for acquittal.

One juror wondered why there was no video of the incident. Didn't casinos have cameras everywhere? We pondered that question for a while before deciding that the video, if any, was inconclusive. Therefore, it wasn't presented as evidence by either side.

Most of the discussion centered on whether McDaniel would have used the knife if Guthrie hadn't swung at him. Based on the judge's explanation of the law, most of the jury thought McDaniel had acted in self-defense, but there were a few diehards who wanted to punish McDaniel for something. After some deliberation, they finally gave up and agreed that he was Not Guilty of the charge of aggravated assault,

After a while, the jury foreman, Sam Luning — a big, gregarious man with reddish hair — said, "Look here, it's obvious McDaniel didn't attack Guthrie until he tried to club him, so let's vote 'Not Guilty' and get the hell out of here."

The jurors nodded, so Luning said, "Let's take a vote and make it official. We will do this as a secret ballot, so nobody can say they got railroaded." He passed out the ballots and pens, collected the votes, and stacked them in a pile. He showed each ballot to the jurors as he unfolded and counted them. All twelve ballots said, "Not Guilty."

We went back to the courtroom and were seated for the last time. The bailiff handed the judge a form signed by foreman Luning. She read it silently, looked at the jury, and handed it back to the bailiff, who returned it to the foreman.

The judge said, "Mr. Foreman, you may read the verdict."

The jury foreman, Luning, loudly read the "Not Guilty" verdict.

Judge Wickham asked, "So say you all?"

We all nodded and said, "Yes, Your Honor."

Judge Wickham thanked us, saying, "Mr. McDaniel is hereby released, and this court is adjourned."

Bagwell slapped McDaniel on the shoulder and smiled.

McDaniel was glaring at Duvall. And Duvall was obviously not happy and was staring at the jurors. But then he jammed his notes into his briefcase and quickly stormed out of the courtroom.

When Judge Wickham released the jurors, I called Craig Clayton to tell him.

"It's over," I said.

"Are you free to leave now?" he asked.

"Yes, can you meet me?"

"Yes, I'm sitting right outside the courtroom."

A quirk in Mississippi gun law allows guns into the courthouse if you have an enhanced concealed carry permit. However, you can't take a firearm into an active courtroom. So Craig was able to get as close to the courtroom as the bench in the hallway outside the courtroom with his weapon. And from there, he watched for anyone who looked like they didn't belong.

We both had previously been targets of assassination attempts and kidnappings. Other members of the protective detail were also in the courthouse and outside. No one looked out of place, but you could never be too careful.

As I came out of the courtroom, Craig nodded toward the stairs, and we walked down to the first floor and out the side door. Agent Donnie Hambleton was waiting in the car.

We pulled away from the curb heading east on State Street and turning left on South Pearl. When we arrived at Wexford House, Donnie pulled around back and let me out.

Craig said, "You're in good hands now with Angie. We'll see you tomorrow at the office."

I nodded and jumped out. Craig and Donnie watched me enter the back door, then slowly made a circle in the broad driveway and pulled back out onto South Pearl, heading back toward the office.

CHAPTER 35

WHEN I ENTERED the back door, Miss Doris was bustling around the kitchen as usual.

She said, "Oh, Mister Grant, I'm so glad you're home. I was worried that court case would keep you there late."

"No, the trial is over and —"

"Hi, hubby!" Angie said as she breezed into the room.

"Hi, honey!" I smiled and hugged and kissed Angie and smoothed her black hair, again admiring her recent haircut — a little shorter than before.

"You don't have to go back to the courthouse tomorrow?"

"No, it's all over."

"Did you put the bad guy in jail?"

"No, he wasn't the bad guy, after all. He is a bad guy, but he wasn't guilty of the assault charge."

Angie gave me a quizzical look. I understood she wanted to know if I had checked out the defendant's memory to see what had happened. I nodded yes, and she smiled.

Miss Doris said, "Well, I'm glad it's over. I would never like to be on a jury with strangers. I'm sure some screwball juror would want to let a guilty person off, and then I'd have to set them straight."

We both laughed. Angie said, "Miss Doris, I'm sure you would."

Miss Doris smiled and muttered, "No guilty person's gonna walk free when I'm on the jury!"

She continued to scurry around the kitchen, with dishes clattering and pans clanking. She stirred a pot on the stove and pulled a pan out of the oven.

She said, "I've got a special treat for you tonight, a coconut cake, your favorite! I mean, both of you like it, not just Mister Grant."

Angie said, "Yes, I do like it, and I know you've been cooking for Grant since he was a little boy, and it's fine that you cook what he likes."

"Thank you, Miss Angie."

Miss Doris continued, "When will Miss Karen come to stay with us again?"

I said, "Maybe when she's not working on a case in D.C."

After our first case had been completed last year, I decided to tell Miss Doris that I was working as a consultant for the CIA. And I also told her who Angie, Karen, and Craig were and what they really did. But I couldn't tell her exactly what I was doing because it was top secret.

It was a big shock for Miss Doris to hear all that, but she almost fainted when I told her that Angie and I were getting married. To my delight, she gathered herself and said that she thought that would be wonderful because she really liked Miss Angie.

Miss Doris never said anything about it, but you could tell she was proud that I was doing consulting work for the government. However, she couldn't imagine what that work might be. And she told me she wouldn't tell a soul, especially her husband, Joe. She said he couldn't keep a secret to save his life.

After our supper of fried pork chops, green beans, mashed potatoes, and applesauce, Miss Doris served slices of the coconut cake. Alex seemed to enjoy the meal as much as we did.

I still considered myself a reasonably slim, taller-than-average man who looked younger than forty-three years. I thought I had to go to the gym tomorrow to work off some of these calories. Angie and I were lucky that the calories had difficulty sticking to us, but it was getting more difficult. Now that Alex was here, he seemed to help get us into the mood to maintain our fitness.

Now that jury duty was over, I wondered what would be next. I'd been able to concentrate on my business since the last case and spend newlywed time with Angie, but I figured this period of inactivity as a CIA "consultant" would end abruptly, but when?

CHAPTER 36

OCTOBER 11
DAKAR, SENEGAL

NAVID WAS TIRED after traveling all day. He had arranged for the hotel to send a car to pick him up at the airport, and the ride to the hotel was uneventful. After he checked in — he was happy to learn the desk clerk spoke Arabic — he looked around the lobby. He saw the restaurant, went over, and looked in. It was relatively empty, though the dinner hour was just beginning. He went to his room and waited to hear from Warthog.

About an hour later, Navid's phone beeped. He saw it was a message from Warthog. "I have arrived."

Navid sent a reply. "Meet at 9:00 p.m., L'Avenue Restaurant, in the lobby. Ask for Mr. Ghorbani."

"See you soon," was the reply.

Fifteen minutes until 9:00 p.m. Navid went to the lobby holding the iPad bag in his left hand, looked again into the almost empty restaurant, and then went to the front desk. He asked the clerk in Arabic to make a reservation for him at the restaurant at a table along the windows under the name of his friend, Mr. Ghorbani.

Then he returned to the restaurant and, when greeted, said, "Ghorbani." The maitre d' nodded and escorted him to a table at the window overlooking the pool and the ocean.

A few minutes later, the maitre d' escorted a man to the table. He looked like a typical American. He was medium height and weight, clean-shaven, and had light brown hair and brown eyes. Navid thought he looked about forty years old. Presumably, this was Warthog. He didn't look Arabic at all.

After the maitre d' had walked away, Navid said, "Are you the famous Warthog?" in Arabic.

The man answered, "Only if you are the famous Scorpion," also in Arabic.

They both laughed.

"You don't look as I expected," Navid said.

Warthog laughed and replied, "Well, you look exactly as I expected, except for your arm. I didn't know about that."

"Yes, it was an unfortunate and permanent injury, courtesy of the Iraqi army."

"I'm sorry," Warthog said.

"Oh, no, it's the source of my terrorist motivation," Navid said. "You know, an eye for an eye."

He studied Warthog's face. It showed a certain kind of hardness. It was like he had a much tougher life than others his age. Yet there was also a keen intelligence in his eyes. It was as if his body had seen a lot of wear and tear, but not his mind. He wondered what was behind his terrorist motivation.

"Where did you learn how to speak Arabic?" Navid asked.

"My mother is, or was, Lebanese. She died a few years ago of kidney failure. She explained how the Israelis, Sunnis, Syrians, and Americans destroyed the lovely country of Lebanon."

"What about your father?"

"He was an American, but he has passed, too. He was a worthless drunk." His face showed anger at the mention of his father, the total opposite of when he described his mother.

"I'm sorry."

"No, I have them to thank for how I turned out, which is not too bad."

"What about your family? Do they know?" asked Navid.

"I don't have any family, my Scorpion friend. This means I am free to fight the devils inside and around me by any means. No risk is too big."

Actually, this declaration by the Warthog made Navid nervous. He did not believe in being so reckless; calculating — yes, but reckless — no.

The waiter came and took their order, then brought the food while they talked.

Navid thought it was ironic that while discussing a proposition that could affect most of the world in one way or another, neither one knew the other's real name.

The only thing they shared was their hatred of Sunni Muslims, the Israelis, and the Americans.

The waiter took their order of roasted fish, vegetables, rice, and tea.

Warthog said, "I traveled a long way. I hope you have something important to offer."

His tone indicated he was not interested in wasting more time with small talk. He wanted to get down to business.

Navid said, "What is the one weapon you wish you could use for a terrorist attack?"

"Either an atomic bomb or a bioweapon with no antidote."

"What would such a weapon be worth?"

"Millions, no doubt."

"And where would you use it?"

"I would use it in the United States. A second choice would be to attack Israel."

Navid leaned forward. "And what if you had more than one weapon?"

Warthog smiled.

"That's an interesting question," Warthog said. "I could cause enormous and irreparable damage in one attack or spread the pain in several attacks. The first attack would be the easiest, and later attacks might even be impossible. So, all things considered, one massive attack would be the best."

Navid said, "Yes, I tend to agree. You would have the element of surprise. After the first attack, it would be lost."

Warthog nodded, eyeing Navid curiously. With a wave, he said, "Well then, quit stalling and tell me what you have."

CHAPTER 37

WHEN NAVID ARRIVED at his shop, Baraz and Farzin were waiting. They were a contrast. Baraz was shorter, darker, and much tougher-looking than Farzin. Maybe because he had been living a rough life in Iraq and Syria, he looked like a man not to be trifled with.

Navid hugged one, then the other with his left arm.

"Father, what was so urgent?" Baraz asked.

"Farzin didn't tell you?"

"No, Father."

Farzin had a surprised look on his face as if he knew he was not to tell anyone, so why would his father even think such a thing.

"We have been assigned a job in Abu Dhabi by the General. It's dangerous, but we will be very well paid. We will disable the Bu Hasa oil field using a truck bomb and drones to disperse radioactive material. The next step is for us to be trained on flying the drones."

"Father, I thought I was to drive the bomb truck?" Farzin said.

"Yes, but I have decided driving the truck is too dangerous, so you will fly a drone."

"But what about the truck?

"We'll unload the truck outside the Camp, fly the drones from there, and then escape. We'll remotely detonate the truck bomb on the road after we deliver the drone bombs, blocking the road to the Camp. And we'll need two more men to fly drones. Baraz, can you handle that?"

"Yes, of course, Father. Several of my men made the trip here with me to visit their families."

"The three of us will learn how to fly the drones as soon as possible, then you can teach the others. I'll call the General to schedule the training. You understand your mother is to know nothing of this."

They both nodded.

Navid didn't care that what he told them about the new plan was nonsense. As far as Navid was concerned, none of this would be happening, but his sons didn't need to know that. Worry threatened to overtake him, but he tamped it down. Warthog had told him he could raise five to ten million for the RDDs and drones, with delivery to the US — a much higher price than Farzad had offered and less risk to his sons. But Warthog needed a few days to ensure his supporters could raise the money, and the wait was more than stressful.

And if Warthog didn't want the RDDs, Navid would tell the General that he had changed his mind and didn't want the job. It would be one or the other — a roll of the dice that could either gain him all that he wanted or cost him everything, or no roll of the dice at all.

CHAPTER 38

NAVID ENTERED THE bookstore on time, nodded to the clerk, and went directly to the back room. He had not slept well. He knew he had to make the most important decision of his life very soon. It was irreversible and had many implications — not all good. But before he could decide, Warthog had to make his decision first.

And he had another problem. He had been arguing with Baraz, who thought it was too dangerous to be involved with radioactive devices. He was only concerned about lethal exposure to radiation, not all the other dire consequences. It was a good thing that he couldn't imagine that Navid had even bigger and more dangerous plans. Navid had finally convinced him that harmful radiation exposure was not possible. He even offered to arrange for Baraz to talk to the General, but Baraz said it wasn't necessary.

The General was waiting for him when he walked in.

"We received the drone training yesterday," Navid said after they'd greeted each other. It was the reason he wanted to see the General. He'd gotten an idea when the Colonel had briefed them on the drones.

"Yes, I heard. But there were only three of you. Don't you need at least one more drone pilot?"

"Actually, we don't. The auto mode wouldn't require a pilot for each drone. But we want one person for each to speed up the setup and shorten the total time to liftoff. So we have two more men we would like to train, but we can do the training ourselves. That's one reason I called. I saw how complex the drone control system was, so I asked the Colonel about reliability. He said it was reliable but that failures have occurred in the past. So I think an extra drone should be supplied as a backup in case anything happens. And we can use it for training, too."

The General thought about the request, then said, "Yes, you're right. You can have an extra drone."

Navid smiled inwardly. Five RDDs and five drones. This would give Warthog the flexibility he wants for any remote attack. He was very careful not to show the General how happy he was. That would make the General suspicious. He took a deep breath.

"Fine, how about I send a truck and pick up the extra drone from the Colonel in the next few days?"

"Yes, I will make arrangements, but I want you to come make the pickup yourself. I don't trust anyone else with our military equipment. I want you to be personally responsible."

"Of course, that is fine."

"Anything else?" asked the General.

"Yes. I want to discuss how the RDDs and drones will be packaged for shipment to Dubai. I want to put them in the same crates I use for shipping rugs. So you can deliver them to me however you like, but I need enough time to repack them — at least a day, preferably two days."

"That's fine with me," said the General. He seemed anxious to get the show on the road.

"And what have you worked out about the initial payment." Navid feared how the General would react, but he needed to know.

"I have approval to make the payment when I turn over the RDDs to you," replied the General. He grimaced more than smiled, but he needed to be sure Navid wouldn't back out.

"I want the payment split between several hawaladars of my choice. This is too much money for only one. And I want the payment in dollars and euros, as I told you before." He was pushing the General again. Navid wanted to use the informal hawaladar network to handle his payments rather than the formal banking system, which the government could manipulate.

"I'll give you the names of the hawaladars in a few days," the General said.

"Yes, of course. That's fine."

Navid knew now that the General had no choice but to do anything he asked.

The General nodded.

Navid understood this was now the point at which the General was his enemy. Still, the General needed him — at least for now. But when he didn't . . . ?

Navid stood, nodded his head, said his goodbyes, and left the store.

❦

The General felt uneasy about the meeting with Navid, though he couldn't exactly put his finger on the reason.

He decided to call Dr. Yazdani.

"Hello?"

"This is General Ghorbani."

"What can I do for you, General?"

The General knew he had to be careful with what he said, even though it was a secure line. He knew the Israelis might be listening.

"Do you have trackers on our toys?"

"Yes, of course, General. We wouldn't want to lose any of them, would we?"

"No, Doctor. We need to have the complete set to play the game."

"Yes, it would not be nearly as much fun, General."

"No, definitely not. I will need access to the tracking software. Colonel Hashemi will follow up with you to ensure it's installed on our devices."

The General felt a little better when he hung up, though a trace of unease still lingered. He would breathe easier when he could see the whereabouts of the RDDs for himself.

CHAPTER 39

CRAIG AND ALEX finished installing the grappling mats in Suite 304, covering the entire floor except for the area near the door, which didn't have enough clearance above the mats to open the door.

I would soon find out if Alex really had expertise in self-defense.

We stood in the middle of the room, just the two of us and my Glock 19. Alex had unloaded it and emptied the chamber so that there was no chance of an accidental shooting. Craig stood outside the suite in the hallway to act as security while we trained.

"Okay, today, let's spend time on disarming techniques for handguns," Alex said.

"All right."

"So more than likely, anyone who points a gun at you at close range is doing it with the intent to take you under their control. If they were going to shoot you from a distance, there's not much you can do from a self-defense standpoint, and they already would have done it. So, they're not planning to shoot you, and they'll hesitate just a split second before they do because they don't really want to. Does that make sense?"

"Yes."

"And if they know anything about you, they won't expect you to fight back. Right?"

"No, I guess not."

"So, the element of surprise would be an advantage for you."

"I guess so," I said. I never expected Alex to be so logical and analytical.

"Now, with me, Craig, and Angie being with you most of the time, it's doubtful you'll ever be in this situation, but you never know, so we want you to be prepared.

"If there's more than one of them, don't resist. The chances of getting away are too slim, and you might die. If you stay alive after being taken captive, rescue is always possible. But if there's only one of them, you might be better off fighting one-on-one because you never know what will happen in a hostage or kidnap situation."

"That makes sense." Though I hoped I'll never be in that situation.

"All right, let's train on disarming in the most common situation."

"You mean I'm going to try to take the gun away?"

"Yes, that's right." *Wow, I can't imagine how I could possibly do that.*

"Point the gun at my face because that's the most intimidating situation. And get fairly close to me because you'll be giving me commands, and you don't want to have to shout, which might draw attention. Put your finger on the trigger, too, rather than in the safe position, just in case you have to shoot me."

Standing about two feet away from him, I did what Alex said.

Alex put his hands up, then said, "Okay, so I'm going to talk to you to focus your attention on my eyes and on what I'm saying, and away from my hands. Tell me to put my hands up, don't move, and shut up."

"Okay, put your hands up, stand still, do what I tell you, and shut up," I say with some ferocity.

"Don't shoot. I'll do what you tell me, just don't shoot me. I'll do anything you say." My attention was automatically fixed on Alex's eyes as he talked, just as he predicted.

But then Alex suddenly turned his body, getting out of the line of fire, and in the same motion, grabbed my right wrist, moving the gun barrel away from him. He put his left hand on top of the gun, then he pulled the weapon toward his body and twisted the gun outward and down with his left hand. My finger caught in the trigger guard and my wrist twisted unnaturally, and I dropped the gun as I fell to the mat, yelping in pain. Alex pushed me away and grabbed the gun.

"Did you see how easy that was?"

I stared up at him in shock. "You almost broke my finger."

"Yeah, that was the idea," Alex said, helping me up. "Now you try it."

I tried to disarm Alex, but I wasn't quick enough. Alex told me to try again, but faster. And then again. Finally, I began to get the hang of it.

When I'd disarmed Alex five times, Alex said, "All right, let's bring in Craig and see if you can disarm him."

"But won't he know what I'm going to do?"

"There are different techniques, so he can't be sure what you will do. But be fast. And one more thing — Craig is even taller than me, so the gun will be a little higher, but the technique is the same. You're just going to have to twist really hard with your left hand and, at the same time, pull down with your right hand on his wrist. That's so you have the gun low enough that you can put some leverage into the twisting of the gun."

Alex went to the door and called in Craig.

"We've been working on a defensive technique, and Grant needs to practice. So I'd like you to hold him at gunpoint and let him try to take evasive action."

Alex handed Craig the gun, and Craig racked it twice, checked the chamber, and pulled the trigger several times to ensure it was empty.

"Okay, so you want me to point the gun at his chest or face?"

"It doesn't make any difference; either is fine."

Craig was savvy enough to know that his height was an advantage. He pointed the gun in his right hand at my forehead and stood a little farther away from me than Alex because his arms were longer.

"Put your hands up, shut your mouth, and don't move," Craig said.

"Don't shoot; I'll do what you say!" I said.

"Shut up!"

"Okay, okay, I will. Just don't —"

"I said —"

Suddenly, I rotated my body out of the line of fire, grabbed Craig's wrist with my right hand, and at the same time, grabbed the Glock slide with my left hand — and pulled the gun toward my body as I twisted it away from Craig. This caught Craig by surprise, and he bent his knees and leaned over, trying to take the pressure off his wrist and finger. I twisted harder, Craig released the gun, and he fell to the mat. I transferred the gun to my right hand and pointed it at Craig with a big smile on my face.

Alex said, "Perfect!"

Craig glared up at me. "Ow! Damn, you hurt me!"

"That's what I was trained to do!" I said, glancing at Alex.

"Well, you did a good job."

Alex said, "Okay, thanks, Craig. You can go back outside now. And thanks for being a good sport."

Craig nodded but didn't look happy as he rubbed his right hand and wrist. He slammed the door as he left.

"Okay, let's try this when the assailant has the gun in his left hand."

Alex showed me the moves, which were just a mirror image of what I had learned before.

I tried it several times. When Alex was satisfied, he said, "Okay, I think that's enough for today. You did well. What do you think?"

"Yeah, I kind of like this. Let's do more when we can."

"I want to train you slowly so you learn each technique completely and can do it without thinking before we move on to something else."

"Okay, that makes sense."

Alex said, "Someday, knowing how to do this might save your life."

CHAPTER 40

DURING THE NIGHT, Commander Moshe Kadosh requested an urgent meeting with Mossad Director Levi Weiss. The Director's assistant told him to come to the Director's office at 10:30 a.m.

"Come in, Moshe. Please sit down, and give me some good news."

"Do I ever ask for an urgent meeting if I have good news?" asked Kadosh.

"I was hoping this would start a new trend, Moshe."

They both laughed. But then the Director's face turned solemn. He felt that he only heard bad news. He expected that as part of his job.

"We have new intel from Unit 8200, sir."

Director Weiss was proud of the Israel Defense Forces – Unit 8200, the equivalent of the NSA in the United States, only smaller. But even the NSA was envious of the expertise of Unit 8200.

"Yes, yes, they always bring me bad news. You would think

if they are listening to phone calls and monitoring e-mail world-wide, they would occasionally find something good, or at least amusing," said the Director. "All right, what is it?"

"Our friend, General Ghorbani, has been in frequent contact with Dr. Yazdani, sir."

"Yes, we always worry when the head of the IRGC-Quds Force is in contact with the Director of the Research Division of the Atomic Energy Organization of Iran. We never like the potential bomb maker to be talking to the potential bomb thrower."

"The General asked the doctor if they had trackers on their 'toys,' sir."

"Well, that can't be good. The General must be worried about control of a radioactive device. What else?"

"He said, 'Yes, of course, we don't want to lose any of them.' That means they have more than one device — whatever they are discussing."

"Anything else?"

"Yes, the doctor said, 'we need a complete set to play the game.' We think this means they have a plan that includes using multiple devices."

"Then it could mean they plan to attack us with a barrage of nuclear weapons. Is that right?"

"Yes, sir, it could mean that. Who else would they attack? Perhaps Saudi Arabia, but we can't take the chance."

"But that would mean they ignored our warning — the elimination of Dr. Soltani."

"It could mean they think they have rogue elements within their government with access to the nuclear devices and the will to act. That's even worse."

"Then whatever is going on, we might need to pre-empt all of their plans by striking first," said Director Weiss.

"But we need to be sure. It might be something else," replied Kadosh.

"What do you have in mind?" asked Weiss.

"We appear to have several choices. Our policy has always been not to strike unless we are absolutely sure we can destroy any and every nuclear device they have. Since we don't know where the devices are, a strike would not be in order. The next best approach is to find out what is going on. We propose to kidnap Dr. Yazdani and find out directly from him. And, his disappearance will likely slow down their plans."

"But if they know we have him, wouldn't that provoke them to do something drastic — and sooner?"

"Yes, but I think we can make it look like we have killed him, but in reality, we will capture him instead."

"Well, if you can do that, you are a magician — even better than Houdini."

"We have a plan, sir. But I need your permission to proceed. I'll need to take some preliminary steps but stop short of actually kidnapping the good doctor until we have final approval."

"Yes, go ahead, but review the plan details with me for final approval. And do it quickly. I'll brief the Prime Minister. In the meantime, direct Unit 8200 to intensify their efforts to learn more about this."

"Yes, sir."

Commander Kadosh rose from his chair and left the office.

Director Weiss shook his head. He wondered if this would eventually lead to all out war with Iran. He certainly hoped not. But he was intrigued by capturing Iran's head nuclear scientist.

CHAPTER 41

OCTOBER 14
NATCHEZ, MISSISSIPPI

IT WAS STARTING as a pleasant, bright sunny day in Natchez. I arrived at the bank building a little later than usual. I had gone with Angie for a workout at the gym first thing that morning. She said she would meet me at the office later.

I walked through the front door of the building into the lobby on my way to the elevator. On my way up to my office, I glanced into the bank to wave to the tellers as usual. But I noticed a man standing next to the lobby entrance, dressed all in black and wearing a black ski mask. It wasn't unusual since the pandemic to see people wearing masks as they went about their business, but not ski masks. And what was really unusual was that he was holding a gun — and it was pointing at me.

I stopped in my tracks and raised my hands.

He said, "Get over here and get on your knees. And keep your hands up!"

I did as he asked but added, "I'm not a bank employee."

He said, "I'm not here to rob the bank. I'm here to kill you."

I was shocked. I was sure it was a bank robbery. But when I looked through the glass doors into the bank, all looked normal.

I tried to think of what I could say or do, but I drew a blank. All I could think was that I needed to remember what I could — to help identify him later. I saw that he had dark hair, but that was about all I could see other than he was medium height and build. Then the reality hit — what I saw wouldn't make any difference if he killed me.

He pointed the gun straight at my face, and I could see his finger start to pull the trigger. All I could do was scream — "Noooooooooo!"

And then, Angie was shaking me. "Grant, Grant! Wake up! What's the matter?"

It took me a few seconds to realize where I was and that my experience was all just a bad dream. I was shaking and sweating. It was so real.

"A bad dream. Just a bad dream, that's all."

"It must have been more than a bad dream — more like a nightmare," said Angie.

I told her all that I could remember.

She asked, "No idea who it was? Or why?"

"No, he didn't look familiar. I have no idea."

"Did you recognize his voice?"

"I don't think so. The mask kind of muffled his voice."

"Grant, do you think this was a random dream or based on some kind of extrasensory intelligence?"

"Honestly, I just don't know."

"I just want you to be safe. That's all I want," said Angie.

I gave her a hug and put her head on my shoulder.

"I love you, too, honey."

I wondered if this dream was caused by my nagging concern that Angie and I were constantly in too much danger? And if it was — what could I do about it?

But if it wasn't a random dream, someone was out to kill me, and I had just gotten a warning or a premonition.

CHAPTER 42

THE GENERAL HAD finally provided the names of several hawaladars he would trust to transfer the one-and-a-half million prepayment to Navid.

Navid didn't know any of the men on the list, but he knew who did. And that was his personal hawaladar, Zubin Deghani, Roya's cousin.

Fortunately, Zubin lived only a few miles away on the other side of Qom. Navid drove to Zubin's shop. Like many hawaladars, his business was jewelry, artwork, and electronics. This was because settling accounts with other hawaladars frequently required fudging on the value of items bought and sold. And many of these items were difficult to value unless you were an expert and knew the exact details and specifications.

Hawaladars usually settled balances by having money transfers in both directions. They typically had years of experience and knew how to make the system work smoothly. But if that wasn't possible in a reasonable period, one could sell something of value to the other for a lower price than the actual value. And if a hawaladar was owed money, he could sell an item to the other hawaladar at an inflated price to settle all or part of the balance.

Hawaladars were experts in the intricacies of importing and exporting, and especially the complexities of the confounding paperwork. They also knew which countries had weak enforcement and used it to their advantage.

Navid entered Zubin's shop. The bell on the door jingled, and Zubin came out from the back room. He had short gray hair and a matching beard. It contrasted with his black shirt, worn untucked, over gray pants and black shoes.

"How are you, Navid-joon?" Zubin asked as he kissed Navid on both cheeks.

"I'm good," said Navid.

"And how is my favorite cousin?"

"Roya is the same as always. You know how she's been since we lost our boys, Kaveh and Javed."

"Yes, yes, a very difficult situation. Please tell Roya I asked about her. What brings you here today? Please sit down." No one else was in the shop, so they stayed in the front and talked, sitting at a small table.

Navid had thought very hard about what he would tell Zubin and what he would ask of him. They had known each other a long time and had family ties. Zubin had often processed cash transfers, large and small, through the hawaladar network for Navid and was well aware of his terrorist organization.

"I have another job for the IRGC and will receive a large payment for the work. The IRGC has given me a list of hawaladars to move the money to me. Their names are Jahan Akbari, Heydar Torabi, and Ashk Davari. Do you know any of them?"

"Yes. They are all very reliable and should be able to handle a large sum for you. But if I had to choose, I would recommend Ashk Davari."

"That's fine. Then I will specify Ashk to receive the payment. However, I want to immediately transfer the money to you and ask you to hold it until I need it. I only need a portion of it initially."

"Do you want me to be your bank? You know I only facilitate transfers. I don't hold assets."

"Yes, I know, but I'm afraid to keep such a large sum at my home or shop. I'm afraid of robbery. Too many people in the IRGC might find out about the payment, and I could be an easy target."

"You could have them deposit the money in a bank."

"I'm afraid I would have no privacy, and it would be a constant worry that somehow the government could take the money from me. The Ministry of Finance controls the banking system, and a word from the right person would threaten my account."

Zubin shook his head once and gave him a long look. "Navid, how much money are we talking about?"

"One and a half million split between euros and dollars in advance, then an equal amount when the job is finished. But another project will bring in even more funds from foreign supporters."

"Now I understand. You want me to transfer and hold large amounts of cash for you, just like a bank. This will be difficult."

"But, Zubin, you do this all the time. You transfer money — to and from — people worldwide."

"Yes, but in much smaller amounts, and I don't hold it in an account for them. Where will this money be coming from — outside Iran? And where will you want to withdraw funds when the time comes?"

"The funds will come from the US. And I'll want to be

able to withdraw funds in several different countries, including Syria, Iraq, Dubai, France, and Senegal."

"Navid-joon, if you weren't such a good friend and married to my cousin, I would tell you it was impossible. But I know you have worked to defend the interests of Iran, so I will help you. But I have to tell you, it will be costly."

"I can understand why it would make you uncomfortable, and I appreciate you helping me. I'll pay whatever I need to pay."

"Why don't you just get paid in Bitcoin or some other digital currency?" asked Zubin.

"Because I can't spend Bitcoins to support my operations in Iraq and Syria; I need real currencies. And who can guarantee that digital currencies are safe?"

"Okay, I understand your concerns. Let's discuss what to do when the first payment is made to Ashk Davari. I think you should create some diversification. Request Ashk to transfer about ten percent to Paris, transfer about twenty percent to Dubai, take twenty percent in cash, and transfer the rest to me. If you don't know what to do with the cash, I will hold it for you. And when you know more about the funds coming from the US, please talk with me again. In the meantime, I'll work out arrangements with hawaladars in the locations you've mentioned."

Navid said, "I also want to set up the hawaladar accounts so that any of us — myself, Farzin, Baraz, and Roya — can claim the money."

"You know that hawaladar transfers are only person to person, right? That's how the system works," replied Zubin.

"Yes, but there must be situations where the person receiving funds dies before they claim the money. What do you do in that case?"

A look of concern crossed Zubin's face, but he said, "Yes, we make exceptions. I'll see what I can do."

"Thank you, Zubin. I'm sorry to ask so much of you. And one more thing — please don't mention any of this to Roya. She gets so upset when she thinks of the danger her children face and blames me."

"Yes, of course."

Navid stood, and Zubin did likewise. Navid awkwardly tried to embrace Zubin and kissed him on the cheeks.

"*Khoda hafez,*" Navid said.

"*Khoda hafez,*" Zubin said as he embraced Navid and kissed him on both cheeks.

As Navid left Zubin's shop, he was pleased. He had made arrangements to handle the payment from the General and at least had begun to plan for the transfer of money from the Warthog. And he still had all his options open.

If the Warthog declined his offer, he could always go ahead with the attack on Bu Hasa. But if he could work out a deal with the Warthog, he was getting all the pieces in place to make it happen. Now, he just had to wait for the Warthog's response.

CHAPTER 43

I HAD JUST gotten into the office when my phone rang. It was a lady who said she lived in New Orleans and was given my name by an antique dealer. She said her name was Mrs. Amelia Lascaux.

"Mrs. Lascaux, how can I help you?" I said.

"Mr. Antoine at the Dumaine Antique Gallery said you could help me. My mother died recently, and I'm trying to dispose of her assets. I mean those that I don't wish to keep. She left me a singing bird box that's been in the family for over a hundred years. Mr. Antoine says it's very valuable, but he doesn't think he has any regular customers who would be interested. He mentioned you as someone who deals in collectibles and might be able to help me."

"Yes, I know Mr. Antoine. Mrs. Lascaux, singing bird boxes are rare but not as popular as music boxes. Have you thought about auctioning it?"

"Oh no, I couldn't do that. I'm afraid I wouldn't get any-where near its true value," she replied.

"I don't have any customers who collect singing bird boxes, Mrs. Lascaux."

"Won't you please just look at it? You might think of some-one who would like it once you see it. Mr. Antoine says you have a very sophisticated clientele, Mr. Markey."

"Well, all right then, Mrs. Lascaux. I will look at it, but no promises."

"When can I see you, Mr. Markey? I am most anxious."

"Could you come to Natchez the day after tomorrow?"

"Yes, I can do that. It's about three hours from New Orle-ans. I could be there at 1:00 p.m."

"That will be fine, Mrs. Lascaux. I'm on the third floor of the First Mississippi Bank building on Canal Street, in Suite 301."

Alex walked into my office through the connecting door as I hung up. He saw the contemplative look on my face.

"Who called? You look puzzled."

"A lady from New Orleans. She wants me to look at a sing-ing bird box she's inherited and wants to sell."

Alex frowned. "Do you know her?"

"No, she was directed to me by an antique dealer I know," I replied.

"I don't like the sound of this," Alex said with a head shake. "How do we know this person is who she says she is?"

Grant shrugged. "I really don't. I suppose I should call the antique dealer and ask him."

"Are you going to see her?"

"Yes, the day after tomorrow."

"I don't think that's a very good idea. What if she's a foreign agent, maybe a Russian? I think I should see her instead. I'll look at her singing bird box. I know something about them. There were quite a few in France that came from Geneva, where the best ones were made. I can tell her if it's valuable and if we might be interested," Alex said.

"Okay, I'll call the antique dealer."

After searching for his phone number, I made the call.

"Hello, Richard? This is Grant Markey. I'm calling about a Mrs. Lascaux. She called me today. What can you tell me about her?"

"Hello, Grant. Nothing, I don't know Mrs. Lascaux. She came into my shop with the singing bird box and wanted to know what it was worth and if I would buy it. I examined it, though, and it looks like a genuine antique. I told her I wasn't interested and couldn't tell her how much it was worth but that you could help her. I know you deal in expensive collectibles. I saw the movement was marked 'Charles Bruguier – Geneve' and did some quick online research. Then I knew it was quite valuable."

"Richard, this is important. Did you volunteer my name, or did she ask about me?"

"I believe she asked if I knew any antique dealers who might know about singing bird boxes. I thought about your collectibles business, so I figured you would know."

"Okay, thanks, Richard. Hope you've been well. Goodbye."

"Goodbye, Grant. Sorry I got you involved in this."

"No problem."

"Well, what do you think?" Grant asked Alex after filling him in.

"This may be a ruse to get a shot at you, or it may be innocent. But it may not all be innocent because maybe she led Antoine to recommend collectible dealers, and hoped he would direct her to you. Then she could use him as a reference. I imagine that was in case you called Antoine and ask him about her. It wouldn't be logical for her to just show up in Natchez or call you about a singing bird box without doing any research in New Orleans.

We could check various sources to see if this lady exists, but I'm willing to bet a Mrs. Lascaux is living in New Orleans, though we won't know if it's her. We'd have to go to New Orleans and snoop around, and we don't have time for that. We'll keep you away from her, and I'll check her out."

"Okay, that makes sense."

CHAPTER 44

TWO DAYS LATER, at precisely 1:00 p.m., the buzzer sounded at Grant's door. But Grant was at Wexford House with Angie, as a precaution. Craig was in the next suite, watching Alex from a hidden camera in Grant's office. Alex checked the screen on the security monitor, saw a woman standing outside, and then opened the door.

"Mr. Markey?" she asked.

"Mrs. Lascaux? Please come in. I'm Alex King, Mr. Markey's partner in the collectibles business. He couldn't make it today but asked me to look at the singing bird box."

Mrs. Lascaux had a very disappointed look on her face. She hesitated for a second outside the door before stepping in with a black leather case in her right hand. It looked like a cosmetics case with a hinged lid and a handle. She had her medium-sized purse strap slung over her left shoulder.

Alex said, "Please sit at the conference table, Mrs. Lascaux."

"You may call me Amelia."

"And you can call me Alex."

He looked her over as she approached the leather swivel chair at the conference table. She was medium height, slim to medium build, and in her mid-forties. She had light brown hair, cut in a bob, and clear, pale blue eyes. "Very attractive" would be a good description of her looks — not a knockout, but definitely pretty. He especially noticed her smile, which was her best feature. She wore a dark blue pantsuit and a cream-colored silk bow tie blouse. He had no reason to consider her a threat, but he couldn't tell whether she had a weapon under her jacket, which made him a little wary.

She placed the leather case on the table and her purse on the floor, then pulled the chair from the table and sat down. She smiled as she looked around the office.

Alex sat across from her in front of a small container holding a selection of mini screwdrivers. There was a large piece of black felt spread out on the table. He reached for the black leather case and asked, "May I?"

"Yes, that's why I'm here." Another smile.

"Have you had this professionally appraised, Amelia?"

"No, the only person who has seen it is Mr. Antoine. And I don't think my mother ever touched it during the last forty years, maybe longer."

Alex carefully opened the leather case. Inside he saw the small singing bird box. It was a gilt silver and enamel box, about 4 inches wide x 2.5 inches deep x 2 inches tall.

"Do you know how she came into possession of it?"

"I believe she inherited it from my grandmother."

"So you don't have any paperwork?"

"Oh, no. Is that important?"

"It might be to a serious collector. Provenance is always important, especially for older, unique European pieces."

"You mean to determine whether they were looted during WWII?"

"Yes, I'm afraid so, Amelia. But it's just as important to examine the item to determine its condition and authenticity."

"I'm sure it was in the family long before WWII. My grandmother, or perhaps my great-grandmother, was the first in our family to have it. And I don't know that either of them ever traveled to Europe."

"They might have purchased it in New Orleans. A lot of antiques came from Paris to New Orleans over the years," said Alex.

"Yes, most likely," replied Amelia.

He thought she sounded honest and that she believed what she said. He was looking for any clue that she wasn't who she claimed, but he hadn't seen anything yet.

"Has it been wound?" Alex examined the brass winding key in the bottom of the leather case.

"Yes, Mr. Antoine wound it and played it once."

Alex studied the case. The slide to start the mechanism was on the front right-hand side of the box. The box itself was silver-gilt with an engraved floral and foliage design. The oval-hinged lid in the center of the top was about half the area of the top of the box. It was decorated with a polychrome enamel painted landscape scene.

Alex took the key and carefully wound the mechanism. Then when he moved the slide to the right, the lid opened, and the bird popped up through the pierced, engraved, decorated grille with its green, blue, and yellow feathers fluttering. It was flapping its wings, moving its beak and tail, and swiveling back and forth, synchronized to the bird's song, which lasted about thirty seconds. Then it dropped out of sight, and the lid closed. The bird's chirping sounded absolutely realistic. The bird was about one inch long from beak to tail.

"It's unbelievable that this mechanism is still performing perfectly after perhaps more than a hundred years," Alex exclaimed.

Amelia nodded. He tried to determine if she was happy or relieved, but he couldn't put his finger on her emotion. Maybe she was glad he hadn't discovered a fake?

"May I open it to inspect the mechanism?" asked Alex.

"Yes, of course. Mr. Antoine opened it also."

Alex put on blue nitrile gloves. He turned over the box, selected a tiny screwdriver, and removed the screws securing the bottom of the case. Alex gently removed the mechanism and set it on the felt. As he expected, the main lever was engraved with the name C. Bruguier and the location of manufacture, Geneve. It also was engraved with the number 330, indicating that it was an early model made by Charles Bruguier and not one of his sons.

Alex also noted that the mechanism was the original chain-fusee type, which was more valuable.

"How does it work?" Amelia asked. Alex thought that was a strange question for her to ask. Was she trying to divert his attention so she could pull her gun?

Alex picked up a screwdriver to use as a pointer. "The mechanism is powered by this spring. When wound, it has a certain amount of potential energy to power the box for only about thirty seconds.

"A chain connecting the housing containing the spring to the fusee, a conical wheel. The fusee is connected by a shaft to the disc cams. When the spring is released, it turns the housing, which unwinds the chain from the fusee onto the cylinder, turning the cams.

"In this device, four rotating disc cams are stacked on each other, which drive the levers. One cam operates the bellows, supplying air to the whistle. Another is for the whistle, which is a single-pipe wind organ. Teeth of various sizes on the cam move levers as the cam rotates. And as the lever moves, rotary motion changes to linear motion, causing the bellows to pump air.

"The whistle has a movable plate at the bottom, which slides in and out to adjust the pitch of each chirp. The other two cams control the levers that move the bird's beak, wings, tail, and body — and also open and close the lid. Does that all make sense?"

"It's complicated, but it sounds simple when you explain it. So what do you think it's worth now that you've examined it?"

"It's very valuable. I'm not an appraiser, but it's worth at least fifty thousand to a serious collector, perhaps more. If I were you, I would take it to the Christie's and Sotheby's auction houses in Dallas to see what they say about auctioning it."

"You and Mr. Markey wouldn't be interested in buying it or finding a potential buyer? I just want to get a reasonable price with the least hassle."

She sounded so sincere.

"I'll talk to him, and we'll be in touch if we're interested. May I take some photos?"

"Yes, of course."

Alex pulled out his phone and took several photos of the mechanism. Then he reassembled the box and took several more shots while making sure to get Amelia Lascaux in the image. Alex also took a video of the singing bird box giving its performance. He then put the box back into the leather case and latched it.

"And how can we get in touch with you, Amelia?"

She reached into her purse and handed him an engraved card titled "Amelia Audet Lascaux" with her address and phone number.

"Thank you again for seeing me, Alex."

He saw her to the door and shook her hand when she left.

After closing the door, he went to the other suite where Craig was waiting.

"Well, what did you think of her?" Alex asked.

"She seemed all right to me," said Craig. "But I want to sweep Grant's office for bugs to verify she didn't plant one. I'll have Lloyd Hart come over and do it right away. Meanwhile, be careful what you say when you're in there."

Craig said, "What did you think, Alex?"

"She was lying," he said.

"About what?" Craig asked.

"The mechanism has been serviced recently. I could see fresh lubricant on it. And I think the paper and animal skin bellows have been refurbished. Nothing over a hundred years old looks that good."

"Why would she lie about that?"

"I don't know. It's a mystery, for sure. Why such an elaborate ruse? And where would they get such a rare antique? I imagine if she was a foreign agent, she would at least try to plant a bug. Maybe when Grant didn't meet with her, and I answered the door instead, she called off whatever she was going to do," Alex said.

"Did she leave any prints?"

"No, she was careful not to touch anything except the door buzzer. Lloyd can check that for prints. But I got her photo, and we can try to identify her."

"Okay, that's all we can do for now," Craig said, running a hand through his hair. "We need to be careful. First, the incident in New York, and now this! Call her in a few days to ensure we can contact her. And we can check out the address she gave us. Something doesn't add up, but I'm not sure what. Maybe they were just probing our security."

"Or maybe she's legitimate, just as she says, though I doubt it," Alex said.

❧

Agent Lloyd Hart came to the office within a few minutes and scanned for bugs. He found one under the edge of the conference table where she had been sitting. He checked for prints on the conference table and the chair, as well as the name card she'd provided, but it appeared she had handled it by the edges. He found nothing usable.

He also checked the button on the buzzer outside Grant's office door, but it was clean. It appeared that she had pushed the buzzer with a handkerchief over her finger and, in the process, wiped off any previous prints as well.

They discovered through a computer search that Amelia Audet Lascaux lived in a home at the Garden District address on the card, but she was a ninety-seven-year-old spinster. And the phone number belonged to a teenager's cell phone in Metairie, Louisiana.

The FBI database used for facial recognition had no match for the photo of Amelia Lascaux, and neither did Interpol.

Craig had stationed Agents Donnie Hambleton and Bill Miller to watch the parking lot and to be available in case of trouble during Mrs. Lascaux's visit. They said she drove a black, late-model Infiniti QX60 SUV. They recorded the license number but later found the Louisiana plates were stolen.

And so, the entire episode remained somewhat of a mystery. Grant and the team assumed she was a foreign agent. They thought they would never see Amelia Audet Lascaux again, but they could never be sure — only time would tell.

After many discussions, they decided to destroy the bug rather than try to exploit it. They suspected the bug was planted by a foreign security service. But which one? They didn't know.

CHAPTER 45

NAVID HAD BEEN dragging his feet on picking up the extra drone. He wanted to hear from Warthog, so he would know if selling the RDDs was going to be a real option.

Rather than waiting longer and risking the General becoming suspicious, Navid took Farzin and retrieved the drone.

It had been six days since Navid met with Warthog in Dakar, and he had heard nothing. He knew it would take time for Warthog to line up the millions of dollars from his donors, but he was still anxious. He couldn't stall the General much longer. But there was nothing he could do but wait. He sighed and shook his head in frustration as he sat in his shop, waiting and thinking.

Navid finally decided to contact Armand, a long-time customer in Paris, the owner of Galerie Drouot. Armand specialized in antique rugs of all types, but especially Persian rugs. His family was Iranian, and he knew Persian rugs very well. Armand was not opposed to supplementing his inventory of antique rugs with new ones smuggled into France by Navid. He contacted Armand using the encrypted Signal messaging app on his phone.

"Armand, I haven't shipped any rugs to you this year. I want to let you know that I have a nice selection of rugs from Kashan, Isfahan, and Qom — similar in size and quality as you have purchased previously. I trust you were satisfied. Therefore, I am attaching photos of the ones I can offer you. These are very high quality, as usual. Please let me know if you are interested. I am planning to make a shipment very soon through Marseille. I hope you are doing well. Sincerely, Navid."

Navid hoped for a quick reply from Armand. He was usually eager to purchase quality rugs at a good price. Navid would offer him an excellent price on this shipment. It was part of his plan.

He put his phone down and wondered how much he should take in cash from his hawaladar, Zubin, after the payment from the General made its way through the hawaladar network. He would need to take cash to make bribes and pay other expenses on his journey, whether to Dubai or elsewhere with the RDDs and the drones.

While he was pondering this question, his phone dinged with an incoming message. He saw that it was from Warthog.

"It has taken time for me to line up financial support from my network. They fully support my purchase of the merchandise, and we can offer $4 million each, half now and half upon delivery. That's $20 million for the five sets plus instructions. That's double what I told you I could raise and the most I can do. Let me know if this is agreeable. Warthog."

Navid re-read the message several times. He noticed Warthog did not specify a delivery date or a delivery location. He assumed Warthog considered those particular details that could be worked out later.

He had a twenty-million-dollar offer from Warthog on a plan with a huge risk versus a three-million-dollar offer from the General. However, to do the General's job properly, Farzin would die. He would not send Farzin on a suicide mission, even if Farzin offered.

With twenty million dollars, he would be one of the most well-funded terrorists in the world. But after stealing the RDDs from the government of Iran, he would be hunted and have to disappear forever. He would have to leave Roya and probably never see her again. But things hadn't been right between himself and Roya in a long time.

Baraz would go with him, but he wanted Farzin to stay with Roya, which meant he would likely never see his youngest son again. But, most importantly, he would get a measure of revenge for the killing of his other two sons. And he would be a revered terrorist, as it would not take long for his name to surface as the person who stole the RDDs. That is, if Warthog successfully employed the RDDs to stage a major attack inside the US.

And if Navid died during this mission, it wouldn't be so bad. He was tired of constantly thinking only about revenge. It had drained his soul. And he was tired of living with only one arm. Altogether, he felt he had more of a burden during his life than any man deserved. And if he passed up this opportunity, something this lucrative would likely never come his way again.

The General had been waiting in the back room of the bookstore for five minutes when Navid finally arrived. After the usual pleasantries, the General said, "Why did you need to see me in person?"

"There are some things I think are better not to discuss by phone." But the General was irritated that Navid called for him to meet him here so often. He thought they had already worked out the details.

"Yes, we always must assume people are listening."

"We are ready to accept the device delivery now. It should be soon, but many things, including the weather, need to fall into place. Then we will package the RDDs and the drones and wait until the time is right to move them to Dubai.

"The SNSC has a final deadline in mind — January 1," the General said.

"Okay but that's still over two months away — plenty of time," said Navid. "The other reason I wanted to see you is to tell you that I have decided to use Ashk Davari as the hawala-dar. I asked around, and he has a good reputation. So please let me know when you make the transfer."

"Yes, of course. As soon as you pick up the RDDs."

"I'll pick them up in the next few days. Who do I call to make the arrangements?"

"You can call Colonel Hashemi in my office. He'll know what to do."

The General showed Navid the Colonel's phone number, and Navid entered it into his phone's contact list.

The General said, "I may not see you again before you leave for Dubai. I wish you all the best. May Allah protect you." He wanted Navid to know that he was tired of the frequent meetings and hoped this was the last time.

Navid said, "Thank you. Allah's protection is all I need." They kissed each other on the cheeks, and Navid left the bookstore.

The General sat thinking. He had an uneasy feeling but could not put his finger on the reason. Navid seemed unusually happy. Was it because the money would be transferred soon, or something else?

CHAPTER 46

AFTER NAVID RETURNED to his shop, he texted Warthog through Signal. "I accept your terms. We can work out the details later. Will provide transfer instructions soon."

In a few minutes, Warthog responded, "Agreed."

Then Navid called Colonel Hashemi.

"Colonel, this is the General's friend, Navid. I'm ready to pick up the merchandise. Please tell me where and when."

"We'll arrange for you to pick up the delivery from Colonel Keshavarz. He'll text you when he's ready. It should be only a day or two."

"Thank you, Colonel." Navid disconnected the call.

Meanwhile, the General sent a message to Admiral Mousavi.

"Please send the authorization to Dr. Yazdani to release the merchandise."

A short time later, he received a message from Admiral

Mousavi with a copy of the authorization to Dr. Yazdani. He frowned as he read the document.

October 17

Dr. Hossein Yazdani

Director

Atomic Energy Organization of Iran – Research Division

Dear Sir,

This is your authority to release the required devices and ancillary equipment to Guardian Major-General Farzad Ghorbani, or his designee, to carry out the order of the Supreme National Security Council as approved.

/signed/

Admiral Ahmad Mousavi

Secretary

Supreme National Security Council

The General was not happy. The Admiral had again taken steps to place the responsibility for the operation, or more accurately, its failure, clearly on the General. If something went wrong, the Admiral could deny that he knew to whom the General had given the RDDs.

The General understood this was how politics worked. If something went wrong, the blame would be his, and his alone. But if it succeeded, he could claim the success primarily as his. Of course, the Ayatollah, the imams, and the SNSC would take their share of the credit, but they all would know that the General was the person responsible.

The General called Dr. Yazdani. He had to be careful of what he said, even though the line was considered secure.

"Doctor, did you see the authorization from the SCNC?"

"Yes, General, I did."

"I recall you are the only one who can set the parameters on the devices."

"Yes, that is correct. And I was going to contact you to discuss this, but you called me first," said the doctor.

"I have decided I need to give as much latitude as possible in case of unexpected complications. So I would like to set the acceptable location parameter to one-quarter mile outside the outer perimeter of the subject area."

"Do you mean beyond the outer checkpoint?" asked the doctor.

"Yes, in case they are unable to penetrate the outer security. And also, please make ground level acceptable for all the devices. Again, I want to give significant flexibility in case of complications."

"In that case, I will disable the automatic function. There's too much chance of a mistake if it's enabled."

"Yes, that makes sense, Doctor."

"I'll make the changes before I release them for delivery."

"Please go ahead and do that, Doctor."

"I will, thank you."

"Goodbye, Doctor."

CHAPTER 47

NAVID RECEIVED A text in the morning from Colonel Keshavarz to say their pickup was ready shortly after he arrived at the shop. Later, he and Farzin watched as the Colonel and his men loaded everything into their truck.

When they'd arrived back at the warehouse, it took Farzin and Baraz two hours to unpack the truck and get the RDDs, drones, and other equipment crated and padlocked.

While Baraz and his men guarded the equipment and Farzin went home, Navid returned to his shop. He sat at a small table in the front room in case any customers stopped by. But there were rarely any customers this time of day.

He needed to think. He had so many pieces to his plan that he needed to review the details to ensure everything was falling into place. Many things needed to happen — and in the correct sequence.

1. SNSC payment to hawaladar Ashk Davari.

2. Transfer of the payment from hawaladar Ashk Davari to hawaladar Zubin Deghani.

3. Provide Warthog the payment instructions, then wait for payment.

4. Withdraw 250,000 euros and 250,000 dollars from Zubin for the trip.

5. Confirm the sale of rugs to Armand.

6. Remove the detonators from the RDDs.

7. Make the diversionary shipment with Farzin and his crew to Dubai.

8. Make the second diversionary shipment of rugs to Armand.

9. Start the long journey with Baraz, and the RDDs, to meet Warthog in the US.

Navid picked up the phone to call Colonel Hashemi first and then Zubin. It was time to get the passcode for his initial payment from the Colonel and confirm with Zubin how to distribute the cash.

CHAPTER 48

NAVID WAS AT the shop before 8:00 a.m., awaiting the messenger the Colonel sent over with the passcode. In the meantime, he texted Warthog using Signal.

"Dubai, hawaladar Mohammad Zarawani. Entire amount. Scorpion."

In a few minutes, he received a response.

"Today will send the initial amount as agreed. Warthog."

That pleased Navid. Now he had another loose end to tie up.

He texted Armand in Paris. "Have you made a decision on your order? If not, I have another customer."

A short time later, Armand responded, "Yes, I will take the entire inventory at the price you offered. Please ship as soon as possible. Will pay using the same method as before."

Things were falling into place. The next item was to deal with the transfer from the General. *Where is that messenger?*

Finally, at 11 a.m., a messenger arrived on a motorbike. He entered the shop, saw Navid, and said, "I have a delivery for Navid Sadeghi."

"That's me."

He pulled an envelope from the pouch around his neck.

"I'll need a signature, sir."

Navid grabbed a pen from the table. He took the envelope from the messenger and laid it on the table. Then he took the clipboard, laid it on the table, and signed the paper.

He said, "Thank you, sir," and quickly left the shop.

Navid struggled to open the envelope with one hand, but he finally got it open by tearing open the end with his teeth.

He pulled out the paper and unfolded it. Written by hand was one word, "al-Faw."

Navid could feel his anger rising. It took a lot of nerve on the General's part to use the location where he lost his arm as a passcode for the money being held by Ashk Davari. He realized it was the General's way of reminding him that he owed his life to him, and therefore, telling Navid that he owed the General his best effort to make this attack successful — no matter the risk — to him or anyone else.

That settled it. He was not turning back now. If Warthog sent the money as promised, that was it — he would screw the General. And if the Warthog didn't send the money, he was now sure he would screw the General anyway by changing his mind about doing the operation. He was pretty sure that he was the General's only option.

CHAPTER 49

NAVID'S PLAN WAS stymied until he heard back from Warthog confirming the payment. But he could, at least, pack up the shipment for Armand, for which Armand had already sent payment.

With a list of the rugs that Armand had purchased, Navid headed to the warehouse near his shop, which he'd been renting for many years. He stored some carpets there, but it was used primarily to stage shipments of supplies for his terrorist operations in Iraq and Syria.

When he arrived, Farzin and Baraz were waiting. The crew was just hanging around — half outside on guard duty.

"We've got a shipment of rugs to pack," Navid said.

Farzin and Baraz frowned and shook their heads. They knew how particular Navid was about packing his rugs. He gave Farzin the extensive list. It had a location number next to the description of each rug. The racks in the warehouse were numbered, which, at least, made the process go much smoother.

Baraz staged the supplies — rolls of canvas, balls of twine, canvas pouches, scissors, duct tape, and mothballs.

Over the years, Navid had perfected a method of shipping Persian rugs and protecting them from damage. They were laid upside down on the floor, folded, rolled against the grain, and wrapped in canvas, with a few mothballs in one or two cloth pouches, depending on the rug size, inside the wrapping. The ends of the canvas wrapping were tied with twine or taped. The canvas was breathable, and the mothballs offered protection against moths during shipment. Then the bundles of wrapped rugs were packed in a wooden crate with a couple more pouches of mothballs.

There were ten crates when Baraz and Farzin were finished and had Navid's approval. They were made of the same plywood material and were about the same size as the crates that they had built for the RDDs, but were horizontal rather than vertical in appearance. They were stenciled with the generic markings Navid routinely used to make shipments to France.

They temporarily placed the loaded crates in the corner of the warehouse, ready for shipment.

"I never thought I'd be packing rugs again," Baraz said with a smile.

"I think we've got a lot of surprises ahead of us," Farzin replied.

Navid was just happy watching them work together. Then the thought occurred to him that this might be the last time, and then he was not so happy.

Suddenly, his phone dinged. He pulled it out of his pocket and checked. It was a text from Warthog.

"Zarawani. Code = Viper." It was the code for the hawala-dar in Dubai.

⌁

"Baraz, Farzin," Navid said, "uncrate one of the drones, remove the RDD, and set it on the table."

After they'd done what he asked, Navid said, "Okay, Baraz, now I need Javad, with his case of tools. But tell the rest of the men to stay outside. The less they know about what we're doing, the better."

Javad Azimi had been with Baraz since before the beginning of al-Haqq. They were buddies in high school and joined the Iranian Army together. Baraz was in the infantry, and Javad became a demolitions expert.

As time passed, they became increasingly disillusioned by Iran's reluctance to fight the Sunni government of Iraq again, which discriminated against its Shi'ite citizens. Baraz and Javad left the Iranian Army when their tour ended and immediately joined al-Haqq with Navid, Kaveh, and Javed, fighting against Iraq.

Javad was slightly taller and heavier than Baraz and even darker, with long hair and a dark beard reaching halfway down his chest.

"Javad, I need your expertise. I hope you haven't lost your touch," said Navid.

Javad smiled as he entered the warehouse and walked up to the table, eyeing the RDD. "I'm always up for a challenge — and this looks like one." Javad walked around, looking at the RDD from every angle.

"Very professional," Javad said. "It looks military,"

He looked more closely at the detonator and examined the stainless RDD case in detail. He ran his hand lightly across the shell.

"Is it warm, or is that my imagination?"

"Maybe a little," Navid said.

Javad got a concerned look on his face. He stroked his beard as he often did when pondering a problem.

"This is something I never expected to see — if it's what I think it is." And he was right.

"Well, now that you've seen and touched it, I need you to remove the detonator."

Javad frowned. "Why?"

"Because it's loaded with electronics. I think it can be detonated remotely by someone other than me, and I also believe it can be tracked. I don't like either of those possibilities; I want total control. I want the detonator removed and our own detonator installed."

Javad looked at the device before him, his forehead crinkled in concern. "It might be booby-trapped."

"No, not a chance," Navid said.

"Why not?"

"Because it does them no good if the bomb is detonated anywhere except where they intend."

Javad thought about it for a few seconds and said, "Yes, that makes sense, but anyone crazy enough to make these devices and give them to you, might just be crazy enough."

Navid said, "No, they're not crazy."

Javad studied Navid for a moment. "Okay, if you're so sure, you can stay here with me while I work on it."

After examining the buttons on the front of the stainless detonator case, he said, "So this is where you turn it on?"

"Yes," Navid said nervously. Visions of the bomb being detonated and blowing them all to pieces went through his head. All that work, and all that money, would have been for nothing.

Javad noticed. "Don't worry, I'm not going to do that. And there's a control module, too?"

"Yes."

"Then bring it to me. I want to ensure it's turned off while I'm working on this thing," Javad said.

Farzin opened one of the smaller crates, pulled out the detonator control module, and brought it to Javad, who looked it over and determined it was turned off.

"Well, can you do it?" asked Navid.

"If it's not booby-trapped, yes. But I'll have to make a guess at the best detonator to replace it. I don't know what's inside the shell containing the bomb. All I'll be able to do, if I'm lucky, is to hook up my detonator to the electrical leads coming out of the shell."

Navid said, "I don't want you to damage this detonator. I want the military to be able to track it, if they have the capability, wherever I send it — and the other detonators, too."

"Okay, but I've changed my mind about one thing. I'd like you all to leave while I work on it. You make me nervous watching me. If you can't give me a wiring diagram, I only need my tools, knowledge, intuition, and a little luck."

Navid, Baraz, and Farzin left Javad alone with the device and waited outside. They sat against the wall in the shade of the warehouse across the street.

When they had been sitting there a few minutes, Navid said, "Farzin, I want you to go and buy a package of numbered container cable security seals — at least twenty-five. You may have to go to several stores to find them, maybe even to shipping companies. If necessary, go to Tehran."

"Yes, Father," he said. He got in one of the SUVs and left to search for the seals.

The others sat quietly or leaned against the building, waiting for Javad to finish his work.

CHAPTER 50

JAVAD TOOK HIS flashlight and carefully examined the connection between the bomb and the detonator. He could see where the two red and yellow wires exited the bomb through special fittings.

Next, he took a stethoscope and listened for any activity inside the bomb and the detonator. He heard nothing and was relieved but knew that didn't necessarily mean anything.

Javad could see where the wires entered the detonator through the same type fittings as on the bomb. About one inch of each insulated wire was visible, connecting the detonator to the bomb. The wires were slack, definitely not under any tension. Again, he was happy to see that. He concluded that the detonator wire connections could only be disconnected from inside the case.

He saw that the top of the case was held with six small stainless screws, so he carefully removed them, one by one, alternating back and forth between each side of the case.

Once the screws were out, he carefully removed the cover.

He wiped his brow and continued.

The inside of the detonator case was crammed with electronics, including what looked like a receiver/transmitter and a fairly large battery. Wires from the bomb were connected to the outputs of a high-capacity pulse generator connected to an electronic switch. Unfortunately, the wires were soldered to the terminals.

He was going to have to cut the two wires. So now he had to make a big decision — which wire to cut first? It probably didn't make any difference, but why take a chance — cut them both simultaneously. No, on second thought, it was impossible to sever the two wires at precisely the same time — and even a microsecond would be too big a difference if it was booby-trapped.

Javad decided to cut the red wire first. He thought it seemed the most likely to trigger a booby trap, so why not do away with the suspense? He took the small pair of wire cutters in his right hand. He steadied his hand as the red wire was positioned between the jaws of the wire cutter, as close to the solder joint as possible — and quickly clipped the wire. There was a pop, or maybe a clicking sound, as the wire was cut — and nothing happened! He carefully put the jaws of the wire cutter around the yellow wire and squeezed the handles. The wire popped as it was clipped, and it dangled harmlessly. Javad let out a sigh of relief.

Next, he removed the four sets of nuts and bolts from the bracket holding the detonator case to the RDD. He carefully lifted the detonator from the RDD and sat it on the table.

He opened the door and waved for Baraz to come in.

Navid followed Baraz inside.

When Javad showed them what he'd done, they congratulated him, giving him big hugs.

Then Navid put his hand on Javad's shoulder and said, "I have four more of these for you to disarm."

Javad said, "As you ask, Navid. I'm ready."

Baraz opened the four other crates. He and Javad disconnected the RDDs from the drones. This time, he allowed Baraz and Navid to watch.

But as Javad was getting started, Navid motioned Baraz off to the side. He said, "I need you to run an errand. Come with me outside, and I'll tell you about it."

After they got outside, Navid said, "I want you to go to the building supply store and buy six 25kg buckets of gypsum joint compound. Also, ten of the smaller 3kg containers. I'll explain more when you get back. Let me tell you that Farzin won't be making the trip with us, and I don't want him to know what's happening. He's going to stay here and take care of your mother. He thinks he's going to Abu Dhabi to carry out a modified version of our original plan. I want him to continue to think that."

"Yes, Father."

CHAPTER 51

ROYA HAD BEEN in this situation many times before, but dealing with her men leaving for a dangerous mission was never easy. This time, at least, she had an early warning from Navid that they would be doing a project for the General. And today, she saw Farzin packing a bag and asked him where he was going. He responded, "Ask Father."

She was in the kitchen cooking dinner when Navid and Baraz arrived. She was angry but on the verge of tears when Navid entered the kitchen.

"So this is it?" she asked tearfully.

"What do you mean?"

"I saw Farzin packing a bag. Are you all leaving to do the General's dirty work?"

"Farzin will be leaving tomorrow, and we'll follow in a few days."

"And will I see any of you again, or will you just be a memory like Kaveh and Javed?"

"Yes, you will see us again. Farzin won't be in danger, and he'll return soon. Baraz and I will be gone longer, but we have a plan and won't be in serious danger, either."

"You're lying, and I know it," she said.

"No, that's the truth!"

He stomped off.

☙

Later, Roya served dinner. Navid was very quiet, and Roya was not talking to him. Farzin and Baraz knew their mother was upset, so they were very quiet, also.

Navid said, "Boys, your mother is worried that something awful will happen to us on this mission. I've tried to reassure her, but she won't believe me. Since we're all here together, I want you to know that if something happens to me, I have given cousin Zubin Deghani a large sum of money to hold for me. If you need money, all you need to do is go to cousin Zubin and ask for it.

"I have told him to allow any of you to withdraw money. The password is 'al-Faw.' That should be easy to remember."

"Do you think that's all I care about — money? Well, you're wrong. I only care about my family!" This time it was Roya who looked disgustingly at Navid and stomped out of the room.

Roya walked to her sister's house nearby. She told her sister that she and Navid had been fighting again, which was nothing new. Roya said she needed a few minutes to let her emotions settle down before returning home, so she sat in her sister's kitchen and drank tea.

She knew that she could do nothing to change Navid's plans, so she had to think about the future. Farzin could run the carpet business with her help if he came home safely and alone. She fully expected Navid to be killed, and probably Baraz, too, as he recklessly followed his father into every dangerous situation. But if they both made it back, she still had hope that someday Navid's bitterness and anger would exhaust itself, and he would return to his former self.

After a while, she felt better, thanked her sister, and walked home. She would not talk to Navid to show him how upset she was with his actions. That was all she could do. She was determined to stay strong.

CHAPTER 52

ALEX WANTED TO go to the shooting range. He said he needed target practice, and I did, too. Craig agreed it would be a good idea but couldn't go. He was busy training on security system software changes over at Wexford House.

And Angie had a hairdresser appointment and didn't want to cancel it.

So it would be just Alex and me going to Pearl, Mississippi, to the Crosshairs Shooting Range.

Since it was just the two of us, Alex wanted us both to wear our weapons. We cleaned our guns first, as always, before going to the range. Then we got ourselves ready to leave.

We took the nondescript black Ford Explorer SUV, usually driven by Agent Miller. He was training with Craig. Alex drove, and I was the navigator.

On our way out of Natchez, Alex said, "Grant, we need to get some gas."

"There's a Chevron station over on US 61, across from McDonald's," I told him.

We turned into the Chevron station, and one island of four pumps was empty, so we pulled in there. Alex opened the door, turned to me, and said, "Pull your gun and cover me. This is where we're the most vulnerable." I thought that was odd for him to say, but I assumed he was just being cautious. I held the Glock 19 in my lap and watched for trouble.

Alex activated the pump and put the nozzle into the tank. Just as he started pumping gas, a white Hyundai sedan came to a screeching halt right in front of our hood, blocking us.

I could see two people in the front seat, wearing ski masks over their faces — just like the man in my nightmare! The man in the passenger seat jumped out of the car. He was tall and dressed all in black, and there was a gun in his hands. That was all I could see.

"Put up your hands," he said to Alex gruffly.

But Alex had other ideas. He had the pump nozzle in his hand. He had taken the nozzle out of the gas tank when he saw something wasn't right.

He was about six feet away from the man with the gun. He pointed the nozzle in his direction and started spraying him with gasoline. Some of it got in the man's eyes, partially protected by the ski mask, and partially soaked his clothes. He could barely see. Alex dropped the hose and leaped over to where the man was bent over, trying to wipe his eyes. Alex kicked him in the left ribs, and he hit the ground.

All I could think was, *Dear God, don't let that gas ignite!*

The other man in the driver's seat came out of the Hyundai with a gun in his right hand. I quickly opened my door and jumped out. He didn't seem to notice me; he was drawing a bead on Alex. He was shorter, stockier, but dressed the same as his friend, ski mask and all.

Alex jumped back behind the fender when he saw the driver pointing the gun in his direction.

I couldn't let him just shoot Alex while I did nothing, so I aimed and pulled the trigger twice. He went down. The man who had been sprayed with gasoline recovered enough to grab his gun. He pointed it at Alex and fired a wild shot that, thankfully, missed.

I swung my gun hand toward the guy on the ground, but Alex had already drawn his Glock. He shot the man multiple times before the guy could get off another shot. The guy on the ground didn't move after that.

"Alex, are you okay?" I shouted.

"Yeah, I'm fine, thanks to you."

"What was that about?" I asked, breathing heavily.

"An attempted kidnapping, I think."

"The cops will be coming," I said. "We need to stay right here."

Alex nodded. It was a close call. He was breathing heavily.

"We need to say it was an attempted carjacking," he said. "If we say anything about kidnapping, that will create too many questions."

"We could say it was a robbery," I said.

"Maybe we just should say we don't know if it was a robbery or carjacking. We were told to get out of the car at gunpoint, and that's all we know."

"Okay, that sounds good to me."

We heard sirens in the distance, but not too far away. The Natchez Police Department was only a couple of blocks down the street. Someone in the gas station had called the police and told them someone had been shot.

The police arrived quickly and called for a second ambulance. Then other officers arrived. They checked the wounded men but said they thought they were dead.

The police officers waited to do anything except to ask us to lay our weapons on the ground and put up our hands. We were put into the back of two different police cruisers.

When the ambulances arrived, they pronounced both men dead.

I felt nauseated and was sweating and shaking. I assumed it was a normal reaction to what had happened.

I couldn't stop thinking that I had killed a man. But he was going to kill Alex and then kidnap or kill me, too. I thought it was clearly self-defense, but would the police look at it that way?

When Natchez Detective Matt Suter arrived, he questioned us separately.

I told him we never saw the suspects' faces. I'm sure Alex told him the same thing.

He asked why we were at the gas station and what we saw and did.

I gave him my version of what happened.

Detective Suter had known me for a long time. He seemed sympathetic and willing to believe me, which was good because it was all true.

They took us to the police station to each make a written statement. They wanted to keep our car to process for any evidence, and they kept our weapons to run ballistic tests to find out who shot who.

I asked, "Will we find out who those guys were? Were they criminals? What's next?"

Detective Suter said, "We'll look for other witnesses and look at the security video. If your story checks out, that will be the end of it, as far as you're concerned. I'll call you in a week or so and let you know if we've got any info on those guys. And we'll let you have your weapons back."

"I guess they weren't expecting us to be armed," I said.

He replied, "I imagine not. Usually, they target single

women for carjacking, so it was probably meant to be an armed robbery. Maybe they were on drugs? If they were, we'd find out from the coroner's report. And we'll find out who they are and what they've done in the past."

The detective paused a moment before he said, "Is Mr. King always so aggressive?"

"He was in the Marines, so I guess he was trained to be aggressive and to defend himself."

"We ran the plates and know that wasn't your car or his."

"Yes, he's new in Natchez and we borrowed the car from a friend."

"How is it that you know Mr. King?"

"He's my new partner in the collectibles business," I said. "He has a similar business to mine in France, and we're going to collaborate. He can source antiques in Europe, and I have the clientele to sell them here."

"I never knew you carried a gun, Grant," said the detective.

"Well, sometimes I'm transporting expensive antiques, and I'm increasingly afraid of robbery. I've got an enhanced concealed carry permit."

Suter nodded his head.

I didn't like the direction of this line of questioning.

Then he looked at me for a long time, deep in thought, but didn't say anything.

Finally, he said, "Until we get back to you, just go about your business. You and Mr. King were lucky today."

I definitely agreed with that.

Two weeks later, Detective Suter called and said the investigation was finished, and we could pick up our weapons and the car. He said the security video matched our statements and was conclusive.

He also reported that the two dead men were members of a gang in Houston that specialized in robbery, carjacking, extortion, murder-for-hire, and kidnapping. They had never been known to operate in Mississippi.

When I heard this, I thought, *That proves this wasn't random. Someone is out to get me. I need to think about what I can do to keep myself and Angie safe. And that nightmare was a premonition after all! This deal with Tony clearly isn't working out, but I don't see a way to quit. This stinks!*

CHAPTER 53

OCTOBER 22
QOM, IRAN

WHEN NAVID, BARAZ, and Farzin arrived at the warehouse in the morning, Navid gave Farzin an envelope of cash to bribe the ship's captain and the officials at the port. The plan was for Farzin to catch the boat to Abu Dhabi at Bandar Lengeh Port and ensure the crates made it to the port warehouse. Of course, Farzin didn't know that the boxes held only the original detonators but not the RDDs, nor that Baraz and Navid weren't joining him like Navid told him they would.

"I'll see you soon, son," Navid said as he awkwardly hugged Farzin.

Farzin hugged Navid and Baraz.

"I'll let you know when I get to Abu Dhabi, and then I'll wait."

"Yes, that's the plan," Navid said.

Baraz and several of his men loaded the box truck with the crates, and Farzin left on his trip.

Navid wiped a tear from his eye. He was sure he would

never see his son again. He watched until he could no longer see the truck when it turned the corner at the end of the street.

Next, Navid texted photos of the crates in Farzin's truck with the seals and the timestamp clearly visible. Navid told the General, "The shipment is on the way."

The General responded, "Excellent!"

Navid assumed they were being watched right at this moment by an Iranian surveillance satellite. He hoped so — at least for a few more hours. And he felt sure the detonator modules were being tracked by the General; he had too much at stake to lose the RDDs.

The next task was to ready the shipment of rugs to Armand. Navid wanted to ensure a decoy shipment for the General to chase once he discovered the RDDs were not in Abu Dhabi.

Two hours later, a second van left the warehouse with rugs bound for Beirut, then to Marseilles for Armand. Farad and Davud were driving the van. They had instructions to take the carpets to the port, as usual, then wait for instructions.

Navid and Baraz, with the rest of their crew, would leave for Latakia, Syria, with the RDDs tomorrow.

As far as Navid was concerned, everything was on schedule.

CHAPTER 54

HURRAS ANSAR AL-HAQQ had years of experience smuggling cargo into and through Iraq and Syria. There were border agents who they had bribed regularly for a long time. At most border crossing points, guards would only casually look into the back of their van, encouraged by a generous bribe not to look too closely. That was where Navid planned to take the RDDs, through Syria, to its major port at Latakia.

However, it was unwise to flaunt anything obviously illegal. As long as the cargo superficially appeared legal, it was allowed to pass with a wink and a nod.

They would form a convoy with the cargo van containing the RDDs in the middle. There were seven men — Baraz, Navid, Javad, and four others. Baraz would drive the lead SUV, Javad would drive the cargo van, and Hassan would drive the other SUV. Navid would ride with Baraz. Javad had installed two hidden compartments under the floor of the cargo van, which held the detonator supplies and C-4 plastic explosive. He'd had to rearrange the AK-47s and ammunition already stored there to make it all fit. The crates with the RDDs, labeled "Handle with Care," were loaded first, then the two crates with the carpets. Finally, all their duffel bags and personal items were packed near the rear doors. They would retrieve their automatic weapons when they entered dangerous territory west of Baghdad.

They only needed to get to Latakia before the General realized what was happening. If they didn't make it first, they would likely die one way or the other.

As they pulled away, Navid's thoughts turned to Roya. He had left his house before dawn. He and Roya had an understanding. After years of frustration and turmoil, they learned this was the best way for them to part when he left on one of his terrorist missions. It was too hard for her — and him — to say their goodbyes, and it usually ended in a fight. So he would leave early while she was sleeping, or at least pretending to sleep.

He hoped he would see her again in better circumstances one day, but he knew that wasn't likely.

Putting that thought out of his mind, Navid turned to Baraz. "What did you tell the others?"

"Well, Javad already knows about the RDDs, so he may have told the others; I don't know. But I told Hassan, Kayvan, and Shahruz we had a very precious but dangerous cargo. And that we were going to sell it to another terrorist organization, but we needed to deliver it to another country, which could only be reached by ship. If we were successful, I told them it would fund our needs for a long time, and they would get a nice bonus. When we reached the ship, we wouldn't demand them to continue the journey, but we would like it if they did. And they would need to decide in a couple of days."

"Very well. It's good that they know that much. They've been loyal, so I think they'll join us on the trip."

Navid settled back in his seat for the long ride. All he could think about was making it to the ship before the General discovered he had been duped.

❧

It was late in the day, and they wanted to cross the border before dark while the traffic was still light. After about eight hours, they reached the border at Khosravi. The border terminal was a huge and modern installation.

Baraz and Navid had passed through this border crossing many times, so they knew the routine. They pulled into the covered checkpoint and stopped at the barrier. A border guard walked up to the SUV.

"Let me see your passports, please," said the Iranian border guard.

"We are with the two vehicles following us. Can you process us all together?" asked Baraz.

"Yes, I can do that," said the guard.

They knew the border guards didn't care what was being taken from Iran into Iraq. They only cared about stopping criminals with warrants for their arrest from leaving the country.

The guard walked back to the cargo van and collected their passports, and then to the SUV bringing up the rear to do the same.

The guard then went inside the checkpoint office to see if anyone in the group was wanted; they were not. He stamped the passports, brought them back outside, and gave them to their owners. He looked into the back of the SUVs.

"I'll have to inspect the inside of the cargo van," he said to Baraz. He wanted to be sure no one was hiding.

"Can I walk back with you and unlock the van?" asked Baraz.

"Yes, of course."

Once Baraz had unlocked and opened the back doors, the guard looked inside with his flashlight.

"What is that smell?" asked the guard.

"Camphor — mothballs. We have a shipment of rugs, and we need to protect them from moths."

The guard nodded and said, "Everything appears to be in order."

Baraz handed him a folded hundred euro bill.

"We appreciate your efficiency," said Baraz.

The guard nodded and opened the barrier to let them pass.

On the Iraqi side, at the Almunthrya Border Crossing Station, there was a completely different situation. Iraq was concerned with keeping out refugees and terrorists from other countries and preventing dangerous weapons and terrorist supplies from entering.

However, after the Americans had left Iraq, the national and regional governments returned to their old ways. Border agents were appointed by patronage, and enforcement was lax.

Baraz and the convoy were directed by Iraqi border guards into an inspection shed about five hundred feet inside Iraq. The facility was old, laid out haphazardly, and appeared dirty and disorganized — in sharp contrast to the Iranian facility.

The Iraqi border officer asked, "What is your business in Iraq?"

Baraz said, "We have a shipment of rugs and want to pass through Iraq on the way to the port at Beirut. These three vehicles are traveling together, providing security for the shipment."

"Let me see your passports."

Baraz handed over their passports, and the guard collected the remaining passports from the other vehicles. He went into a small office in the corner of the shed. He scanned their information into the Iraqi border control system. None of them were on any watch list forbidding entry into the country. And

Iran was one of the countries whose citizens were not required to have a visa to enter Iraq. He stamped their passports and handed them back to Baraz.

"I'll need to inspect the cargo," said the guard.

"I'll have to unlock the van," said Baraz. The guard nodded.

Baraz unlocked the van and opened the doors. The guard peered in with his flashlight.

"Why are the crates locked?"

"Because the rugs are valuable."

"And why do the crates have holes in them?"

"Because the rugs need to breathe."

"What's that smell?"

"Camphor — mothballs."

"Okay, you may proceed."

Baraz said, "Thank you, my friend," as he handed him a hundred euro bill. The guard nodded and smiled.

As the convoy pulled away from the border crossing station, Navid breathed a sigh of relief. He was still very worried that the General might find them out. You never knew when something might go very wrong.

CHAPTER 55

THE CONVOY SPENT the night in Khanaquin, leaving after they ate breakfast at a small cafe in a neighborhood that was an enclave of Iranian immigrants. They had already installed Iraqi plates to help them stay under the radar around Baghdad and into Al Anbar Governorate.

As they were readying to leave Khanaquin, Baraz received a message from Farzin. "The cargo is in the warehouse." Baraz handed Navid his phone. Navid handed it back and said, "Tell him to wait for further instructions and that we'll see him soon." Baraz nodded and sent the message.

They were only a little past Baghdad when Navid said, "I've changed my mind. I don't think we should wait any longer to get our weapons from the van. Let's find a place to stop just west of Ramadi. There's been too much going on in Anbar Province lately. And we aren't exactly welcome there."

Baraz nodded.

Four hours later, they passed through Ramadi after they crossed the Euphrates River. Once they were through the town, they approached a bombed-out and deserted industrial area. Baraz pulled off the road and through a paved area filled with rubble and potholes. The cargo van and the trailing SUV followed. Baraz stopped behind a partially destroyed building.

Baraz and Navid got out of their SUV. They called over the rest of their group.

"We're going to get our AK-47s from the cargo van. Also, ammunition and some grenades. We don't know what might happen during the rest of our trip. We're going to be stopping in Ar-Rutbah for food and gasoline. We know it's not a safe place, so I want you — Hassan, Kayvan, and Shahruz — to ride together with your weapons in the trailing SUV. Park away from us when we stop in Ar-Rutbah, and keep out of sight as much as you can. Then hang back when we leave until we approach the border crossing. And watch for anyone following us. You may need to bail us out of trouble."

The convoy entered Ar-Rutbah, the largest town in Anbar Province. Ar-Rutbah was a Sunni stronghold and was even briefly occupied by ISIS. There were still terrorist gangs operating in the area, of which Baraz and Navid were keenly aware. This was their last chance for food and gasoline before entering Syria.

They stopped at a gas station on the western outskirts of Ar-Rutbah. Many trucks often stopped there for the night as the station also served food.

After filling his gas tank, Baraz pulled into a row of vehicles near the building. The cargo van parked next to him. The second SUV hung back, filling its tank in the island of pumps farthest from the cargo van. Then they parked several rows away but with a clear view of the SUV and the cargo van.

Baraz went into the building and ordered food to go. He brought it back for himself, Navid, and Javad, and they sat in their vehicles and ate. Meanwhile, Kayvan went into the building and brought back food for himself, Hassan, and Shahruz. They finished their food quickly.

Baraz and Javad drove their vehicles from the lot onto the highway, heading west toward the border crossing. Baraz noticed that two panel trucks seemed to be waiting for them to leave and, after he and Javad passed, the trucks pulled out behind them. He could see in his rearview mirror that Hassan waited until the panel trucks were well down the road before he left the lot.

Only a mile or so down the road, Baraz said, "I think we've got a flat." The tire pressure icon had started flashing. He began to slow down, looking for a place to pull off the road.

A few hundred yards farther, Baraz pulled off into a gravel parking lot in front of a row of abandoned and bombed-out shophouses.

During the ISIS battle against Iraqi and American forces, many buildings where ISIS took refuge were bombed and hit with rockets. Shophouses, each with a storefront downstairs and an apartment upstairs, were popular with ISIS because they could store their equipment downstairs and live directly above. They forced out the owners and took them over for their own use.

Javad pulled in behind Baraz and waited to find out what was happening.

The panel trucks pulled in, one stopping in front of Baraz and one stopping next to him, blocking his SUV.

Baraz couldn't see Hassan, but he hoped his friend had noticed what was going on. Baraz didn't have a good feeling about these panel trucks.

He reached over and got a flashlight from the glovebox

since it was getting dark, then climbed out of the SUV to check the tires. He had his Glock in his waistband, just in case. Navid also had his handgun ready and had gotten out of the SUV on the passenger side. He stood next to the door, ready and waiting for whatever happened next.

Baraz saw that the back left tire was flat. He suspected the trucks' occupants had something to do with that; most likely, an icepick, or something similar, forcefully stabbed into the tire, causing a leak.

He decided to act normally until he saw that things weren't normal. As he walked around and opened the tailgate to retrieve the tools to change the tire, he noticed two men getting out of each panel truck and walking toward him.

"Flat tire?" said the biggest man of the bunch. He had shaggy black hair and a full beard. He was wearing faded military fatigues, as were the others. But the most noticeable feature was a scar across the right side of his nose that disappeared under his beard.

"Yes, it looks that way," said Baraz.

"You need any help?" said the big man.

"No, I can handle it," said Baraz.

"We'll stay until you change it, just in case you need help," the big man added.

Baraz shrugged his shoulders as he pulled out the tools.

The other men casually surrounded Baraz.

Navid stood on the other side of the SUV.

Baraz started cranking the mechanism to lower the tire from the bottom of the Land Cruiser. After it was on the ground, he crawled underneath and disconnected the chain. Then he pulled the tire out from under the SUV and picked up the jack. He set up the jack, loosened the lug nuts slightly, and then raised the wheel off the ground with the jack. He removed the lug nuts, removed the tire, and placed the spare on the hub.

Then he put the lug nuts back on, tightened them, and lowered the SUV to the ground. And then, he put the jack and the tools away. Meanwhile, the men from the panel truck stood quietly and watched.

While he was doing all this, two of the men left the group and walked back to the cargo van. They told Javad to get out and join them while Baraz changed the tire. One of them held a gun on Javad. After checking to see if Javad had a weapon, they marched Javad over to the SUV.

"Can you give me a hand with this tire?" Baraz asked the big man. The big man motioned to one of the others, who helped Baraz put the tire in the back of the SUV.

Baraz shut the tailgate; he saw Javad but didn't see that Javad had a gun stuck in his back.

"Okay, thanks for your help," he said to the big man as he walked toward the driver's door.

"Wait a minute," said the big man. "We want to be paid for our help."

Baraz and Navid knew this meant trouble.

"Okay, how much?" asked Baraz.

"We want your SUV — and your cargo van."

"We'll gladly pay you, but we can't give up our vehicles."

The big man pulled his handgun and pointed it in Baraz's face. At the same time, the others drew their weapons. Baraz raised his hands and saw Navid do the same with his one good arm.

As several of the big man's associates searched them and took their guns, he wondered where Hassan and the others were.

The big man said, "And we'll take your money, too. I recognize your Persian accents. We don't like foreigners, much less Shi'ites. Give me the car keys."

Baraz handed the key fob to the big man, and Javad did the same with the cargo van fob.

"And give me the key to the lock on the cargo van," said the big man.

Baraz nodded, and Javad fished in his pocket, got the key, and handed it over.

The big man waved his weapon toward the shophouses. Baraz and Javad looked at each other, then began walking in the direction the big man indicated.

There were six shophouses in each of the three buildings in a long row, and an alleyway between each of the buildings to allow access to the back doors of the shops.

The big man lined them up against a building and began shouting how he hated Shi'ites and would take pleasure in killing them. His associates kept Baraz, Navid, and Javad at gunpoint, standing about fifteen feet away. It seemed obvious they were going to execute them. Still, the big man wanted to mentally torture them first with the anticipation of death. Baraz was fine with that. It gave Hassan, Shahruz, and Kayvan more time to get to them. He only hoped they realized what was happening.

Without warning, loud reports of gunshots and the characteristic rattling and clanking sound of an AK-47 — "ack, ack, ack, ack" — rent through the air.

Baraz, Navid, and Javad instinctively hit the ground. When the sound stopped, Baraz was surprised to find he was still alive. He looked up and saw Hassan, Kayvan, and Shahruz checking the bodies. The big man and his associates were all quite dead.

Baraz said, "Check the bodies for keys." He helped Navid to his feet.

"Kayvan, Shahruz — bring their vans back here. We need to load their bodies in their vans and then get the hell out of here."

Hassan handed them the keys.

After the bandits' vans were pulled around behind the

shophouse building, they loaded the bodies and locked the van doors. Baraz threw their keys into the mass of burned-out vehicles around the shophouses. He unloaded their weapons and threw those, too.

Baraz said, "Let's head for the border and get across before anyone discovers what happened here." Navid nodded and walked toward their SUV as fast as he could.

A little over an hour later, the convoy approached the Al-Waleed border crossing on the Iraqi side of the border. It was obvious the guards only cared if persons with outstanding warrants for criminal activity were trying to cross into Syria. A bribe of a hundred euros each to two border agents made the process go smoothly. In about twenty minutes, they were on their way.

There was a small border station located about a half mile inside Syria, but they were even more lax, and another bribe made it a quick process. Baraz knew a large gas station in Al-Tanf where he hoped they could fix the tire.

Al-Tanf was fifteen miles past the Syrian border station. It was a small town on the main Bagdad-Damascus highway, so it had more facilities than would otherwise be expected. It was already dark. There was a large, brightly lit, twenty-four-hour truck stop, and Baraz pulled in with the others in the convoy behind him. By this time, it was after 9 p.m.

He pulled up to one of the maintenance bays and climbed out of the SUV. He saw a mechanic working on a small truck inside the garage, so he walked in through the open door.

The mechanic looked up.

Baraz said, "I've got a flat tire I need to fix."

"I'll take a look at it," said the mechanic, wiping his hands on an oily rag.

They walked out to the SUV. Baraz opened the back of the

SUV, and the mechanic lifted out the tire onto the ground. He rolled the flat tire into the maintenance bay as best he could.

"Did you pick up a nail?" he asked.

"I don't know. I couldn't tell where it was leaking."

The mechanic grunted and put an air hose on the tire valve to pump it up. Then he squirted soapy water on the tire and looked for bubbles. After he spun the tire around a few times, he said, "It's leaking here," pointing to the sidewall. "No nail or screw. It looks like a small puncture."

Baraz thought, "*Yeah, an icepick, just like I thought.*»

"I can't fix a hole in the sidewall. But I have a used tire the same size that's good enough for a spare."

"How much?" asked Baraz.

"How about two hundred euros?" asked the mechanic.

"Yes, okay," said Baraz. He was willing to pay a lot more.

The mechanic pulled the tire off the rim and put the used spare on.

Navid said to Baraz, "Let's stay in the parking lot tonight. We can get gasoline and food and use their facilities. We can take turns standing watch during the night and leave early tomorrow. We'll get to Latakia tomorrow if all goes well."

But Navid worried they wouldn't make it to Latakia in time to catch the next ship heading west. If so, they would have to wait. And that would increase the risk of being caught by the General before they could get away with the RDDs.

Baraz nodded and went to tell the rest of the men.

When he returned, Navid said, "Give me your phone."

He had one more thing to take care of before he totally broke contact with Farzin.

He opened the Signal app and sent a message to Farzin.

"Come home, son. The plan has changed. Leave the cargo there. Just come home."

Farzin replied, "Yes, Father."

At least he had taken steps to protect his youngest son. That would at least be some consolation to Roya. He hoped that would count for something.

CHAPTER 56

COLONEL HASHEMI KNOCKED on the door to General Ghorbani's office. "Come in," responded the General as he looked up from his computer screen.

"Sir, I have urgent news. We're tracking the RDDs on the way from Qom to Abu Dhabi. The ship has arrived."

The General looked at him impatiently. "Yes, that's what we expected."

"But, sir, we also had satellite surveillance on the warehouse where the RDDs were stored in Qom. Our surveillance technician reported that a second van left the warehouse heading in the opposite direction only two hours after the RDDs left for the port. He has continued to track it. The van is now in southwestern Iraq, almost to Syria."

"So what? Navid is in the rug business." said the General.

"But if Navid and the rest are all on the ship with the RDDs, who's driving the second van, where is it going, and what is it carrying?"

"All right, keep the surveillance on the second van, and let me know where it goes. I'll ask Navid for a report."

The Colonel saluted and left the General's office.

The General texted Navid, "Please provide an update," and waited for a reply. After a half hour, the General started wondering why Navid was not responding. Was it because he couldn't receive text messages on his phone in the UAE or was he in that van and not answering? All he could do now was wait, and he began to think more seriously that he was being double-crossed by Navid. He hoped he was wrong.

CHAPTER 57

THERE WAS A knock at the back door. Miss Doris wondered who in the world would be coming to the back door in the middle of the afternoon instead of the front door? She wasn't expecting a delivery. If it was that peddler again, she would let him have it.

She wiped her hands with the dish towel and went to the door. She saw their yard man, Willie Johnson, standing there.

"Willie, what do you want? Don't you know I'm cooking dinner for Mister Grant and Miss Angie?"

"I'm sorry, Miss Doris. May I come onto the back porch? I have something important to tell you," said Willie.

"All right, Willie, but make it quick. I don't have time to waste with you."

Willie stepped up into the screened back porch. He was wearing his khaki work clothes, had his work gloves hanging out of his back pocket, and was holding a big straw hat in his hand. Willie was a slim black man who'd been doing yard work for Grant and others in the neighborhood for about fifteen years. Miss Doris considered herself his boss when he was working at Wexford House.

"Thank you, Miss Doris. I'm so sorry to bother you."

"Get on with it, man," said Miss Doris.

"Well, there's this woman . . ."

"Wait a minute. I'm not helping you with your personal problems, Willie."

"No, no, you misunderstand, Miss Doris. This woman says she's an agent of US Customs & Border Protection."

"What, now? What are you saying?"

"There's this lady, and she's been asking me questions about Mister Grant and Miss Angie. Well, about everybody that lives and works here at Wexford," said Willie.

"Well, land sakes. What is she asking about, and why is she asking?"

"She says Mister Grant and Miss Angie are smugglers, Miss Doris!"

"What? Is she crazy?"

"She wants to know everything about the comings and goings here, who lives in the carriage house, and everything!"

"And just when was this? When she was asking, I mean?"

"She's been asking me every week for the last month or so. She showed me a badge and everything, Miss Doris. She said I would get in trouble with the law if I didn't help."

"And what have you told her, Willie?"

"Nothing, Miss Doris, because I don't know anything. I'm just a yard man. But she tells me I need to find out."

"And how are you supposed to do that, Willie?" asked Miss Doris.

"She says I should ask you, Miss Doris."

"Well, look here, Willie, I'm not gonna share any of Mister Grant's business with you or anyone else!"

Willie stepped back and put his hands up as if to protect himself. Miss Doris sounded aggressive.

"I know, I know," he said.

"And when are you supposed to see her again, Willie?"

"I don't know, she just shows up at my house. I don't like spying on Mister Grant, Miss Angie, or you, so I thought I better tell you about it."

"You were right to do that, Willie. We know Mister Grant wouldn't do anything like that." Miss Doris scoffed. "And I bet that woman isn't even a real agent."

"But the badge, Miss Doris. It looked real."

"She coulda got that out of a Cracker Jack box, and you wouldn't know the difference! I'm gonna tell Mister Grant and see what he says to do. And you don't say anything to that woman when you see her. And don't tell her you talked to me. Because if she's a fake, she might shoot you dead, do you understand?"

"Yes, ma'am. I won't tell her anything. And I'll let you know if she comes to see me again."

"All right, Willie, now you go back to work. You did the right thing by telling me. Now keep quiet about it."

"Yes, ma'am."

He wiped his brow and left the porch.

Miss Doris watched him return to the yard and start raking up leaves.

"My, oh my," she said to herself. She knew that secret government work would bring trouble to Grant. I better tell him just as soon as he gets home.

CHAPTER 58

LATAKIA (POP. **380,000**) was by far the largest seaport in Syria, though not large by global standards. It was strategically located, only twenty miles from Turkey and less than a hundred miles across the sea from Cyprus. For years, Latakia had been controlled by Syrian government forces and protected by Khmeimim, a Russian airbase adjacent to the Bassel Al-Assad airport outside Latakia.

For years, Navid has been using Latakia as the primary port to smuggle rugs to Europe. He was known to many officials in Latakia as a supporter of the Syrian government through his al-Haqq organization, which had been fighting ISIS and other Sunni elements who opposed Assad. And with one arm, he was considered a heroic survivor of the Iran-Iraq war.

Baraz and Navid decided to stay at the Al-Samman Hotel, near Hutteen Square, right across from the port. One significant advantage of this hotel was that they could park their vehicles behind the building, so guarding the cargo van in shifts would be much easier.

Navid and Baraz visited the harbormaster, Aram Bakir. His office was in a small white concrete block building at the entrance to the port facility. His secretary announced to Mr. Bakir they had arrived and were ushered into his office.

Bakir stood up from his desk wearing a rumpled tan suit. He was a short, fat, swarthy man with dyed black hair and a bushy black mustache. He came around the desk with his hand extended and a big smile on his face.

"Mr. Navid, my one-armed friend. It's so good to see you!" He shook Navid's left hand.

"Mr. Aram, it's been too long. You are looking well," replied Navid.

"Is this your son?"

"Yes, this is Baraz. He has taken over most of my operation. I'm almost retired now."

Bakir looked Baraz up and down and said, "Yes, he looks just like you when you were younger." He pumped Baraz's right hand.

Baraz smiled.

Bakir motioned for them to sit down, which they did on two couches in the corner of the office. He asked, "What can I do for you, my friend? Another rug shipment to France?"

"No, I have a shipment of valuable cargo that needs to go to the US. And I have to make the delivery personally. So, I am looking for a ship that can take the cargo and us to escort it."

Bakir frowned. "Where in the US do you need to make delivery?"

Navid said, "I prefer a small port anywhere along the Gulf of Mexico or on the Atlantic coast."

Bakir thought a moment and said, "You are in luck. A ship here in port today, the M/V Zervas, makes stops in the Mediterranean, then crosses the Atlantic to the Dominican Republic. After a few more stops, it eventually returns here. But from Santo Domingo to the US, I'm not sure. But I know the harbormaster in Santo Domingo. I will see what I can arrange."

"Can you secure cargo space on the ship and arrange for us to be brought aboard as crew? We'll have seven crates, and there are just three of us."

Navid was referring to the five crates with the paired RDDs and drones, one crate with the batteries and charging equipment, and one crate with Javad's electronic components and tools.

"The cargo won't be a problem. We will just need to create some paperwork. But we'll have to get new passports for you as Lebanese citizens. I can arrange for them today. All it takes is money." He smiled.

"I can handle the costs if within reason," said Navid.

"I'll have to talk to the ship's captain. He won't like adding crew, but money talks. And I'll need all of you to come back here at 1:00 p.m. this afternoon to have photos taken for your new IDs. I'll have them ready for you in the morning."

"Yes, we'll be back at 1:00 p.m. Thank you, my friend."

After they were outside, Baraz asked Navid, "Why did you say there were only three of us?"

"I've changed my mind about taking the others. I only want Javad to go with us; we need him. If we bring too many others with us, it'll draw too much attention. If we can't secure the cargo with just three of us, we can't do it with six. Tell the others that after we're on the ship, we want them to take the vehicles and wait for us in Homs. Give them enough money to last for six months. After Davud and Farhad tell you the rugs have shipped from Beirut, tell them to go home — back to Iran, and wait."

"Okay, Father, as you say."

❧

The next morning, Mr. Bakir was waiting in the guardhouse with a man of impressive bearing wearing a khaki uniform and an officer's cap. His dark hair transitioned into a short, white beard on his broad, tanned face.

Navid and Baraz greeted Mr. Bakir while Javad and the others waited in their vehicles.

Bakir said, "Let me introduce you to Captain Doukas."

Captain Doukas hesitated before shaking Navid's left hand and then shook hands with Baraz.

He said in Arabic, "I welcome you to join me on the M/V Zervas. My ship is not new, but she is a good ship. With modern technology, we crew differently now than when it was new, so we have space for you in the officer's quarters. My request is that you stay away from the crew. They don't need to know our arrangement."

Bakir said, "I've also been in touch with Señor Arturo Rodriguez, harbormaster of Santo Domingo. He may be able to help you once you land there. He is part of a group of like-minded harbormasters who work together to facilitate services for clients like yourself."

"Thank you. We look forward to meeting Señor Arturo."

Bakir smiled. "Captain Doukas speaks Arabic in addition to Greek and English. So he will be your interpreter when you meet with Señor Arturo, who speaks English as well as he does Spanish."

Bakir continued, "I have given your new passports to Captain Doukas. He needs them for the port authorities at each stop. You will get them when you disembark. In the meantime, here are copies you can inspect."

He handed Baraz the copies.

"How much money did Mr. Bakir give you for our arrangement, Captain?" asked Navid. He had no doubt that Bakir was an honest man. This show was purely to ensure the Captain knew Navid expected honest dealings. And it could only enhance Bakir's reputation as an honest man. A win-win, in Navid's mind.

"He gave me twenty-five thousand euros. I assume that was the full amount?"

"Yes, I was just confirming that Mr. Bakir is still as honest as he has been in the past."

Bakir smiled but gritted his teeth as he wiped his brow with his handkerchief.

After a moment of uncomfortable silence, Bakir pointed to a golf cart nearby and said, "Follow the Captain and me to the Zervas."

Navid watched as the crates were unloaded from the cargo van, placed on pallets, and strapped down. Finally, the pallets were loaded into the top level of the forward hold. The three levels of the hold were separated by removable plates. Once the pallets were loaded, Navid headed to the gangway and embarked on the ship. The Captain met him at the top of the gangway and took him to his cabin.

There was a benefit to having the Captain escort them onto the ship. They could bring their duffel bags of weapons, money, and detonator supplies without inspection.

Only one problem worried Navid — Captain Doukas held their passports!

CHAPTER 59

THE GENERAL WAS uneasy that he had still not heard from Navid. He had been thinking of all the possible reasons, some too terrible to comprehend.

The General pressed the button on his intercom and called for Colonel Hashemi.

"Yes, General?" The Colonel entered his office.

"Where are the RDDs now, Colonel?"

"They are still in the warehouse in Abu Dhabi, sir."

"Nothing from Navid or his sons?"

"No, sir."

"Let me know if anything changes, Colonel."

The General pondered his options. He had to decide how much longer to wait before taking action. Fortunately, the Admiral had not yet asked for an update.

Navid might have been waiting to make a move until all the conditions for the attack were favorable. It didn't appear the weather was now a problem, but he wasn't there on the ground to see for himself, so he had to accept that as a possibility. He knew that wind was an important factor, maybe the most important, and the wind could be different even in nearby locations. He had to trust Navid, but he didn't like it.

He could only take one practical step — to contact his agent in Abu Dhabi, Yousef Nair. He would provide the trucks to Navid to make the Bu Hasa attack. The General had actually talked to Yousef about this last week so that he would know the operation had been approved by himself personally. Surely, Navid or Farzin would have contacted Yousef by now to make arrangements. Yousef had no knowledge of the RDDs, but he knew the Iranians had evaluated the Bu Hasa defenses, so an attack of some kind would not be a complete surprise. The General had insisted that Farzin should only be known to Yousef as Abdullah, and he remembered to be sure not to slip and use Farzin's name when talking with Yousef.

The General decided to call Yousef directly instead of asking the Colonel to do it. He used his secure phone line — at least secure on his end. The Iranian technology switched the call through several nodes to obscure its source and disguise his voice.

"Hello?"

"Have you heard from Abdullah?"

"Yes, he called me three days ago. He said he wanted an Al Sayyad food service truck and another unmarked one. And he wanted a small warehouse to use as a staging area. He said he thought he would need the trucks today, but I haven't heard from him again. I'm wondering if something is wrong."

"I just sent you a link to download a file to your phone." The link opened the tracking program so Yousef could see the location of the weapons. He told Yousef to follow the tracker to the place, find the crates containing the weapons, open them, and send him photos of what he had seen.

There was a slight pause where the General assumed Yousef was looking at the program. Then Yousef said, "Sir, the cargo is in a government-run warehouse. I can't get in there without the proper paperwork, and I can't just start opening the crates when I do. The best I can do with proper paperwork is to claim the cargo and take it to another location for inspection. I need you to find Abdullah and get the paperwork."

"Okay, I'll let you know when I do. Wait for instructions."

"Yes, sir!"

When he'd hung up, the General summoned the Colonel.

"Yes, sir?" he asked as he entered the General's office.

"Send for my car. I'm going to Qom, and you're going with me. I'll explain on the way."

The General realized that if things went wrong, the Admiral and others in the SNSC would blame him and maybe even accuse him of working with Navid to steal the RDDs. So he decided from this point he needed witnesses who could testify about what he did when he suspected the RDDs might be missing. And the Colonel would be his key witness.

He was angry at himself for trusting Navid.

When they arrived at Navid's house, the General said, "Come with me."

They stepped out of the car, went to the front door, and knocked.

Roya answered the door. She didn't say anything for a moment when she first saw the General.

"Roya, it's been a long time."

She replied, "Yes, Farzad, and when I see you, there is always trouble. What do you want?"

"Roya, please," he said, palms wide in supplication. "I can't be blamed for what Navid does. He makes his own decisions."

"Yes, but you allow him to make bad choices."

"This is Colonel Hashemi. Are you going to invite us in?"

Roya looked over the Colonel for a moment. "Yes, of course. Come in."

They entered the small living room.

She said, "Please sit down," gesturing toward the couch and an oversized upholstered chair in the corner. "Now, what is it you want?"

"I've lost contact with Navid, Baraz, and Farzin. Have you heard from them or know where they are?"

"Navid and Baraz left here four days ago. Navid said they were working on a mission for you. Farzin left a day earlier."

"Have you heard from them?" he asked.

"I haven't heard from Navid and Baraz, but Farzin is here."

"Here? Now?"

"Yes, and yes."

"Will you get him, please?" asked the General.

Roya stood from her chair and walked slowly down the hallway toward the bedrooms.

In a moment, she returned with Farzin.

"Farzin, why aren't you in Dubai or Abu Dhabi?" asked the General.

"I took the cargo to Abu Dhabi. I was supposed to wait for my father and Baraz to arrive in a few days before proceeding. But I received a message from them saying to come home, so that's what I did," said Farzin. "And I'm waiting to hear from them."

"Did they say anything else?"

"No."

"Do you have the paperwork for the cargo in the warehouse?"

"Yes, I have it."

"Then please give it to me. I need to retrieve the cargo," said the General.

"Just give me a minute," said Farzin.

He returned in a minute or two with several documents.

The General looked over the paperwork. It all looked to be in order.

He hesitated about what to do next. He wondered if Farzin was telling him everything, but Farzin seemed as confused as he was. And if he arrested Farzin, it would set off a chain reaction that could turn out badly. No, he decided it was better to try to sort things out by himself, with the Colonel's help.

"Farzin, let me know immediately if you hear from them. And don't leave Qom without talking to me first."

Farzin nodded.

The General turned to Roya.

"I'm sorry you have such a poor opinion of me. That's all I can say."

Roya looked at him sternly. "Navid owes you his life. You take advantage of that. You should consider whether that is fair to his family."

The General looked at her, nodded, and turned away, walking to the car. The Colonel tipped his cap and followed behind.

CHAPTER 60

COLONEL AMIR HASHEMI was waiting for Yousef at the Millennium Central Al Mafraq Hotel near Musaffah Port. He was in civilian clothes, holding a brown briefcase in his lap as he and Yousef drove to the port warehouse.

The General decided he would attract too much attention if he traveled to the UAE. So, he sent the Colonel. His job was to inspect the crates and confirm the RDDs were safe.

As Yousef parked in front of the warehouse office, he said, "Wait here while I show them the paperwork and arrange the pickup."

The Colonel assumed they would take the crates directly to the small warehouse and open them for inspection. But would the crates be safe to leave there?

Yousef came back to the truck, waving another document.

"When I give them this at the dock, they will bring the cargo to the truck."

The crates appeared to be in good condition when brought

out for loading. After the crates were in the truck, Yousef pulled away from the dock.

"We'll go to the warehouse and open the crates if you like. I brought some tools, but they look fine to me."

They arrived at the small building on a side street near the port in a few minutes. Yousef had paid a premium to rent the space for one month from the owner, who had placed an online ad.

Yousef pulled the truck in front of the warehouse's roll-up door. The truck had a powered liftgate, which allowed them to quickly lower the crates to street level. They worked together, each grabbing handles on opposite sides of the containers to move them, in tandem, into the warehouse. Yousef then grabbed his tools from the truck, brought them into the warehouse, and closed the roll-up door.

"Where do you want to start?" asked Yousef.

"Let's open this one," replied the Colonel.

"And unless you have the combination to the lock, I'd suggest we open the back of the crate," the Colonel said.

Yousef nodded, got out his power screwdriver, and started working on the back panel. After he removed the screws, they tried to take off the plywood sheet, but it wouldn't budge. Yousef pulled a small pry bar from his tool bag. He moved the plywood enough that they could see it was fastened with adhesive to a sheet of thick foam inside the crate, secured along the inside corners.

"We're going to have to pull on the plywood until something gives," said the Colonel.

Fortunately, Yousef had several pairs of work gloves in his tool bag. They pulled on the plywood until the foam broke loose in several places, then they finally freed the plywood with most of the foam still attached.

Inside, they saw white plastic buckets — two much smaller

ones sitting on top of a similar, larger one. On top of the smaller buckets was something wrapped in burlap.

The Colonel removed the burlap bundle and unwrapped it. It was a relatively thin stainless steel case. It had a few buttons along the edge, and a green LED light was illuminated.

Yousef said, "What's that? Is it dangerous? Will it explode?"

The Colonel examined it carefully. "No, the light just shows that the battery is charged."

He sat the detonator control on the floor. They pulled the white buckets from the crate.

They both saw the markings that said "Gypsum Joint Compound" in large letters.

"Should we open them?" asked Yousef. The Colonel nodded.

Yousef grabbed the pry bar and opened the lid on the large bucket. It contained gypsum joint compound. He did the same with the smaller container. It was filled with the same material.

"Is this what you expected?" he asked the Colonel.

"No, it's not." He was already thinking about the General's reaction.

"Should we open the other crates?" asked Yousef.

The Colonel was shaking. He was pretty sure he knew what this meant. But he needed to let the General know right away and get instructions.

"Not until I make a phone call," said the Colonel.

He went outside, climbed into the truck, and dialed the General's number.

"Yes, Colonel?"

"They're not here!"

"What do you mean? The tracker says they are in the warehouse," the General said.

"Yes, the control boxes are here, but nothing else. They replaced the other merchandise with buckets of gypsum joint compound, probably so that the crates weighed the correct amount. At least, that's what we found in the first crate. Should we open the rest?"

"Yes, open the other crates; we must be sure."

"What should I do with them?"

"If the others are the same, gather up the control boxes. Yousef can dispose of them, preferably offshore in deep water."

"What about everything else?"

"I really don't care. Just leave them there. But if Yousef thinks it's better to dispose of them somehow, go ahead."

"And after that, should I return to the office or wait for instructions?"

"You might as well come back. And don't say anything to anyone."

"Yes, sir."

CHAPTER 61

THE GENERAL SAT stunned at his desk. Multiple thoughts raced through his mind. Where were his RDDs? Where was Navid? And why would Navid go to the trouble of placing the gypsum compound in the crates? The only explanation was to fool Farzin. Therefore, Farzin wasn't in on the plan — or was he?

The General could feel his hands shaking and perspiration forming on his forehead. He experienced fear and hate at the same time. He was nauseated and felt faint; he thought he was having a panic attack. If he had really lost the RDDs, it probably meant his life. The Supreme National Security Council would not be happy, and they would quickly demand a scapegoat.

He calmed down and thought there might still be one chance. If Dr. Yazdani was as clever and devious as he surmised, perhaps he had provided a way to track the RDDs themselves — or, just as likely, track the drones.

He called the doctor to check.

When he'd told him the merchandise was missing,

Dr. Yazdani said, "But our tracker shows all of it is sitting in a warehouse in Abu Dhabi."

"Unfortunately, only the control modules."

"That is a big problem, General."

"Yes, I know. I'm hoping you may have provided a secondary method of tracking — perhaps the drones?"

"Not that I am aware of, General. But I will talk with the engineer who installed the tracker. Perhaps he added something without telling me. Let me call you back."

"I will be waiting."

In a few minutes, Dr. Yazdani called back.

"Unfortunately, we have no alternate tracking."

"Yes, that is very unfortunate."

"Do you know where the merchandise might be?" asked the doctor.

"No, but I will check with a few people who may know, and I'll get back to you," said the General.

"I'll be available to help in any way I can."

"Thank you, Doctor."

The General remembered that a second van had been seen leaving the warehouse, heading toward Syria. He would take a risk and ask for an update from the surveillance technicians. It might raise suspicion, but what else could he do?

CHAPTER 62

Miss Doris told me about the woman who said she was a US Customs & Border Protection agent and was pumping Willie Johnson for information.

Wanting to talk to Craig and Karen when I got to the office, I turned to Alex and said, "Sorry, Alex, I've got to talk to Craig about top-secret information on a case we're handling."

Alex said, "I understand. I'll just wait in Craig's office."

We got Karen on the phone, and I told them all that Miss Doris had told me.

I said I thought they should arrest her the next time she appeared at Willie's home.

But Karen disagreed. "We don't know what this is about, but it seems this is some kind of a plot against you, Grant. I doubt this woman is working alone, so let's see if we can find out who she's working with or working for before we arrest her."

"Yes, that's a better idea, especially if it's another foreign intelligence service. We need to know which one," I said.

We decided to stake out Willie's home until she contacted him again, and then we would put a tail on her and see where that led. And then we could decide what to do next.

Craig assigned Agents Sterling Brown, Roman Muzik, and Russ Chandler to handle the stakeout.

And so the stakeout was set up, and we waited for the woman to reappear.

CHAPTER 63

WHEN COLONEL HASHEMI returned from Abu Dhabi the next day, the General told him he'd gotten a report that the second van that left Navid's warehouse had gone to Beirut but was now back at the rug warehouse.

The General and the Colonel arrived at the warehouse about two hours after they received that news. He wondered if maybe Navid was back in Qom. He would force him to turn over the RDDs and arrest him if he was.

The white Renault van was parked outside, but the warehouse was locked.

"Let's go to Navid's shop." Their driver drove them to the shop, a short distance away.

They entered the shop, and Farzin, sitting at the table studying some paperwork, looked up as they entered.

"The van is back at the warehouse. Where is your father?" asked the General.

"I haven't seen him," said Farzin.

"Didn't he take the van to Beirut?"

"No, I don't think so."

"Then who did?"

"I believe he asked Davud and Farhad to take a shipment of rugs to the port in Beirut to ship to a customer in France," Farzin said.

The General frowned. "And what customer is that?"

"His name is Armand. I'll have to look up his address." He picked up a ledger book and flipped through the pages. "Armand Ahmadi. He owns Galerie Drouot, 32 Rue Drouot, 75009 Paris, France. He's a regular customer."

The Colonel entered the contact information in his phone.

"Have you heard from your father?" asked the General.

"No, I'm still waiting."

"Have you heard from Baraz?"

"No."

"Let me know when you do," said the General.

"Yes, of course."

They turned and left the shop.

The General asked the Colonel, "What do you think?"

"I think he's telling the truth. I believe Navid wants to keep Farzin completely in the dark. He's probably doing that for his wife. She's already lost two sons."

"Maybe so," replied the General angrily.

His only option now was to follow the money. That might lead him to Navid, but if not, he might recover some of the money anyway.

When they got into the car, the General told the Colonel, "Get the hawaladar, Ashk Davari, on the phone. We need to find out what happened to the one-and-a-half million payment."

The General was furious and scared at the same time. He had to decide what to do next. He had no idea.

CHAPTER 64

LEVI WEISS, DIRECTOR of Mossad, had received an urgent request at midnight for a meeting with Moshe Kadosh first thing this morning. Levi was grumpy in the morning, and most people stayed away from him until at least 9:00 a.m. So at 6:30 a.m., he was not in good humor, sitting at his desk wondering what this urgent meeting was about. There was a knock at his door.

"Come in."

Commander Moshe Kadosh said, "You remember when we talked of our suspicions about nuclear devices in Iran?"

"Yes. What is it?"

"We have news from our informant in the Atomic Energy Organization of Iran. Do you remember Dr. Rahim Ghanbarzadeh, known as Dr. G?"

"Yes, yes. What information has he provided?"

"He says Iran has lost control of five RDDs packed with enough Cs-137 to contaminate the entire city of Tel Aviv."

Weiss frowned. "How did this happen?"

"He says our friend, General Ghorbani, got approval to attack a location in the UAE in response to signing the treaty with us. The IRGC gave the RDDs to a proxy terrorist group that was paid to carry out the attack, but the terrorists stole the RDDs, and they don't know where they are."

"Didn't they have tracking devices on the RDDs?"

"Yes, but the tracker was in the detonator box, and the terrorists were able to detach the detonator box from every RDD. The IRGC thought the RDDs were in the UAE but found out only the detonator control boxes were there. Dr. G was the one who set up the tracking devices, and they are in a panic to find the RDDs. Unfortunately, they have no other means to track. They lost the devices about ten days ago, so they could be anywhere by now."

"Does Dr. G know the identity of the terrorist group?"

"No, he says General Ghorbani, Admiral Mousavi, and Dr. Yazdani are the only ones who know."

"Then the RDDs could be headed to Israel or already in Israel."

"Unlikely, but yes. I believe we would detect the radiation when, and if, they try to bring the RDDs across the border."

"But what if they brought in the RDDs underground, through a tunnel, with help from the Palestinians?"

"Yes, that is possible."

"Then we have to find out who has them," said Director Weiss.

"Remember the plan to kidnap Dr. Yazdani?"

"I do."

"I think we ought to activate it now."

"How much time do you need?"

"Only about a week. We've been making preparations just in case."

"Yes, I approved and paid for your unusual 'preparations,'

if you recall. I will inform the Prime Minister. You can assume you have approval unless you hear differently from me before 4:00 p.m. today."

"Yes, sir."

Director Weiss sat with his head in his hands. Five RDDs. Location unknown — and in control of Iranian terrorists who hate Israel. Enough Cs-137 to contaminate all of Tel Aviv. And all this before 7:00 a.m.

CHAPTER 65

SAMAN SASANI CAME to the UK when his mother, Shirin, fled Iran after the violent demonstrations during the White Revolution in 1963. Her husband was killed in the riots instigated by Ruhollah Khomeini in opposition to the reforms pursued by the Shah of Iran.

Shirin's other son stayed in Iran with her parents, who blamed her for her husband's death because of her insistence on participating in the demonstrations. She was barred by the government from returning to Iran and eventually lost contact with her parents and her other son.

Shirin eventually married another Iranian refugee named Hassan Sasani, a London doctor. Hassan adopted Saman and began calling him Sam.

Sam Sasani was an excellent student and became a mechanical engineer. He designed agricultural machinery and married a woman named Fariba, also an Iranian immigrant. They settled in the industrial city of Birmingham, where he worked for a company manufacturing agricultural equipment.

Sam and Fariba lived happily until they both developed severe health problems. Unfortunately, Sam had made several bad investments that put them in financial jeopardy and gave a bleak outlook to their retirement. They never had children; they only had each other.

Fariba had been fighting breast cancer for several years. Then Sam was suddenly diagnosed with vCJD, also known as variant Creutzfeldt-Jakob Disease, which is almost always fatal within about a year. Creutzfeldt-Jakob Disease is thought to be contracted by eating beef from cows infected with Mad Cow Disease. And the UK was the center of Mad Cow Disease.

A human interest story in the Daily Mail described the Sasani family's plight. A week later, a knock at their door changed everything.

Fariba answered the door. A tall, nicely dressed woman with short black hair, wearing a dark blue suit, stood on the small porch, holding a dark brown leather portfolio in her left hand.

"Mrs. Sasani, I am Ela Vaknin, Public Affairs Officer at the Israeli Embassy in London. May I talk to you?"

She handed a business card to Fariba, who read it and said, "Yes, come in."

Fariba led Ela into the small living room and gestured toward a chair.

"Please sit down, Ms. Vaknin."

"Thank you, Mrs. Sasani. I won't take much of your time. We keep up with the local news in each country where we have embassies, and I read the article in the Daily Mail. We are so sorry to hear about your and your husband's health problems. We may be able to help.

"We are concerned that the infectious prions that cause

vCJD may be developed into potent biological weapons and used against Israel and other countries. We have been doing research into treatments against prion infections. However, cases are so rare that it limits our research.

"We have an offer for you to consider. Suppose you and your husband agree to relocate to Tel Aviv. In that case, we will provide the best treatment possible for your cancer and for your husband as he struggles with vCJD. We have several treatments in development for vCJD. We would like to test them on patients without other treatment options.

"We will provide housing and a generous stipend for as long as you live. The only requirement we have is that when your husband dies, for whatever reason, he donates his body for medical research.

"I have all the details shown here in this document. I will be happy to explain it to your husband. If you agree, sign the offer document, which you can cancel within thirty days, and we will send you to Tel Aviv immediately. You can make the final decision while you are in Tel Aviv and after evaluating what we offer."

Fariba said, "Sam is not doing well. I will explain and show him your offer letter. If he is interested, I will contact you."

A few days later, Ela Vaknin met Sam. She was very convincing, telling him he could have hope of surviving if he went to Israel for treatment at Herzliya Medical Center, Israel's largest private hospital. And she provided information on breast cancer survival rates for those treated at the same medical center. In the end, Sam and Fariba agreed to go to Israel.

Ela accompanied them on their first trip, escorting them to the hospital in Herzliya, north of Tel Aviv. And while they were talking with the doctors, Ela drove to Mossad Headquarters in nearby Glilot to check in with her boss, Director Levi Weiss. Director Weiss was pleased the Sasanis had accepted the offer.

❦

Unfortunately, Sam only lived for about fifteen months after beginning treatment at Herzliya Medical Center. Per the agreement, his body was given to the hospital for research. Fariba fared better. Her cancer was in remission, and she was allowed to return to London after two years. Israel continued to pay her a monthly stipend as long as she lived.

The Mossad organization always prided itself on thinking and planning years ahead, which paid off this time. They now had the bodily remains of Dr. Hossein Yazdani's identical twin brother. Mossad had been assessing and planning how to compromise Dr. Yazdani since he became the head of Iranian nuclear research.

And the Mossad planned to use the remains that contained identical DNA to Dr. Yazdani's when the time was right. The clock was ticking, and the right time was coming soon.

CHAPTER 66

NOVEMBER 1
TEHRAN, IRAN

EVERY MORNING, DR. YAZDANI left his home in a chauffeured car with an armed bodyguard accompanying him to his office at the Tehran Nuclear Research Center in Amirabad. The best route was directly through the center of Tehran using the Tohid Tunnel.

The only thing that could throw off the plan was if the doctor was sick and stayed home. A Mossad agent, Yair Bekher, was watching the house to see if the doctor was picked up at his usual time. If so, then the rest of the plan would be initiated. If today was a no-go, then tomorrow would work just as well.

A few minutes after 7:00 a.m., the black Mercedes stopped at the gate to Dr. Yazdani's home on Kafiabadi Street. The guard opened the gate, and the car pulled through.

Yair Bekher had a clear view of the gate from where he was parked several houses down. He was tired of waiting and needed to use the bathroom, but he knew he couldn't leave his post. So he just gritted his teeth and waited in pain.

After about five minutes, the gate opened, and the black Mercedes pulled out and turned in his direction. As the car passed, Yair saw a person in the back seat, obscured by the heavily tinted windows. He assumed it was Dr. Yazdani. He radioed to Uri Davidoff, "Plan A, Step 1, Plan A, Step 1."

Uri understood that absolutely verifying that Dr. Yazdani was in the car was impossible. However, they had watched the doctor's house and office for several days and were sure that no one other than the doctor had ridden in the back seat of the Mercedes. There was always a risk of a mistake with an operation like this. But he thought the Iranians were too complacent to switch their routine.

The black Mercedes worked its way over to Yaman Street, then onto the Chamran Highway, the expressway heading south into the center of Tehran. A white sedan pulled in behind them and followed them onto the highway.

Traffic was moderate but increasing as they passed under the Hashemi-Rafsanjani Highway. In the passenger seat of the white sedan, Uri Davidoff radioed ahead, "Plan A, Step 2, Plan A, Step 2".

At that moment, a black hearse and an ambulance pulled onto Darya Boulevard and then onto the ramp to enter Chamran Highway. They were about a half mile ahead of the doctor's Mercedes.

The hearse driver, Mossad agent Ariel Yehezkel, radioed, "Plan A, on schedule, Plan A, on schedule." Uri responded, "Plan A, Step 3, Plan A, Step 3."

Three white box trucks entered Chamran Highway at the next expressway entrance and stayed in the slow lane, waiting for the Mercedes to pass.

Uri Davidoff could see the location of the hearse and ambulance on an iPad, using tracking devices they had installed earlier. The black Mercedes was now only about five hundred feet ahead of them. And the three box trucks were less than a thousand feet further ahead. The noose was tightening.

As the caravan approached the Kordestan Expressway, Uri radioed, "Plan A, Step 4, Plan A, Step 4." At that moment, two agents on motorcycles entered the ramp onto the Chamran Highway.

During the next quarter mile, the critical steps were executed as planned. The black Mercedes passed the three box trucks. The box trucks then pulled in behind the white sedan. The white sedan, with agents Erez and Davidoff, passed the doctor's Mercedes and moved into the far right lane next to the ambulance. The hearse kept pace with the ambulance in the far left lane. The doctor's black Mercedes was right behind them. They were all now traveling at the posted speed limit.

The caravan was lined up as follows: the ambulance, hearse and the Mossad's white Mercedes side-by-side-by-side in the lead, followed by the doctor's black Mercedes, followed by the three box trucks, followed by two motorcycles.

The two motorcycles were in the lane on the far right as they approached the Tohid Tunnel. The tunnel had two tubes, one in each direction, each with three vehicle lanes, plus a motorcycle lane on the far right. The tunnel ran for almost two miles carrying traffic north and south through the most congested part of the city.

The tunnel had two great features for an operation like this. Once a vehicle was in the tunnel, there was nowhere to go except to the other end. And no one except those inside the tunnel could see what was happening.

When the ambulance, hearse, and white sedan entered the tunnel, Uri radioed, "Plan A, Step 5, Plan A, Step 5."

At that moment, the box truck drivers pushed hard on their brakes and stopped, with flashers on, just inside the tunnel, blocking all lanes except the motorcycle lane. The two motorcycles passed the trucks and accelerated to catch up with the black Mercedes.

When the black Mercedes was halfway through the tunnel, Uri radioed, "Plan A, Step 6, Plan A, Step 6."

The driver of the black Mercedes noticed that the traffic had dropped back, and he wondered why. But just as he started to say something to the bodyguard sitting next to him, he saw that the three vehicles in front of him were stopping, too, and that the ambulance had started flashing its emergency lights.

As he came to a screeching stop, the motorcycles pulled up on either side of the black Mercedes. The driver and bodyguard in the black Mercedes turned to look out their windows just as the motorcycle drivers pulled out their Sig Sauer P226 pistols and shot them dead through the closed windows. A few higher-level Iranian officials had armored vehicles with bulletproof glass. Unfortunately, despite his importance, the doctor was not at that level.

Dr. Yazdani realized what was happening and frantically checked to ensure his doors were locked. He crouched down, hoping the assailants wouldn't know anyone was in the back seat, but realized that was unlikely.

Meanwhile, Uri Davidoff was out of his car and approaching the doctor's window. He pulled on the door handle and realized it was locked, as he expected. He shouted, in perfect Farsi, "Unlock the door, or I'll shoot you through the window."

Dr. Yazdani unlocked the door, and Uri opened it. "Get out of the car."

Agent Erez jabbed a hypodermic injector into his neck as the doctor emerged from the back seat. The doctor immediately started to feel the effects of the chloral hydrate/flunitrazepam solution. Agents Davidoff and Erez helped the doctor as he staggered to the back of the ambulance. The gurney was already out of the ambulance, but a body was already lying on it.

The bodily remains of Sam Sasani had not been used for research purposes. Nor had they been cremated, embalmed, or buried. Instead, he had been preserved cryogenically. But not to eventually bring Sam back from the dead; it was to preserve his DNA. The Mossad had a plan, and now they would carry it out, with every meticulous detail thought out.

They had watched Dr. Yazdani for years. They saw his rise through the ranks of Iranian scientists and predicted that one day he would be their top nuclear scientist, which he now was. If anyone knew the secrets of the Iran nuclear program, it was Dr. Yazdani. And now he might possess the information that would allow the Mossad to locate the missing RDDs, and protect Israel.

The recent treaty between Israel and the UAE would simplify one part of their plan. Many Iranians were living and working in the UAE. So it was not unusual when an Iranian died in the UAE to ship the body back to Iran. There was a well-documented procedure, and it happened regularly. And the UAE treaty arrangement with Israel would make it easier to ship a body from Israel to the UAE.

The body of Sam Sasani had been gradually brought out of its cryogenic state. It was warmed to 33F and held at that temperature for twenty-four hours. In the walk-in cooler, the Mossad technicians dressed the corpse in clothing as close to what Dr. Yazdani typically wore as they could approximate — a black suit, white shirt, and they even had an Iranian-made belt and black lace-up shoes. They then placed the body in the insulated coffin. It was monitored and maintained at the critical 33F temperature when the lid was closed.

Sam's casket was taken to the Tel Aviv airport, where a private jet transported it to Dubai. The flight took only three and a half hours. Once the plane arrived in Dubai, the Mossad agent escorting the casket took the papers to DXB Airport Security and Border Control. The paperwork showed the body being transferred from Dubai to Tehran to be met there by representatives of the Ghannad Funeral Home. The security officer had been expecting the transfer. He looked briefly at the forged death certificate and stamped the papers without so much as a question.

The hearse crew had the casket out of the back on another gurney, and the coffin was open. Sam Sasani was lying in the casket, still very well preserved, only slightly warmer now. The agents lifted him from the casket and carried his body to the black Mercedes. They placed him in the back seat.

As that was happening, the body on the other gurney was loaded into the casket. Then the doctor was laid on the emergency medical gurney, unconscious, and the gurney was loaded into the ambulance.

The hearse and ambulance drivers each took a five-gallon container of gasoline. They poured them into the black Mercedes, mainly into the back seat onto Sam's body, but also into the front seat.

Once that was done, they all returned to their vehicles, and Uri fired a rocket-propelled grenade into the black Mercedes. It exploded, with a fireball erupting, generating a thick cloud of black smoke.

After the explosion, the ambulance, the hearse, and the white sedan sped away, exiting the tunnel's south end within about a minute. The strong ventilation system in the Tohid Tunnel would soon spew smoke to the outside. It would only be a few minutes until the police and fire department arrived.

At the tunnel's north end, the three box truck drivers were shouting, "Fire, fire!" as they left their vehicles, made their way out of the tunnel, and disappeared into the crowd of cars and drivers sitting in the stopped traffic on the expressway. They eventually found their way to the intersection of Nosrat and Jamalzadeh Streets. A van was waiting to take them back to the warehouse.

When the fire department and police arrived, the black Mercedes was a smoldering hulk. They extinguished the few remaining flames and began trying to identify the car and the occupants. They also started interviewing witnesses. The problem was that no one really saw anything. But there were the three abandoned box trucks. That was really all they had.

Eventually, they determined the car belonged to the Iran Nuclear Research Center. The Center reported that Dr. Yazdani, the driver, and the bodyguard were missing. The police recovered the remains of the three bodies and took them to the morgue to be identified. There wasn't much to work with.

When the incident was reported to the General, he immediately assumed that Israel had assassinated another Iranian nuclear scientist. Still, he wondered why they had done it at this particular moment, especially with the RDDs missing. Did they know?

The hearse went back to the warehouse. The Mossad agents took the borrowed body out of the insulated casket. They placed it back into its original coffin borrowed from the funeral home. Then they returned the hearse and the casket to the Ghannad Funeral Home in their original condition.

The ambulance took the doctor, still unconscious, directly to the airport, accompanied by a trained nurse who was also a Mossad agent. A Medivac jet was waiting to take the doctor to Dubai. The paperwork was in order, and transporting a seriously ill patient for medical treatment in Dubai wasn't unusual. After a two-hour flight, the jet touched down in Dubai and taxied on the tarmac next to another Medivac jet, waiting to fly to Tel Aviv. The forged paperwork was in order, and no one in airport security batted an eye as the patient was transferred.

Three and a half hours later, Dr. Yazdani was in Tel Aviv. He was taken by ambulance to the Herzliya Medical Center and placed into a private room in the secure ward used exclusively by the Mossad. He was still unconscious.

CHAPTER 67

NOVEMBER 2
PUERTO DE LAS PALMAS, CANARY ISLANDS

NAVID, BARAZ, AND Javad killed time on the ship by watching the ocean, talking, or sleeping. They tried to keep to themselves during mealtime. The crew knew they were paying passengers, obviously a side deal of the Captain, and he had made it clear not to engage with them.

They'd made sure to stay on the ship even when docked. Baraz and Javad had argued with Navid about that, but he hadn't relented. Navid wanted to get off the ship so much he couldn't stand it, too, but it wasn't worth the risk of being spotted. Navid figured they only had another two weeks before they were in the clear in the US.

A serious topic of conversation between them was the detonator.

"What have you decided about the detonator, Javad?" asked Navid.

"I'm still thinking about it," he said.

"What is there to think about?"

"Well, what's the most important factor? The reliability of the detonator or the ability to set it off remotely?" asked Javad.

"I'm hoping to be able to use the drones to allow as wide dispersion as possible," said Navid.

"I think reliability must come first," Baraz chimed in.

"Are you unsure if you can detonate the explosive device remotely?" asked Navid.

"Theoretically, I can. But I've never done it with the available equipment, at the distance you want."

"What's the alternative?"

"The most reliable alternative, assuming you don't want to be close enough to use a wire to detonate it, is to do it with a timer. I can guarantee that will work."

"But then, most likely, that means a ground detonation. It will be almost impossible to coordinate drones to be in the correct position at a specific time, and there won't be much margin for error."

"Yes, I'm afraid so."

"Let me think about that, but the final decision will be made by our customer," said Navid, "And maybe he'll have his own demolition expert."

"I'll try to think of other alternatives," said Javad.

"Yes, please do," replied Navid.

"But doesn't our responsibility end when we deliver the RDDs?" asked Baraz.

"They expected the RDDs would come with the original detonators, though I told them there might be the possibility that we couldn't guarantee it. For the amount of money they're paying, we are responsible for providing a workable option," said Navid.

He knew they would need to decide very soon if they were going to deliver the RDDs with or without detonators.

CHAPTER 68

THE SURVEILLANCE ON the woman who said she was a CBP agent led them to Houston. Agents Brown, Muzik, and Chandler watched her for four days, then moved in with local FBI agents and arrested her after consulting with Craig and Karen.

Agent Chandler gave a verbal report to Craig.

"Actually, the woman lives outside Houston in an upscale neighborhood in Katy, Texas. It took a few days to figure out who she is.

"Her name is Maaike van Leersum, the daughter of Dutch immigrants. But the interesting thing is that she is married to Wu Ming, the Black Jade crime family head in Houston.

"Maaike van Leersum denies everything — even denies being in Natchez or talking to Willie Johnson. The FBI brought in Wu Ming for questioning, but he also denies knowledge of any activities in Natchez."

The FBI obtained a search warrant for their home and found the fake CBP badge and forged credentials. But Maaike pleaded complete ignorance about why the credentials were in their home, claiming Agents Brown and Chandler must have planted them.

The case file was sent to Craig and Grant. By this time, they had told Alex that suspicious activity at Wexford House was being investigated. When Alex saw the file, he said, "That's Amelia Lascaux!" Craig agreed. Alex pulled out his phone and showed Grant the photos of her sitting in his office with the bird box.

Craig passed that information to the FBI agents investigating Maaike van Leersum and her husband.

✧

Maaike van Leersum continued to deny everything, including impersonating Amelia Lascaux. But she was charged with impersonating a CBP officer under 18 USC § 912, with a penalty of up to three years in federal prison. That was the best they could do.

They had no evidence against her husband, but their best guess was that he had contacts with the MSS, the Chinese intelligence service. And he also had connections with other organized crime gangs.

If Wu Ming was in contact with the MSS, they were most likely planning some kind of operation against Grant, perhaps as payback for disrupting the plan to attack the US financial system; that was Grant's first case with the CIA.

If nothing else, this would set back China's plan for a while, and the US government was now aware of its intentions.

Grant was sure they were somehow involved in the attempt to kill or kidnap him at the gas station since they now knew the two dead men were gang members from Houston. But there was no definite link to van Leersum, Wu Ming, or the Black Jade gang.

CHAPTER 69

Mossad Director Levi Weiss finally called his counterpart, CIA Director Tony Russell. Although Director Russell had only been in his position briefly, Weiss had known him for many years, as they both delighted in frustrating Russia's operations in the Middle East.

"Mister Director, thank you for taking my call today," said Weiss.

"Yes, it's been a while since we've spoken," replied Russell.

"I need to make you aware of a situation. You might be able to help us. And there is the remote possibility that you will be affected, too."

"What happened?"

"We have a confidential informant in Iran's nuclear research organization. He tells us that Iran has lost five nuclear devices."

"Atomic weapons? We thought they were at least a year or two away," said Russell.

"No, I mean dirty bombs."

"How much radioactive material?"

"He says enough to contaminate the entire city of Tel Aviv."

"When did they lose them?"

"About two weeks ago. They planned to use the RDDs at an oil field in the UAE to punish them for signing the treaty with us. They had given them to a proxy terrorist group, but now they're missing. He says the Iran military is in a panic."

"What have you done to verify this and locate the RDDs?"

"We kidnapped their top nuclear scientist, Dr. Hossein Yazdani. If anyone can help us understand the situation, it's him."

"I thought he was killed in Tehran a few days ago?"

"We made it look that way, but we have him."

"What has he told you?"

"Nothing. He's unresponsive."

"Maybe we can send an interrogation team to assist you."

"We don't need more interrogators. We need a mind reader." Weiss laughed.

"You mean he's unconscious?"

"Yes, he's in a coma."

"Hmmm, well, that's a problem."

"Yes, we're working on it, but we haven't been able to wake him yet."

"How can we help?"

"We know you have operatives all over the Middle East. If they keep their ears open, they may pick up information on where the RDDs are being kept. We expect the terrorists will have Israel as a target, but so far, we haven't heard from them. We are expecting an extortion attempt — a swap of a huge amount of money for the weapons. The other possibility is that they hate Israel enough to detonate them with no warning."

"Why don't I come to Tel Aviv with a few specialists? We can discuss the options. Have you told anyone else?"

"No, we don't want to create a panic. And if the word gets out, it may precipitate an attack by the terrorists. We need time to find them."

"We'll get there as soon as possible, maybe in two days," said Russell.

"We'll be waiting for you."

CHAPTER 70

THE ADMIRAL REQUESTED an update on the Bu Hasa attack for the SNSC. All the General could think to tell him was that Navid was waiting for the right moment. He hoped the Admiral would not become suspicious that things had gone wrong, but he knew his time was running out. He decided that he better assess his options, and then do something — anything.

Where the hell is Navid? he wondered. He was already thinking of making his escape now before the Admiral figured out both the RDDs and Navid had disappeared. He and the Colonel had talked to Navid's hawaladars, and it seemed that Navid took all the cash with him. And it made sense to the General that the only reason Navid would do that was if he had fled with the RDDs.

The General sighed. If he did nothing and Navid used the Iranian RDDs elsewhere, the General would be arrested and court-martialed as an accessory to Navid's crime. And the most likely penalty would be death by hanging. The SNSC, and specifically the Admiral, would never take the blame.

Another option for the General would be to defect to another country. The United States, Israel, and the UK were the most likely prospects. All of them would be interested in the information he could provide about the inner workings of Iran, agents operating in their country, and other sensitive information about the Iranian intentions for the nuclear program.

He could flee to a remote country and attempt to disappear, maybe somewhere in South America or Africa. But he would have to take enough money to sustain himself, and he didn't have that much. He could only speak Farsi and Arabic fluently, so he would be almost helpless in places where the primary language was English or Spanish unless he had local help.

And finally, there was Russia. They were an ally of Iran when it suited their interests but frequently went their own way. He had good relationships with the Russian intelligence services and military. They worked together in Syria and coordinated efforts in other Middle East operations. He could provide them with inside information about the Iranian military and intelligence operations. And he reasoned that they would protect him — otherwise, they would have no ability in the future to attract other defectors or spies.

Yes, maybe Russia would be his best choice. That is, if they would accept him as a defector. And he would be taking a big risk just to find out.

And there was something else bothering the General — actually, two things. First, he couldn't understand why Dr. Yazdani's killers would burn the car. If Dr. Yazdani was dead, why wasn't that enough? It required the coroner to identify the body from DNA and dental records. But that was the second thing — the doctor's dentist was missing the dental records of several hundred patients, including Dr. Yazdani.

The General couldn't spend any more time thinking about the doctor. He had an important decision to make. The General thought it over and called the Colonel into his office.

"Yes, sir."

"I want to go to Damascus. That's where our best chance might be to catch up with Navid. If he isn't in the UAE or here, he must be in Iraq, Syria, Lebanon, Jordan, or Israel. Getting help from our contacts in Syria would be the best place to start. And I want to be directly involved."

"I will make the travel arrangements, sir."

CHAPTER 71

FROM THE BLUFF overlooking the Mediterranean, the sparkling sea was a deep marine blue. I had never seen such beautiful water. Angie and I were sitting on the terrace of the former US Ambassador's residence on Galel Techelet Street in Herzliya, a suburb north of Tel Aviv.

When the US Embassy moved to Jerusalem, the Ambassador's residence in Tel Aviv was sold to an American billionaire. Fortunately, the new absentee owner made it available to the US Ambassador, Arthur Debowy, when he had business in Tel Aviv, which was frequently.

I saw Tony emerge from the villa, walking briskly across the terrace. He joined Angie and me for breakfast.

"I hope you had a good rest last night. It was a long flight," he said.

"Yes, jet lag is a killer," I said, smiling.

"Where are Alex and Sharon?" Tony asked.

"They'll be down in a few minutes," Angie said.

"Have you seen the doctor this morning?"

"No," I said. The doctor Tony mentioned was Lt. Col. Gerald Budi, a neurologist from Walter Reed Medical Center, who specialized in treating comatose patients with brain injuries.

Karen Spencer had relayed to us that the Israelis had called Tony for help locating some dirty bombs the Iranians had lost. I had mixed feelings. I was to look into the mind of someone in a coma. I've never attempted this, so I didn't know if it was possible. I was worried the expectations were too high, but I'd do my best.

Alex made the trip as my personal bodyguard, along with Angie and Craig. And Karen had insisted that Sharon provide disguises while I was in Tel Aviv. She convinced Tony that it was too dangerous to allow me to be so highly visible on this trip when the time and effort to provide disguises for me was so small.

Sharon had disguised me with a wig of curly light brown hair, a mustache, and large tortoiseshell glasses. And she had fitted me with soft contact lenses that changed my eyes from blue to brown. I was impressed by how much my looks had changed.

"You, Alex, and Craig will be part of my security detail today," said Tony. "You'll be Agent Mark Grant again."

"Okay, that's fine. When do we leave?"

"Director Weiss said he would pick us up at 10:00 a.m. Angie, you'll have to hold down the fort here with Sharon," said Tony.

"I could think of worse places to hang out," Angie said as she took in the view through her oversized dark Gucci sunglasses.

Just as Tony and I started to leave the table to wait for Director Weiss at the front door, Ambassador Debowy walked out onto the terrace, talking with several of his staff, who were listening intently. He was maybe a touch shorter than average but with exceptionally broad shoulders, dark wavy hair, and a thick mustache. He had an air of authority and a ready smile. He was the perfect representative of the United States, exuding strength, intelligence, confidence, and charm.

President William Cameron had decided to place a career diplomat as the Israeli Ambassador rather than a political appointee. So he moved Ambassador Debowy from Bangkok to Jerusalem.

"Good morning, Tony," said the Ambassador.

"It's good to see you, Arthur. And thanks for allowing us to stay here."

"I'm a guest, too!" He laughed. "While you're working, I think I'll join this lovely lady for breakfast and find out what's happening back in the US."

Angie smiled and, as he sat down, toasted the Ambassador with her glass of orange juice.

CHAPTER 72

Dr. Budi waited with the rest of us in the front hall of the Ambassador's residence. Tony asked him, "Well, what are you expecting to see, Doctor?"

I was anxious to hear what the doctor had to say. He had slept most of the flight, and talked with Tony during the remaining time.

The doctor was a friendly, handsome fifty-year-old with dark wavy hair and a constant smile. But he was also one of the top trauma doctors in the US. He had dedicated his life and career to treating soldiers and other military personnel with neurological injuries. He was usually in uniform or wearing a white coat. Today he was dressed in casual clothing.

"The patient will be in intensive care. He'll be hooked up to an assortment of sensors and tubes. And he'll be unconscious. That's what I expect."

"Is there any hope to bring him out of it?" asked Tony.

"It depends on the cause and his condition. I've seen people come out of a coma just fine," said the doctor.

I hoped the doctor was right — and that it would happen soon.

A white Mercedes van pulled into the compound and stopped in front of the entrance. A security agent hopped out of the front seat and opened the back door. Director Weiss climbed out.

"Levi, so good to see you," said Tony, shaking hands with the Director.

"Yes, you too, and thank you for coming," replied Director Weiss.

"Let me introduce you to my entourage. This is Dr. Gerald Budi, one of the top trauma doctors in the US. He'll examine the patient. He's very experienced with these types of cases. And this is Agent Mark Grant. I've assigned him to be my point person on this case. And here are Agents Alex King and Craig Clayton. They're providing my security on this trip," said Tony.

Director Weiss shook hands with all of us.

I studied Director Weiss closely. He looked like an ordinary guy, not a killer, as how the head of Mossad was always portrayed.

"The hospital is only a few miles from here. The Mossad has a private ward where the patient is being treated," said Weiss. He motioned us toward the van. We boarded and left the compound, heading south.

After a short drive, the van pulled up to a side entrance to the Herzliya Medical Center. A security agent jumped out, went to the door, and entered a code into the keypad. The door popped open, and he motioned for the van passengers to enter.

When we entered, we found ourselves in a security screening area. After Director Weiss talked with the officer on duty, we were allowed to pass through another set of doors marked "Research – Restricted Area."

I felt it might be easier to get in here than out.

Once inside, we were met in a conference room by a woman in a white coat with a stethoscope hanging from her side pocket.

Director Weiss said, "This is Dr. Lisa Haritonovich, our top neurologist. She's in charge of the patient."

Dr. Haritonovich smiled and shook hands with Tony, Dr. Budi, and me. Alex and Craig stayed in the background scanning the surroundings.

The Israeli doctor was in her forties, relatively short, with medium-length blonde hair. She gave the impression of being very intense and professional.

"I've been waiting to meet you, Dr. Budi. I hope you can help us figure out what to do with the patient," she said.

"I would like you to give me your summary of his condition and then allow me to see the patient," he said.

"Yes, I will be happy to do that. The patient has been with us for almost six days. When he arrived, he was unconscious. His vital signs were all normal and stable, and we began running tests to determine why he was not responding. His GCS score was a 3, indicating a deep coma.

"Here are the results of his blood work. You will notice that the blood sugar was completely normal, ruling out hypoglycemia. There were no illegal drugs found in his system. However, there was a residual amount of the chloral hydrate/flunitrazepam solution, which initially rendered him unconscious. However, he should have regained consciousness with the drugs at that insignificant level.

"We immediately ran CT and MRI scans looking for a brain hemorrhage or abnormality — none were found. The EEG showed a very low level of brain activity, consistent with being in a coma. And we used electromyography to determine if there was nerve damage, which there was not.

"Since then, we have taken more X-rays to determine if there is evidence of trauma to the skull, which might have produced a hematoma not visible externally. However, we could not find anything."

"Have you ruled out 'Locked-in Syndrome'?" asked Dr. Budi.

"Yes, there is no response to stimuli in the EEG, which would be expected with 'LiS.'"

"Has there been any change at all since he was admitted?"

"No, nothing," she said.

"May I see the MRI and CT scans?"

"Yes, of course."

Dr. Haritonovich pulled up the scans on the large computer screen. Dr. Budi looked closely at each scan.

"No signs of cerebral infarctions or cerebral neoplasms. The pons looks normal. There is no obvious cause," said Dr. Budi. "I would like to see the patient now."

"Yes, he's in the next room," said Dr. Haritonovich.

Tony, Director Weiss, Dr. Budi, and I followed her.

She led us next door.

I took a deep breath. This was my time.

Dr. Yazdani was lying in bed with tubes and sensors attached to his head, torso, and limbs. His eyes were closed, and he looked like he was resting peacefully.

Dr. Budi studied the monitors, especially the EEG screen. He opened the patient's eyes and checked the pupils. He squeezed a finger and watched the monitor for any reaction. There was no response.

As Dr. Budi worked, I studied Dr. Yazdani closely, wondering if I could make a connection and extract any information from his memory. I closed my eyes and chose the day before the abduction, but nothing clearly came to me, though I thought the doctor was talking to someone in a uniform. I wondered if I could do better if I could concentrate without distraction.

"Is there anything you can suggest, Doctor?" asked Dr. Haritonovich.

"There is one technique that we have found useful. We stimulate the patient with familiar sounds, such as music they like. If possible, a family member talking or reading to them. In this case, I would suggest you have someone read to him in Farsi and maybe play Iranian and classical music. I would keep this up for an extended period. It may help bring him out of the coma. Otherwise, he is in good health, so I am optimistic. Director Weiss, could you advise me of updates from Dr. Haritonovich?"

"I can transmit the doctor's reports to Director Russell."

"That will be fine."

Dr. Haritonovich led the group out of the room and down the hall to the exit.

I stopped and took a final look at Dr. Yazdani before I left the room. I wasn't sure what I would be able to do if he stayed in a coma.

We all said goodbye and loaded into the van.

"Do you have any other leads on the whereabouts of the RDDs?" asked Tony.

Director Weiss said, "Unfortunately, no. We are on high alert along all our borders, but we're not being specific about the type of threat to avoid panic."

"That makes sense. We'll keep in close touch. It's important we avoid a radioactive attack by terrorists anywhere," said Tony.

Director Weiss nodded, though I noticed a look of worry flash across his face.

After we were back at the Ambassador's residence, Tony pulled me aside.

"Were you able to connect?"

"Not exactly. I'm getting something, but it's cutting in and out. If he regains consciousness, I won't have a problem. But until then, I can't say," I said.

Tony frowned. I knew he would be pestering me for results in the coming days.

"Let's get back to the US. There's nothing more we can do here," Tony said.

CHAPTER 73

Señor Arturo helped Navid, Baraz, and Javad secure passage from Santo Domingo to a suburb of New Orleans — Belle Chasse — with a man named Captain Broussard on an unusual type of ship, a dredger. The vessel had been working in the Santo Domingo harbor. And now, Señor Arturo was very anxious to receive his payment.

Broussard watched while the stevedores moved the crates from the truck to the deck of the dredger named *The Goliath*. Baraz and Javad took their duffel bags onto the ship while Navid waited with Señor Arturo. The Captain showed them where their cabins were located. They stowed their gear and moved the crates into one of their cabins on the main deck level.

Baraz came back to the gangway and gave Navid a thumbs up. Navid opened the duffel in which he'd packed the cash from Zubin and handed Señor Arturo his fee of twenty thousand dollars. Señor Arturo smiled and tipped his hat to Navid, and he nodded to Señor Arturo.

Navid boarded, and Captain Broussard was waiting at the top of the gangway. He told Baraz he wanted to collect his payment in private, so they went inside one of their cabins. Navid opened the duffel and counted out the twenty-five-thousand-dollar payoff. He handed it to Captain Broussard, who smiled and stuffed the bundles under his shirt and into his pants.

"We'll be leaving port in a few minutes. The tugboat has already attached the towing cable. I suggest you watch the disembarkation from the mess hall on the second deck. It has windows and a good view. But don't walk out on the deck. This ship is not designed for sea conditions, and you might get thrown overboard," said Broussard. "I'll see you at 6:00 p.m. for dinner," he murmured as he walked away with the stacks of bills making lumps in his clothes.

Navid felt safer now, being off the freighter and onto this type of working ship. It was certainly not the type to be suspected of carrying cargo from the Middle East. But he still worried that the General might find him, even here.

At dinner, Captain Broussard sat with them and tried to make conversation. He mentioned the thousands of tons of silt he had removed from the channel in the Santo Domingo harbor. Baraz listened and translated for Navid and Javad, who were interested in hearing about the dredger.

"What language is that?" asked Broussard.

"Lebanese," said Baraz. He had anticipated this question and decided to speak to Navid and Javad in Arabic, not Farsi. He thought it would be less of a problem to be identified as Lebanese than Iranian.

Captain Broussard grunted and said, "I knew it was one of those Middle Eastern languages." And he didn't say it in a friendly way.

The rest of the dinner was quiet, without much conversation.

Javad was still uncertain about the detonator design. His only sure option was to use a timer. But he even had uncertainties about this. The most pressing question was how he would attach the detonator to the RDD. And the other was how to keep it from being easily disarmed.

He asked Navid, "Can I work with one of the RDDs to figure out the detonator details?"

Navid thought about it and said, "Yes, as long as you're careful. It's important that we don't do anything to create a problem that prevents delivery to our customer."

"I think it will be best if I work on it in my cabin, where I have more room," said Javad.

Navid looked at Baraz, who nodded.

"Okay, we'll help you move one of the crates to your cabin," said Navid.

Baraz and Javad moved the crate to Javad's cabin. Navid opened the combination lock, and Baraz helped Javad remove the RDD and the attached drone from the container. Once the crate was empty, they returned it to the cabin where the others were stored.

Javad thanked them, and they left. Javad sat on the bed, looking at the RDD and the drone. He felt the entire operation depended on him developing a detonator to satisfy the customer. He was determined to make it work, even if the design might be dangerous.

He knew one thing. Navid and Baraz had always counted on him, and he wouldn't disappoint them. The biggest problem was that he couldn't test his design. And he only had a limited number of timers and switches to work with. So the design needed to be simple and reliable.

He sat on the bed and thought about the options. And he didn't really like any of them.

∽

Navid was anxious to notify the Warthog of their destination. What if they arrived in Belle Chasse and no one was there to meet them? What would they do?

"Baraz, let me have your phone. I need to contact our customer," said Navid.

Baraz handed it to him.

Navid opened the Signal app and sent Warthog the following message: "Will arrive, Belle Chasse, near New Orleans, approximately November 16, aboard dredger, *The Goliath*. Meet us there. Will need a large van or small truck. More details later."

A short while later, he received a reply.

"Will meet you in Belle Chasse."

CHAPTER 74

NOVEMBER 10
DAMASCUS, SYRIA

THE GENERAL AND Colonel Hashemi flew from Tehran to Damascus on one of IranAir's two Airbus A330 aircraft. They were dressed in civilian clothes to maintain a low profile. The three-hour flight was uneventful, but the General always worried when flying close to Israel. The General had decided that using an Iranian military plane would raise too many questions at home and in Damascus.

During the flight, Colonel Hashemi looked out the window. The General sat on the aisle next to the Colonel because he hated to be confined in a window seat. He also didn't feel like talking during the flight and made sure the Colonel knew it. When the Colonel tried to start a conversation, the General opened a magazine and began reading. The Colonel knew when the General didn't want to talk. The General finally put down the magazine and looked out the window, too, watching the color of the Syrian desert change from amber to ochre as the sun descended in the west.

They were traveling to Damascus to meet with the leader of a major terrorist group in Syria, supported by Iran and protected by the Syrian government. They hoped he would know the whereabouts of Navid. Actually, the General knew the chances were minimal. So he planned to seek asylum while he was in Damascus, but it would be tricky.

Colonel Hashemi followed protocol when making the travel arrangements by notifying the Syrian government of their travel plans and asking for expedited clearance at Damascus International Airport passport control.

When they landed in Damascus, Syrian security personnel met them at the plane and took them to a small office where their passports were checked and stamped, away from the normal flow of passengers.

They were escorted around passport control and waved through customs. At the exit to baggage claim, they were met by Iranian security personnel from the embassy. The security personnel were part of the IRGC, so the General and Colonel were their commanding officers.

The officer in charge was Captain Jafari, accompanied by a sergeant and a corporal. The Captain saluted when he saw them, which seemed silly because they were not in uniform.

When they were close enough to speak, he said, "I am Captain Jafari, and my men and I will escort you to the embassy, sir."

The Colonel said, "The General and I thank you."

"The Ambassador is waiting to receive you," said the Captain.

They were loaded into a van and driven from Damascus International to the Iranian embassy in the southwestern quadrant of the city, right on Fayez Mansoor Street. Unlike Iranian embassies in other major cities, the building was not in its own compound but was situated right along the main street, making security very difficult.

When they arrived at the embassy, Ambassador Zanganeh was there to greet them.

"General, we are honored to have you visit us!" said the Ambassador.

"The Colonel and I are happy to be here," replied the General. He hated all these niceties.

"I understand you asked to stay in the embassy per official security protocol while you are in Damascus," said Zanganeh.

"Yes, the local hotels are too difficult to secure. We appreciate your hospitality in allowing us to stay here."

"How long will you be staying?"

"I believe the Colonel told you we would be here for two nights, but that could change on short notice."

"That is fine, and in keeping with security procedures, we will dine here at the embassy tonight," said the Ambassador.

"Thank you, may we meet you at 7:00 p.m.?" asked the General.

"Yes, of course."

The Ambassador entertained them with an excellent dinner and stories about his experiences being stationed in many countries, including the UAE. The General was polite but bored to tears. Mercifully, the Ambassador ran out of stories at about 11:00 p.m.

General Ghorbani couldn't wait until tomorrow. It was the day his future would be decided.

CHAPTER 75

GENERAL GHORBANI AND Colonel Hashemi had an appointment scheduled for noon. They slept late and had breakfast in the embassy dining room. The Ambassador and his wife had already left for a morning event at Damascus University.

The General was on edge, and the Colonel knew the signs. The General ignored him and was preoccupied, pushing his food around on his plate.

"Do you have confirmation from El-Sayed?" asked the General.

"Yes, he will be there at noon."

"Is he asking again what we want to talk about?"

"No, he is being respectful and not asking any questions," said the Colonel.

"He'll find out soon enough, and we don't want the word to get out ahead of time, or we'll lose any chance of finding them," said the General, still frowning. He wiped his mouth with his napkin and stood up.

"The security detail wants to leave here at 11:15 a.m. to take us to the restaurant," said Colonel Hashemi.

"I'll be ready a few minutes early," said the General, who was never late.

He went to his room and lay on the bed to rest and to think until time to leave. He hoped and prayed that Aahad El-Sayed would know where to find Navid and Baraz. El-Sayed knew them well.

El-Sayed was the Lebanese leader of Hezbollah operations in Syria. Iran provided financial support to Hezbollah, and Ghorbani had known El-Sayed for many years. They had both spent decades fighting the influence of Israel in the Mideast, and the battlefield in recent years had been in Syria and Lebanon. El-Sayed, General Ghorbani, and Navid Sadeghi had all been heavily involved during that time.

If El-Sayed knew where to find Navid, the General's troubles could be contained and resolved quietly. If not, then all hell would break loose, and soon.

He knew he would need to make a decision shortly. The critical moment might have arrived. He would find out today at lunch. And he thought, *If I go back to Iran without knowing where to find Navid, I could face death. How could Navid do this to me? After all, we were friends. Where are Navid's loyalties?*

A few minutes after 11:00 a.m., the General made his way to the main lobby of the embassy. Captain Jafari was there with five of his men. They were all dressed in civilian clothes, as were the General and Colonel. It was not acceptable for them to wear uniforms in Old Damascus. The Damascus police would be called, and there would be trouble.

In the Middle East, it was commonplace for meetings of important people, especially when violence was a possibility, to take place in public places. Therefore, neither side had an advantage. Though Hezbollah and the IRGC were allies, there was still concern about the safety of the two principal participants in this meeting, with each side wary of the other; Aahad El-Sayed was especially concerned. He was more concerned about potential third parties, such as the Mossad. It was agreed to meet in a private room at the Al-Madarah Restaurant in Old Damascus. This location was considered public enough, with armed security details from both parties waiting in the wings in case of trouble.

Colonel Hashemi arrived in the embassy lobby at 11:15 a.m. sharp. General Ghorbani was glad to see him; he was tired of making small talk with Captain Jafari.

They piled into two black Mercedes SUVs for the ride across town to the Bab Touma area of Old Damascus. They made their way down the narrow streets and stopped in front of the restaurant at 11:50 a.m. Captain Jafari jumped out of the vehicle with two of his men, looked up and down the narrow street, and then entered the restaurant. The General and Colonel waited in the SUV until one of the Captain's men gave them the okay that the restaurant was secure.

After receiving the all-clear signal, General Ghorbani and Colonel Hashemi entered the restaurant, escorted by a member of their security detail. They went directly to the private room designated for their meeting, not even noticed by the diners enjoying their lunch.

Captain Jafari had made the reservation and had asked the owner for two more tables with seating directly outside the private room. One table for him and his men and the other for the Hezbollah security detail. While the General and the Colonel went inside the private room, the Captain and the others stationed themselves at the tables outside.

At exactly noon, two white Toyota SUVs stopped in front

of the restaurant. The same routine was played out. The Hez-bollah three-man security detail entered the restaurant, surveyed the main dining room, and asked to be shown the private room. They nodded to Captain Jafari as they passed his table. When they entered the private dining room, they nodded to the General and Colonel and checked the setup. They quickly checked the drawers in the sideboard for weapons. Finding none, they left and brought Aahad El-Sayed and his lieutenant into the room.

When El-Sayed entered the room, the General stood and greeted him by saying, "Mar Habā."

El-Sayed responded, "Mar Habtén," and smiled.

They shook hands and kissed each other three times on alternate cheeks, starting with the left cheek, as was customary in Lebanon. The General then introduced Colonel Hashemi, who El-Sayed had not met in person. And then El-Sayed introduced Ghawer Aboud, his aide. The ritual was repeated with greetings and kissing.

El-Sayed looked like any ordinary man on the street. He was an average Lebanese or Syrian, with black hair and a full black beard. He wore black pants, a white shirt open at the neck, a black vest, and black shoes. Aboud was dressed exactly the same, except with a tan vest.

The owner came into the room to take their food order when they were seated. He had two waiters behind him with trays containing tea, hot water, and all the accoutrements. He suggested they try the yalanji, makdous, muhammara, mahshi, and kibbeh bil sanieh.

The General said, "Fine, fine." El-Sayed nodded.

They drank tea and exchanged pleasantries while the wait-ers quickly brought platters of food in.

The General noticed that El-Sayed waited until Aboud sampled each dish before he ate anything.

"Do you suspect poison?" asked the General.

El-Sayed smiled. "Let's just say I don't like strong spices, and Aboud makes sure the food is suitable for me." They all laughed, even Aboud.

They ate and talked about old times and how things have changed.

After a few minutes, the waiters brought in the main dishes — mahshi, kibbeh bil sanieh, and more pita bread.

Aboud again sampled everything, to the General's amusement, and then they all ate while they talked.

After the meal, El-Sayed drank strong Syrian coffee and smoked an Alhamraa brand cigarette, the local Marlboro knock-off. At Aboud's request, the restaurant owner brought a hookah water pipe, his choice of mint-flavored shisha, and three red-hot charcoal cubes. Aboud puffed away, and a cloud of pungent shisha, mixed with the swirl of cigarette smoke, created a thick haze over the table. The General was annoyed but didn't say anything; he needed El-Sayed's cooperation. No, actually, more than cooperation. He needed El-Sayed's help.

"General, let's get down to business. I'm sure you did not come to Damascus just to have lunch with me. Hopefully, you are not unhappy with how we have spent the money you generously give us to fight the Jewish state."

"No, we are very happy with your constant harassment of Israel," replied the General.

"Well, then, what is it?"

"I'm hoping you can tell me where I can find Navid Sadeghi and his son, Baraz. You know them — they are the leaders of Hurras Ansar al-Haqq. They're working on something for me, but I've lost contact with them and am worried."

El-Sayed hesitated momentarily and took a puff from his second cigarette. Then he said, "Yes, I know them. But I haven't seen Navid in several years. I saw Baraz last year but haven't seen him since."

"Yes, but have you heard anything of them recently?"

El-Sayed shook his head. "Nothing specific, but I have heard rumors they are involved in something big. You know some of their members are friends of my men, and they talk. You know how it is these days when everyone has a mobile phone."

The General felt that his last hope was gone.

"So, you don't know where they are?"

"No, but I can ask around. I don't think they're in Syria, though. I would know if they were."

"If you hear anything, please let me or Colonel Hashemi know as soon as possible," said the General. He tried to mask his emotions.

El-Sayed nodded. "Yes, of course."

"Now we must leave to attend to other important business, but first, as you are my guests, we will pay the owner for our fine meal," said the General.

They all stood and began the ritual of saying goodbye, with handshakes and kisses all around, with the traditional Lebanese goodbye, "Ma'e Ssalēmet," repeated by all of them.

During the ride back to the embassy, the General blankly stared out the window.

As they neared the Iranian embassy, the General finally snapped out of his trance, having come to a decision. Strangely, he felt refreshed, like a load had been taken off his shoulders.

CHAPTER 76

Captain Jafari waited in the embassy lobby for the General. After about an hour, the General descended the stairway in his full-dress uniform. The Colonel was completely unaware the General was leaving the embassy.

The Captain ushered the General outside to the waiting Mercedes SUVs and guided him to the second SUV in the caravan. In tandem, the vehicles pulled out of the embassy onto Fayez Mansoor Street. They headed north toward the Russian embassy on Khattab Street, about two miles away.

The Russian embassy was also on a main street but was a much larger complex of several modern buildings. One of them was a tall office building.

The caravan pulled into the entrance to the Russian embassy, and Captain Jafari opened the car door for the General.

"You can wait here for me," said the General, who then turned and entered the main building.

Once inside, the General was immediately confronted by a Russian guard, who was confused to see a visitor in a full-dress uniform from a foreign country.

He said in Arabic, "What is your business?"

The General replied, "I am Guardian Major-General Farzad Ghorbani, Commander of the Islamic Revolutionary Guard Corp of the Islamic Republic of Iran. Please tell the Ambassador that I am here to see him."

"Do you have an appointment, sir?"

"No, but he will see me."

"Yes, sir, please wait."

In a few minutes, the guard returned with a lady following behind.

"I am Katerina Ivanovna, the Ambassador's secretary. How can I help you?" she asked in Arabic.

"I am here to see the Ambassador on urgent business. I am authorized to speak only with him."

She nodded and waved her hand for him to follow as she walked back down the hallway. She led him to an elevator and went up to the third floor.

She took him to a suite of expensively appointed offices in the back corner of the building. She walked into an expansive outer office and showed him a set of double doors leading to an inner office.

"Ambassador Barinov will see you now," she said as she opened the door and directed him inside.

The Ambassador, Alexei Barinov, was sitting behind his ornate desk when the General entered. He immediately rose to greet his guest. Barinov looked like many Russian bureaucrats, about average height, slightly overweight, and wearing a baggy blue suit. He had thick brown hair, pale blue eyes, a round face, and a somewhat bulbous nose. He was slightly older than the General.

"General, so good to see you again. I believe the last time I saw you was in Moscow." The Ambassador was fluent in Arabic, and so was the General.

"Yes, Mr. Ambassador, that is true. The conference discussed how our countries could work together in Syria."

"Please sit down. What can I do for you today, General?"

"I came here to defect — to seek asylum, Mr. Ambassador."

Ambassador Barinov looked confused. "But, General, when a person defects, they go to the enemy!"

"Mr. Ambassador, Iran has no friends, only enemies of varying degrees."

"Why do you want to defect?"

"Because an operation went bad, and I will be blamed. There will be serious consequences for me and for Iran. And it might affect Russia. I would be willing to help Russia avoid the worst — if my safety is guaranteed."

"That is all you can tell me?"

"Yes, I will share the details only with Director Belyaev and General Galkin."

Ambassador Barinov leaned forward in his chair with his elbows on the desk. He put his hands together in front of his face, interlacing the fingers, and rubbed his nose with the index fingers as he thought.

Then he said, "Please wait here. I will make a phone call." He got up from the desk and walked to the outer office.

The General waited impatiently. He needed to know if the Russians would grant him asylum. If not, he didn't know what to do. Neither the US nor the UK had embassies in Damascus, and certainly, Israel did not.

The Ambassador reentered his office. He told the General, "Director Belyaev wishes to see you to discuss your situation. He wants me to accompany you to Moscow. He says he has spoken to President Drozdov and will grant you asylum, assuming you fully cooperate with him. We will go to the airport when the plane is ready."

"And what does 'fully cooperate' mean?" the General asked.

The Ambassador spread his arms wide and shrugged his shoulders. "I'm only the messenger."

General Ghorbani hesitated a moment. He wondered what they might ask him that he could not share. Then he thought about what might happen if they sent him back to Iran.

"Yes, fine. I need to send away my security detail. May I write a note to be delivered to the Captain?"

"Yes, of course."

The General wrote the following note in Farsi:

Captain Jafari,

I will be staying a while with the Ambassador. Please return now to the embassy, and I will let you know later when to return here for me.

/signed/

Major-General Ghorbani – Commander IRGC-QF

He folded the paper, wrote "Captain Jafari" on the outside, and handed it to the Ambassador. He had intentionally written the note ambiguously, just in case he changed his mind later.

The Ambassador gave the note to his secretary and told her to deliver it to Captain Jafari.

An hour later, the secretary informed Ambassador Barinov that the plane was heading to Damascus International. She told him the security detail was ready to take him and the General to the airport.

The General had already changed clothes at the Ambassador's urging. He supplied him with the civilian clothing of a security officer who lived in the embassy. He told the General, "There are spies and informants everywhere, and I doubt you want your government to know what you're doing — at least not yet. There's no reason for your government to know you are traveling to Moscow. And the Director asks that you surrender your phone. We will keep it here in our safe."

The General handed the phone to the Ambassador, who gave it to his secretary for safekeeping.

They loaded into three of the embassy's SUVs. The convoy headed to Damascus International with the diplomatic flag flying on the lead vehicle while they rode in the third SUV in line. The airport was twenty miles southeast of the city, and it took them about an hour to make the trip.

Once they arrived, they drove to the plane parked on the tarmac, away from the terminal.

The plane was a Falcon 2000EX, a mid-sized business jet. It was based at Khmeimim Air Base near Latakia to shuttle high-level military officers and government officials between Moscow and Syria.

The caravan pulled up to the airstairs at the plane. The Ambassador and General stepped out and quickly climbed the airstairs into the cabin. The pilot and co-pilot greeted them, as did the cabin steward. They were all Russian military personnel.

It was a stressful flight for the General. His mind was full of thoughts about what he could, should, or shouldn't tell the Russians about the RDDs and his involvement in the plan.

If the devices were detonated in Russia, he wondered if they would hold him responsible, with dire consequences.

He held out hope that the RDDs could be recovered with the help of the Russians, and then he could return home to Iran with no consequences. It was getting easier to deceive himself.

And then he shuddered, thinking about living the rest of his life in Russia.

His mind raced from one scenario to the next, each worst than the last.

CHAPTER 77

AMBASSADOR BARINOV WAS sent back to Syria on an overnight flight, landing in Damascus at 6:00 a.m. He went directly to the embassy and awaited instructions.

At 8:00 a.m., the Ambassador received a message from Director Belyaev. It contained a message the Ambassador was instructed to deliver to the Iranian embassy at 10:00 a.m.

It read as follows,

Ambassador of the Islamic Republic of Iran to the Syrian Arab Republic

The Honorable Amir Zanganeh

Ambassador Zanganeh,

Major-General Farzad Ghorbani has requested the Russian Federation to grant him political asylum. The Russian Federation has conditionally approved his request. We are discussing with the General his reasons for defection, which include an Iranian security threat potentially dangerous to the Russian Federation and its people.

Sincerely,

/signed/

Alexei Barinov

Ambassador of the Russian Federation to the Syrian Arab Republic

At 10:00 a.m., a courier entered the Iranian embassy and delivered a diplomatic envelope addressed to Ambassador Zanganeh.

When Ambassador Zanganeh opened the letter and read the message, all hell broke loose.

He immediately called the Minister of Foreign Affairs, Salar Mazanderani, in Tehran — his boss. The Minister called Admiral Mousavi and told him. The Admiral called the Ayatollah, who was enraged, demanding that Russia turn over the General to Iran.

Ambassador Zanganeh called Ambassador Barinov.

"Mister Ambassador, I must insist that you turn over General Ghorbani to our security detail immediately," Zanganeh said.

Ambassador Barinov replied, "I am sorry, but I cannot do that. He has been granted asylum. Actually, the General is already in Moscow."

"But, Ambassador, Russia and Iran are allies. The General cannot defect."

"Well, he did. And he has shared very concerning information that Iran should have already told Russia. Is this how you treat your allies?" Barinov asked.

"Thank you, Ambassador Barinov. I will communicate your

response to Tehran," Zanganeh said as he abruptly hung up the phone without waiting for a reply.

In one of the three wings of the SVR building's second floor, there were suite accommodations for field agents, sometimes used for important visitors. It was much easier to house them in the SVR facilities than to try to provide security for them at Moscow hotels.

At 9:00 a.m., a room steward brought breakfast to the General's suite. Ghorbani was still tired, as he was unable to sleep very well. He picked at the food, which was not entirely to his liking.

Then an hour later, there was a knock at the door. The General answered it, and General Alexei Galkin walked in and sat on the couch.

"General Ghorbani, is everything satisfactory with your accommodations?"

"Yes, everything is fine," Ghorbani said, deciding not to complain about the food.

"Then I will continue with a few questions the Director wants you to answer. Let's start by asking you to share everything you know about Iranian intelligence operations in Russia, including the locations and names of your agents," requested Galkin.

General Ghorbani hesitated before answering, as he considered how much detail he should share.

"General, you are wasting time trying to filter the information you are about to provide. It is too late for that. The Iranian government has already been notified of your asylum. I have here a copy of the shared document." He handed a copy to the General.

The General read the short document carefully, his stomach churning. He realized then that he could never return to Iran.

He envisioned the angry reaction inside the Iranian government to his defection. He was now considered a traitor, and he knew it. He wondered how long the Russians would call him "General"? He figured he had already been stripped of his rank. He started to ask Galkin but then thought better of it.

He told Galkin, "Bring me some paper and pencils, and I'll write down what I can remember." Galkin nodded and left the suite.

While the General waited for Galkin's return, the question that had kept him awake all night returned with a vengeance. *Where the hell is Navid Sadeghi?*

CHAPTER 78

WHEN I ENTERED the kitchen for breakfast, Miss Doris was bustling about as usual. She was busy frying bacon in one pan and making hash brown potatoes in another.

"Good morning, Miss Doris," I said.

"And the same to you, Mister Grant. Will Miss Angie be having breakfast this morning?"

"Yes, she'll be down in a minute."

"All right, then let me get you some coffee," she said with a smile. "And what about Mister Alex?"

"I don't know. I imagine he'll be here quickly when he smells the bacon," I laughed.

Angie walked into the kitchen, looking fresh and ready for the day. I watched as Miss Doris looked her over and nodded with approval.

"Would you like some tea, Miss Angie?" asked Doris.

"Yes, and only fruit this morning, please."

Miss Doris looked at her disapprovingly. "You need to keep up your strength, Miss Angie."

"Yes, I know, but keeping my figure is important." She laughed.

I smiled because I was happy Angie and Miss Doris got along well.

"Mister Grant, can I ask you something before Mister Alex gets here?"

"Yes, of course, Miss Doris. What is it?"

"You remember my friend, Pearl Stevens?"

"Yes, she cares for old Mister John Curlee, right?"

"Yessir, and he's in pretty bad shape," she said. "He's talking about selling Iyyakchush Plantation. His children moved away, and Pearl moved in to care for him after his wife died. But now, living so far out in the country isn't a good idea with him being in bad health. And she doesn't know what she'll do if he sells the plantation."

"Yes, it sounds like a bad situation," I said.

"I was hoping you might buy the place, Mister Grant," said Doris.

Angie looked at him with a frown. "Who's John Curlee?"

"A friend of my father. He lives on his family's plantation north of Natchez, close to the Pontotoc Bluffs Plantation I inherited. You know, that property along the river," Grant said.

"I love that place. We don't get there enough. The view is so beautiful, overlooking the Mississippi," she said.

We didn't go more often because Pontotoc Bluffs Plantation didn't have a plantation house; it was just raw land. It was beautiful, overlooking the river, but just land.

"How long has Mr. Curlee lived there?" she asked.

"All his life, I guess, except when he was an Army paratrooper. His family grew cotton, but he eventually sold all the farmland except fifty acres surrounding the house, which over-looks the river."

Angie nodded and asked, "What's it like? I mean, the house?"

I shook my head, racking my brain. "It's hard to remember all the details; I haven't been there in years. It's a large white clapboard house that sits about a hundred feet from the edge of the high bluff towering over the river. The side of the house facing the river has a deep porch on both floors with tall columns running along the entire length. The columned porches wrap around the front, the sides, and the back. The rear of the house is identical to the front. A breezeway on the north side attaches the kitchen and servants' quarters to the house. There are quite a few bedrooms, a large parlor, a dining room, and a library. And, of course, there's a carriage house."

"It sounds wonderful," Angie said, her eyes lighting up at the mention of the library, which I knew she'd like. Cozy rooms where you can curl up and read were right up Angie's alley.

"Yes, we can take a ride out there if you want. I'll call Mister John and ask if it's okay to stop by," I said.

"Why's it called Iyyakchush Plantation?" she asked. "What does it mean?"

"My father told me Iyyakchush means 'claw' in Choctaw. Mister John's great-grandfather said the Choctaw tribe used to hunt black bears on his land to get the claws for bear claw necklaces."

Alex entered the kitchen at that moment, ready for break-fast. "What about bear claws? That sounds interesting."

"I was explaining the name of a plantation near Natchez that Angie wants to see. We'll ride out there as soon as I can arrange it with the owner," I said. "Doris, we'll see what Mister John says about selling. But it would be an awful lot to take on."

Miss Doris nodded. "Yes, but there's nothing like it, and you love the river view so much."

"Yes, if you give me the phone number at Iyyakchush, I'll call Mister John."

"I'll write it down for you," said Miss Doris, grabbing a small piece of note paper and a pencil.

CHAPTER 79

LATER IN THE morning, I sat at my desk wondering what else I could try with the patient. Tony had been badgering me daily about getting information from Dr. Yazdani.

The doctor was still in a coma, and I couldn't make a solid connection to his memory. Just bits and pieces of information were coming through, like a radio or television cutting in and out. If the doctor could just come close to waking up, I'm sure I would be able to learn more about the RDDs, but not now.

The phone rang. It was Tony — again!

"Hello, Tony. No, nothing from the doctor. We'll just have to be patient."

"Grant, we can't just wait around. How about seeing if any other important people know anything. How about President Rostami or President Drozdov? You saw them in New York, right?" asked Tony.

"Yes, I suppose I could give them a try."

Now that this was an active case, I couldn't say no like before.

"All right, do that and let me know. We're all getting very nervous here," said Tony.

I assume when Tony said "we," he meant himself and President Cameron.

"Okay, Tony, I'll let you know. But give me some time."

"Grant, don't drag this out. Let me know as soon as you can."

Once we hung up, I decided to start with President Rostami. I reasoned that the radioactive material belonged to the Iranians, so they would most likely have helpful information. I knew Israel had been told on October 29 that the RDDs disappeared on October 19. I also knew that Dr. Yazdani had been captured on November 1, and the CIA was notified by Israel on November 4. But I also knew President Rostami might not know the RDDs were missing. With so many questions about timing, I started checking Rostami's memory today and working backward; this would take some time.

I didn't have to work long before learning something interesting. President Rostami had received a call from Admiral Mousavi this morning to tell him that General Ghorbani had defected to Russia. They were upset and trying to decide who would tell the Ayatollah. But they didn't mention why the General had defected, only that it was a significant security breach.

This was the first time I had heard of General Ghorbani. I made a note to ask Tony who he was.

Then I moved next to see what I could determine from the recesses of President Drozdov's mind. Again, it didn't take long to learn that Drozdov had been involved in granting asylum to General Ghorbani. But now I learned that the General had information to share about the missing RDDs if they would give him asylum. President Drozdov readily agreed.

I felt this was important, so I called Tony.

"Hello, Grant. What did you find out?"

"President Rostami is quite upset to learn that a General Ghorbani defected to Russia."

"What else?"

"President Drozdov granted asylum to General Ghorbani and was told that the General had information to share about missing RDDs that might even be heading to Russia."

"Good, good. Now we're getting somewhere."

"Who is General Ghorbani?"

"He's head of the Iranian Revolutionary Guard Corps — or he was until he defected," said Tony.

"What does this mean?" I asked.

"It appears that General Ghorbani screwed up. He's scared and running away. It also means he doesn't know where the RDDs are, or he would still be trying to get them back."

I said, "I've never encountered General Ghorbani, so I can't get information from him."

"Okay, sit tight, and I'll tell you what to do next. Check back with Drozdov and Rostami daily in case they have new information. And keep checking Dr. Yazdani. He's probably the key to this, as the Israelis correctly determined."

"Okay, Tony, I'll do that," I said, then hung up.

Now that the work for Tony was out of the way, I decided to call out to Iyyakchush Plantation. I pulled the folded note from my pocket, opened it, and dialed the number.

The phone was answered after three rings. "Iyyakchush Plantation, Pearl speaking."

"Pearl, this is Grant Markey. I'm calling to speak to Mister John. Is he available?"

"Yessir, Mister Grant, he is. Doris told me you might be calling. Hold on and let me get Mister John on the phone," she said.

After about a minute, I heard the phone click as if someone had picked up an extension.

"Hello, this is John Curlee."

"Hello, Mister John, this is Grant Markey."

"Hi, Grant. It's good to hear from you. It's been a long time. What can I do for you?"

"I told my wife, Angie, about Iyyakchush Plantation and hoped to bring her out to see it. She's from California and unfamiliar with Natchez but loves old antebellum houses."

"Yes, I would be pleased if you would visit me. But don't wait long. I'm not doing well and might have to move into town soon. I'm thinking of selling the place," Mister John said.

"We could come out tomorrow if that's all right with you."

"Yes, of course. Come out around 3:00 p.m., and we'll have tea."

"I might bring my business partner, Alex King — if that's okay."

"Yes, fine."

"All right, we'll see you then."

"Goodbye, Grant."

"Goodbye, Mister John."

My conversation with John Curlee brought back old memories, and I was now looking forward to visiting Iyyakchush almost as much as Angie.

With my personal security increasingly threatened, I realized Iyyakchush would probably be a more secure location for us than Wexford House.

CHAPTER 80

NOVEMBER 14
NATCHEZ, MISSISSIPPI

I DROVE WITH Alex in the passenger seat and Angie in the back. We passed Pontotoc Bluffs Plantation, passed over the Gilliam Chute, and finally arrived at the entrance to Iyyakchush Plantation, where the Mississippi River made a sweeping turn from the south to the east. It wasn't that far out to Iyyakchush Plantation, but it was mostly on gravel roads.

I stopped and read the old hand-painted sign on the mailbox post with three lines of lettering, "Iyyakchush," then in smaller letters, "ca. 1842", and below that, "J. M. Curlee."

I turned in, drove through the open gate, and continued down the long gravel driveway shaded by large oak trees, the house not yet visible.

We continued along the long driveway, which curved to the right and eventually emerged into an expanse of lawn that gave us the first view of the house.

Angie said, "Wow, lovely!" I could see she was excited, and I was also curious about what we would find.

The house was as I remembered it but had some features I had forgotten. We were arriving at what I called the east front of the house — it was opposite the west side that faced the river.

We saw that the house had a large square belvedere perched at the center of the hip roof, with a railed walkway around it. I noted that the building had five tall brick chimneys, two on each end (the north and south) and another tall chimney at the far wall of the one-story kitchen attached on the north side. The roof had three dormers that helped give the structure a symmetrical appearance.

The driveway swept around and made a circle in the east front of the house. We stopped the car at the front door, which was significantly above ground level and across the generous depth of the porch, accessed by a broad set of ten steps. We stepped out of the car while admiring the plantings of boxwoods, rambling roses, and azaleas. There were also ancient magnolia trees at the corners of the house.

We climbed the steps, and when I knocked at the door it was immediately opened by Pearl, who had been waiting for us to arrive.

She said, "Please come in, Mister Grant," and to Angie and Alex, "I'm Pearl Stevens. I take care of Mister John. And I'm a friend of Miss Doris Webb," she said proudly.

I introduced Angie and Alex to Pearl, and she led us into the house and along the central gallery.

"Let me escort you to the drawing room. Mister John is waiting for you," she said. We followed her along the gallery toward the front of the house while admiring the formal dining room, the library, and the antique wallpaper, chandeliers, and other antebellum decorations and artwork. At this point, we still had yet to see the river.

Pearl ushered us into the south parlor, where Mister John was waiting. Pearl hurried over and helped him to his feet.

Though he used a cane to steady himself, he stood ramrod straight, just as he did when he was a paratrooper many years ago. He smiled as we shook hands.

"It's been so long since I've seen you, Grant. And this must be your wife, Angie, and your business partner, Alex?"

"Yes, Angie and Alex."

They all shook hands.

I handed him a small package. "I assumed you still smoke your pipe, so I brought you a pouch of tobacco."

"That was very thoughtful of you. Yes, I still smoke, and my doctor lectures me whenever I see him. But now that I'm over ninety, I think he's given up." John motioned toward the Victorian couches, which perfectly complemented the room. "Please sit down. Pearl will bring us some tea and cookies."

Once they sat, John said, "After we have tea, you can look around as much as you want."

"Mister John, you said you might be moving soon?" I asked.

"Yes, my health isn't good, and it takes so long to get medical help in an emergency. I'm considering selling if I can find anyone foolish enough to buy the place. I've been talking to a real estate broker. He tells me it would be worth a fortune in Natchez, but way out here, it's just a white elephant."

"Don't your sons want it?"

"No, Mike's in Dallas, and Jimmy's in Los Angeles. They're city boys now. They just want the money. They don't care about this place, and I don't blame them. Grant, do you remember coming here when you were a little boy?"

"I remember we used to come out here on the Fourth of July after the parade in town. You invited a lot of people for a big picnic and fireworks."

"Yes, that's right. I held my last Fourth of July party about thirty years ago. Do you remember what you told me after you came down from the widow's walk?"

I shook my head. "No, I don't. When was that?"

"It was on the Fourth of July. I think you were about twelve years old."

"Maybe I'll remember later."

Mister John nodded and smiled.

Pearl brought the tea and cookies, and Mister John related stories about living at Iyyakchush and how the river dominates everything.

When we finished the tea and cookies, Mister John said, "Grant, show Angie and Alex around the house and yard. Take them out to see the river. It's a nice day, so you can go up to the widow's walk on top if you want, but be careful."

Pearl walked to the front door with us. She said, "You can walk out to the fence. If you want to go up to the widow's walk, you go up to the second floor, then there's a door near the center of the gallery leading to stairs that go up to the attic. Then there's a ladder up into the belvedere, and you'll see a door leading outside. It's not windy today, so you should be safe up there."

We walked across the expansive yard, framed by a fence line on both sides, covered with rambling roses. There were more boxwoods, azaleas, and magnolias along this side of the house, and also plantings of rhododendrons and hydrangeas.

We looked down onto the river when we reached the wrought-iron fence at the bluff's edge. The river was maybe a half mile wide and muddy, as usual. There were several barges in the distance, heading downriver. We could see the bend of the river right in front of us but not much farther to the right or the left. Across the river in Louisiana, the ground level was much lower, and the farmland was obviously vulnerable to flooding.

Angie turned and said, "Let's go up there," pointing to the belvedere. I saw how happy and excited she was. I nodded, and we walked back toward the house, admiring its unique beauty.

But Alex wasn't looking at the house; instead, he was studying the grounds. I suspected he was looking with an eye on security.

The second floor's stairway was on the gallery's south side. When we reached the second floor, Angie walked the entire length of the gallery, looking into the bedrooms, then returned to where Alex and I were waiting. Large windows at either end of the gallery were nearly as tall as the high ceiling. There was a door across from the stairs, which Angie opened, only to find more stairs leading to the attic.

We climbed the stairs, with me taking the lead and Angie and Alex following. The stairs took us up into the attic, and I saw the ladder, which I remembered went up to the belvedere.

"Let me go all the way up first. Then I'll let you know if it's safe," I said.

I clambered up the ladder into the belvedere. It was dusty but appeared to be in good repair. I saw an old binocular case hanging on a hook, so I got them out and put the strap around my neck. I tried the door, which led out onto the roof. It opened, and I carefully stepped out. The roof felt solid, so I returned inside and said, "It's okay. You can come up."

When Angie and Alex reached the top, they looked out the dirty windows of the belvedere. Angie said, "I can't see anything, and I don't like cobwebs," as she moved to the door and stepped out onto the roof. Alex and I followed.

A waist-high wrought-iron railing bordered the entire flat part of the roof. We walked toward the railing at the front and looked out over the river. The view was spectacular. We were at least forty feet higher than ground level and could see in all directions up and down the river. The sun was shining and it felt hot, with heat reflecting off the roof. Fortunately, there was no wind, which would have made it dangerous, but a little breeze would have been nice. We took turns with the binoculars. I could tell Angie was already in love with the place.

I stood there and looked out over the landscape, bringing back memories from so many years ago. I wondered what I had told Mister John. There was only one way to find out. So while Angie pointed out things of interest to Alex, I tried to concentrate on Mister John and the Fourth of July when I was twelve.

And then I began to have visions, and what I saw was . . .

Mister John was talking with my father and an older man on the front porch. He looked up and saw me coming out the front door, walking hurriedly toward them. Mister John asked, "Did you go up top, Grant? How did you like it?"

"Mister John, I saw a riverboat on its way from Memphis to New Orleans! When I grow up, I want to live here so I can watch the river every day!"

They all laughed, and my father patted me on the shoulder; I laughed, too.

And now, I chuckled again, remembering that moment.

CHAPTER 81

WHEN WE ARRIVED back in the south parlor, Mister John was waiting. "How did you like it up top, Angie?" he asked.

"I loved it," she said.

"Was the view as you remembered, Grant?"

"Yes, even better. And I remember what I told you."

Mister John smiled. "Would you be interested in buying?" he asked.

I looked at Angie. She smiled and nodded.

"Yes, I might, but it's a lot to take on. And I can't move out here anytime soon, as much as I'd like to," I said.

"I don't have the time to wait for a buyer. I'll make you a good offer. The place would be worth millions in Natchez, but way out here, I'll only ask one-and-a-half million."

I rubbed my chin and looked at Angie. She nodded again.

I hesitated. Buying this place would mean I'd have two large homes. It was a lot for the two of us, but I could afford them. And Angie liked it so much. And sometimes, we just needed to get away from Wexford House. Plus, there was more privacy and probably better security. Lastly, an opportunity like this might not come along again.

"Are you saying you'll sell as-is, fully furnished?" I asked.

"Yes, what am I going to do with all this furniture?" Mister John said.

"Well, then I agree if Angie agrees." I looked at her expectantly.

"Oh, yes," she said and hugged me.

"I'll have my attorney, Oliver Briggs, draw up the paperwork if that's okay with you, Mister John?"

"Yes, that's fine. I want to be out of here in a week." Mister John extended his hand. I shook it and grinned.

Angie exclaimed, "Oh, Grant!" and gave me another big hug and kiss.

I was happy. And Alex smiled, too, so I assume he approved.

Mister John rang the bell to call in Pearl and gave her the news. She raised both hands to her face and said, "Oh, my!"

I told her, "Miss Pearl, nothing changes for you. I want you to stay here and look after the place. We'll come out on the weekends, mostly, at least in the beginning. Is that all right with you?"

"Yes, sir, Mister Grant." Pearl's face lit up, and her eyes welled up with tears. I was sure they were tears of happiness.

"Well, then you just help Mister John get ready to move into town."

We said our goodbyes and drove away from the house and out of the long driveway. When we were almost to the main road, we saw a car in the distance blocking the driveway. We saw Craig Clayton and Donnie Hambleton leaning against the car when we got closer.

When Craig saw them coming, he said something to Donnie, and they both got into the car, pulled out onto the main road, and waited. I stopped the car next to Craig, and Alex rolled down his window.

"Did anyone suspicious drive by?" asked Alex.

"No, just a farmer in an old pickup truck. We got the plate number if you want to check it out," said Craig. Alex thanked him and rolled up his window.

Our car passed by them, and they dropped in behind.

"I asked them to follow us," Alex said in response to my questioning look. "From your description, I figured there was only one way in and out of Iyyakchush, which is both good and bad for security. I didn't want to take any chances."

"Good idea," I said.

Craig and Donnie followed us all the way back to Wexford House.

When we arrived, I told Craig I'd bought the place, and he'd have to figure out how to secure it.

He said, "It'll probably be easier to do there than here," and smiled.

CHAPTER 82

JAVAD HAD BEEN thinking about and sporadically working on the detonator design. Whenever he felt he had a solution, Javad later realized there was a problem he had not anticipated. He scrapped many different concepts for the detonator before he hit on one that satisfied all his criteria.

He decided that the most straightforward option was to leave the RDD attached to the drone and use the drone's batteries to power the detonator. He rewired the drone with power from all six batteries connected in parallel. But he ran the wires to the detonator via several different pathways, providing redundancy. The batteries would give a severe jolt to detonate the C-4 inside the RDD. Now the question was how to construct the timing mechanism, so it was foolproof and couldn't be easily disarmed.

Javad decided to use multiple timers connected in parallel. And he had enough electronic components to design a complex circuit to confuse anyone trying to disarm it. He set it up so that if someone tried cutting any one of the wires running from the timers to one of the detonator switches, it would instantly detonate through the other switch. And it was impossible to cut all the battery and switch wires at precisely the same time. Plus, he added dummy wires to confuse anyone trying to disarm it. He used an improvised case to attach the electronics to the drone's frame.

The design was as foolproof as you could get. Unfortunately, you couldn't change your mind and disarm it once it was set.

Javad tried to disarm it himself in various ways, but always with the device disconnected from the RDD. He monitored what was happening on his different voltage, amperage, resistance, and capacitance meters. Once satisfied, he told Navid and Baraz not to worry; they had a working detonator prototype to show their customer.

Navid was happy with Javad's work, but Baraz was upset. He didn't want anything to do with being responsible for setting the detonators. He anticipated that the Warthog would have Javad reproduce the detonator setup on each RDD. In other words, they couldn't just make the delivery, get paid, and leave; they would be involved in the attack.

CHAPTER 83

THE SHORT TRIP up the Mississippi River had been uneventful. *The Goliath* entered the river from the Gulf of Mexico through the Southwest Pass and worked its way up the river about seventy-five miles to Belle Chasse. It took almost a full day due to the strong current flowing downriver.

Navid sent the Warthog a message through Signal. "Will dock in Belle Chasse tonight."

Warthog replied, "Will meet you at ship. Using the name Charlie Bass."

Navid told Baraz and Javad to pack everything up and get ready to go.

People were waiting at the dock when *The Goliath* docked in Belle Chasse. The crew had been gone from home for quite a while, and their families, most of whom lived in New Orleans, were there to meet them.

Navid leaned against the rail, watching for the Warthog. Baraz and Javad were in their cabins guarding their belongings and the RDDs. He would be relieved once they were off the ship and safely away from here.

Finally, Navid saw Warthog, driving a white SUV, stop in the parking lot adjacent to the dock. A large cargo van pulled in beside him. Warthog scanned the dock, looking for Navid, waving to him from the ship.

They waited until the crowd at the dock dispersed. Then Navid went to the cabins to tell Baraz and Javad.

Baraz grabbed his belongings, and Navid took the duffel stuffed with cash to pay Captain Broussard.

Once Navid had paid him, Broussard thanked him and asked if he needed help disembarking. Baraz answered for him, saying no — not if his friends could come aboard and help unload. The Captain agreed.

The Warthog came aboard and shook hands with Navid.

"Captain, this is Mr. Bass," Baraz said as he shook hands with the Warthog for the first time. The Captain shook hands and then quickly turned and walked away, responding to a call from a deckhand.

Bass waved to his men to come aboard. They each pushed a hand truck, expecting to unload some heavy objects.

Bass said to Baraz and Navid, "This is Babak Farrokhzad and Ebi Rahimi. They are true believers. They also speak English, and Arabic, as well as Farsi."

They went to the cabin where Javad was lying on his bed, looking tired. He had repacked the RDD with the completed detonator prototype back into its crate.

Babak and Ebi started moving the crates while Navid, Baraz, Javad, and Bass carried the duffel bags.

After they made their way down the gangplank, Bass told them to wait there while he drove the box truck onto the dock. It had a power liftgate, and they used it to load the crates.

Babak and Ebi made two more trips with the hand trucks to retrieve the remaining crates from the cabin.

Bass motioned Navid, Baraz, and Javad to the SUV, which he drove, while Babak and Ebi climbed into the truck's cab. The amazing thing was that no customs or border official was stationed on the dock, only an attendant who operated the fueling station. *The Goliath* was considered a harmless vessel, a regular visitor to Belle Chasse.

Baraz asked Bass, "Where are we going now?"

He replied in Arabic, "I've rented a place for us to use."

They drove about three miles to the western outskirts of Belle Chasse into an old industrial area. They finally pulled into what looked like a used car lot with an old concrete block building that obviously was a vacant auto mechanic's shop.

They climbed out of the truck, and Bass unlocked the door to the shop. There was a waiting room, an office, a storeroom, a bathroom, and a three-bay garage. They raised one of the garage doors and unloaded the truck.

Bass said, "We'll be working and sleeping here, keeping a low profile." Navid saw sleeping bags and other personal supplies in the office.

Once everything was inside, the Warthog said, "Let me see the merchandise."

Navid told the Warthog that Javad had devised a detonator and installed it on one of the RDDs. He also apologized for removing the original detonators but explained that he needed to do it because of the tracking devices. Bass nodded, accepting his explanation.

Baraz opened the RDD crate with the detonator and asked Javad to explain how it worked. After hearing the explanation, Bass was satisfied, though obviously disappointed that he couldn't use the drone because the detonator design by Javad was based only on a timer, not remote detonation.

"Babak is my demolition expert. Please show him how to build the detonator and explain everything about its operation," said Bass.

Navid agreed and told Javad to start working with Babak.

Javad and Babak left the room to begin assembling the detonators.

Baraz told Bass, "Now that we've made the delivery, we're ready to be paid. We also need to determine where we can go from here. We think South America would be a good place to get lost for a while, perhaps Venezuela, Argentina, or even Cuba."

Bass looked at Navid and said, "Plans have changed. I'm not going to pay until these RDDs have actually been detonated. We don't know if they'll work, and we've already paid you a fortune — upfront. So you'll stay with us until we make the attack. Then we can get you into Mexico, maybe even South America — we'll see what we can do."

Navid suddenly realized how careless and foolish he had been to trust the Warthog so completely, but even more so, not to at least try to make concrete plans for escape. But the reality was that they would have to rely on the Warthog; they knew nothing about the US.

To Baraz, Navid said, in Farsi, "We don't have a choice. We can't make him pay, and we don't have resources here to help us escape. So let's play along, get paid, then get the hell out of America as fast as we can."

Baraz said, "I agree. I don't like it, but I don't see a good alternative. Besides, we agree with him on the need for an attack — that's also our goal."

Navid turned back to Bass and said in Arabic, "Okay, we understand. But we need help leaving the country when this is over."

Bass said, "You'll have it."

Around 5:00 p.m., Bass left in the SUV and returned a little later with food. He brought Indian food to share with everyone. Javad and Babak took a break from installing the detonators and joined the others. Compared to the menu on the ships, this food was ten times better. Though Navid and Baraz enjoyed it, it seemed to make Javad ill.

CHAPTER 84

NOVEMBER 17
BELLE CHASSE, LOUISIANA

JAVAD WAS NOT feeling much better in the morning, but he worked with Babak, and they installed detonators on two more RDDs. By this time, Babak was knowledgeable enough to work alone on the RDDs, and Javad rested but was getting much sicker.

When Javad's sickness had progressed to nausea, diarrhea, and fever, Bass said, "Javad needs to see a doctor. I'm going to take him. The rest of you can stay here, so Babak can keep working. Help me load Javad into the SUV."

It took Bass, Baraz, and Ebi to load Javad into the back seat of the SUV, where he slumped over. He was barely responsive.

Bass took Javad to Ochsner Medical Center – West Bank, only three miles away, in Gretna. Finally, they arrived, and he ran into the emergency room. He racked his brain, deciding what to tell them at the hospital. Bass decided the best course was just to act dumb.

"I have a man in my SUV who is very ill. I don't know

what's wrong with him. I hired him to do some work for me, but he became ill today."

The medical staff ran out and unloaded Javad onto a gurney. They took him into the back and started checking his vital signs.

Meanwhile, at the desk, the clerk was trying to register the patient.

"What's his name?"

"It's Javad, but I don't know his last name. He doesn't speak much English."

"Where does he live?"

"In Belle Chasse with his brother. That's all I know."

"And what is your name, sir?"

"Charlie Bass." He had already decided he needed to share his alias. He knew that police were routinely stationed in emergency rooms and didn't want to draw more attention to himself than necessary. He thought there was a chance he would be asked to show his ID and maybe even questioned about Javad by the police.

"I assume he has no insurance. Will you be responsible for his bill?" asked the desk clerk.

"No, but I'll try to find his family and bring them here," said Bass.

"Let's see what the doctor says," said the desk clerk. "He might not even be sick enough to stay." Bass was highly skeptical of that remark but knew hospitals were reluctant to accept patients with no means to pay. However, legally they could not turn anyone away who needed medical attention.

"I'll park my car and come back in to wait," said Bass, but he had no intention of hanging around. He could call later to inquire about Javad's condition. The check-in clerk nodded, barely paying attention, as she was already starting to register another patient.

❧

The doctors and nurses were puzzled. Javad was feverish, nauseous, and had diarrhea, but they couldn't find any cause. He couldn't speak English, so they couldn't ask him, and he was barely conscious. They were not happy to learn from the desk clerk that Bass had left, as he might have been able to give them more information.

They ran a whole battery of blood panels and other tests, but they were inconclusive. However, several suspicious and related results were low blood and platelet counts. They retested and saw that the blood and platelet counts were progressively getting worse.

Finally, one of the doctors speculated it might be radiation poisoning. However, there was no evidence of it, such as a radiation burn. They decided to start giving him Neupogen to counter bone marrow damage and increase his blood count. They also gave him a dose of Prussian Blue and potassium iodide in case he had ingested radioactive particles. Otherwise, they could do nothing except treat his symptoms: ondansetron for nausea, acetaminophen for fever, and fluids for diarrhea.

As required by protocol, the hospital reported to DHS that they were treating a patient for potential significant radiation exposure. Further, the patient was a Middle Eastern man who didn't speak English. This set off alarm bells in Washington, D.C.

CHAPTER 85

IT WAS ALMOST noon when Karen Spencer arrived in Natchez after the two-hour drive from Jackson-Evers airport. She came directly to my office in the First Mississippi Bank building.

She knocked on the door of Suite 301, and after seeing her through the peephole, I let her in.

"What are you doing here?" I asked.

"I'll tell you as soon as you gather everyone," she said.

As soon as we all were in my office, Karen began, "I'm sorry I couldn't let you know I was coming — orders from Tony. He wanted me to talk to you in person. Yesterday something happened that alarmed the security establishment.

"There was a report of a Middle Eastern man, whose name we think is Javad or Jawad, we aren't sure, was admitted to a hospital in New Orleans with radiation poisoning. We know a large amount of radioactive material has gone missing from

Iran. It's possible, then, that one or more RDDs are already in the United States, and he was working with them.

"DNI Nelson, FBI Director Lambert, and Director Russell want Grant to visit this man in the hospital and find out anything he can about the whereabouts of the RDDs, the plan to use them, and the people involved."

I thought, *Please don't let him be in a coma!*

"FBI Director Lambert has agreed to give you all temporary FBI Special Agent status. When you arrive, you'll meet the New Orleans FBI Special Agent-in-Charge, Farouque Khattak. He's at the hospital.

"The patient is at Ochsner in Gretna, Louisiana. It's only about a three-hour drive. I suggest you leave as quickly as you can. Call Tony directly, then me when you find out anything. I'll go back to D.C. and wait. We don't want any of this to leak out, okay?"

They all nodded.

"And your FBI credentials are in this case," she added, handing it to me.

Craig said, "Go home and pack some clothes, and I'll pick you all up in an hour. And Grant, bring your weapon, too."

I opened the case with the credentials, which included FBI badges. I noticed that my credential said "Special Agent Mark Grant," the same as before.

❧

Craig drove as fast as he could, and we arrived at Ochsner before 4:00 p.m. When we arrived at the hospital, Special Agent Khattak was waiting. Craig assigned Alex to watch the waiting room. The rest of us went just inside the treatment area.

Craig introduced everyone and asked, "How's the patient?"

Khattak said, "He's hanging on but getting worse. Maybe you should talk first with the doctor."

He took us to the hospital room. I saw Javad lying in bed with his eyes closed, tubes running from the bags hanging on the intravenous pole to the catheter in the back of his right hand. The monitors showed his pulse rate, respiratory rate, blood oxygen, and heart telemetry.

The doctor was there, standing next to the bed. He had a badge on his white coat that said, "R. Bedinghaus, M.D., Emergency Medicine."

"Dr. Bedinghaus, these agents are from headquarters. What can you tell them about the patient?"

"He's very ill, and his organs are shutting down. We think it's radiation poisoning, but we aren't completely sure. We can't communicate with him. And as you can see, he's barely conscious."

"Do you know how long ago he was exposed? And did he ingest any radioactive material?" I ask.

"Actually, we don't know. We think it was from prolonged exposure to radiation, probably gamma rays. We don't see any evidence that he swallowed any radioactive material. He probably has experienced symptoms for several days, maybe more. You might learn more if one of your agents can speak Arabic, though we have already tried with our local interpreter. The patient wouldn't respond."

We all looked at Agent Khattak. He said, "I speak Urdu, not Arabic."

"Agent Grant speaks Arabic. Let's leave him with the patient and allow him to see if he can learn anything," Craig said.

Agent Khattak nodded, and they all filed out of the room, leaving me alone with Javad.

I stood next to him and closely studied his face. I thought I saw his eyes moving back and forth under the closed lids. I hoped that he wasn't in a coma like Dr. Yazdani.

I called out, "Javad! Jawad!" His eyelids fluttered but didn't open.

I decided to see if I could access Javad's memory from two days ago when Dr. Bedinghaus thought he might have begun to experience symptoms.

I began to get images. Javad was talking with another man in Farsi, not Arabic. They were working with electronic components on a table in front of a stainless cylinder attached to a drone. Javad was showing the layout and connections of the electronics.

"After the timers are set, there is no way to disarm them, so you must be sure exactly when you want the device to detonate. As I explained, if any of the wires are cut, even if all are cut simultaneously, the device will explode," said Javad.

"What if the timer is reset?" asked the man.

"No, the same thing will happen. If one timer stops, the circuit will sense a voltage change and set off the detonator," said Javad. "And don't forget what I told you about the dual timers and the display."

I studied the other man working with Javad. He was also Middle Eastern and wore a uniform shirt with a logo embroidered on the pocket that said "Preston Lubricants." There was a name embroidered above the pocket — it read "Bobby."

At that moment, an alarm went off on one of the monitors. Nurses came rushing in, followed by the doctor. The nurse in charge said, "You'll have to leave now."

I went out into the hallway, where the others were waiting. I asked Agent Khattak, "Do you know anything about a company called Preston Lubricants?"

"No, I've never heard of them."

"I think Javad could potentially be in danger. Can you get some agents up here to guard him?" I asked.

I thought the people who now had the RDDs might decide

they didn't want this man to talk, though it seemed they wanted him to have medical care. I thought we shouldn't take any chances if he survived, and we could question him later.

"Yes, I'll get some agents stationed here," said Agent Khattak.

We found a table in the corner of the Ochsner cafeteria where we could talk.

"I think they're going to detonate the RDDs soon. Javad was showing another man how to set them. But I have no idea where they are or where they'll set them off.

"The other man was Middle Eastern but wore a uniform shirt with a 'Preston Lubricants' logo and the name 'Bobby' embroidered above it.

"Agent Khattak says he's never heard of Preston Lubricants, so maybe it's not located around here. I Googled it on the way to the cafeteria and found nothing. But I have an idea," I said. "There's one person I can think of who might know something about Preston Lubricants. His name is Leroy Allen McDaniel, and fortunately, he lives in New Orleans."

"Who is that?" asked Angie.

"He's the defendant at the trial on which I served as a juror. He was an employee of Orleans Petroleum Products Company in New Orleans. If anyone knows, he will. We just need to find him — and fast," I said. "And one other thing, we're going to need to tell Alex what's going on."

Craig said, "Okay, I'll tell him. He needs to know what we're getting into."

CHAPTER 86

As soon as we were back in Javad's room, we asked Agent Khattak to locate the home address of Leroy Allen McDaniel. The agent made a phone call, gave the person at the other end instructions, and asked for a quick answer.

About ten minutes later, Agent Khattak received a call with the information he wanted.

"Leroy McDaniel lives at 420A Chalmette St., Harvey, Louisiana. That's only about fifteen minutes from here," said Agent Khattak.

Within thirty minutes, Craig pulled up in front of the house. We sat in the car, looking around, trying to determine if anyone was home.

We had filled in Alex on what was happening. "Just let me know what I need to do," he said.

The house was what's known locally as a "double shotgun." It was a long rectangular structure built on concrete block piers. It had a covered front porch with two front doors, and the house was divided right down the middle. There was nothing to indicate whether anyone was inside.

Alex and Craig exited the car and went to the front door of 420A, which was on the left side. Craig knocked and called, "Mr. McDaniel, are you there?" There was no response. He knocked again.

Finally, he saw a curtain move, and someone looked out. Craig held up the FBI identification and said, "FBI, Mr. McDaniel."

The door cracked open, and McDaniel peeked out. "What do you want?"

"We need your help, Mr. McDaniel," said Craig.

After a moment, he opened the door. "Come in and tell me how I can help."

They entered and sat on a couch in the small, narrow living room.

Craig took the lead.

"Mr. McDaniel, we have a case involving national security, and we don't have much time. We know you work on the river for Orleans Petroleum Products, and your knowledge may be able to help us."

"I don't work there anymore," he said. "They decided to make all their deliveries by truck and got rid of all of us river rats."

Craig said, "In any case, you still have knowledge that may be able to help us. What do you know about Preston Lubricants?"

McDaniel said, "Preston Lubricants is located over around Houston. Well, they used to be. They merged with another outfit and now call themselves Lone Star Petroleum Distillates. They have a few boats that make deliveries to refineries and other factories along the coast and up the river."

"Mr. McDaniel, did you know any of the men who work there?"

"I knew a few of them, but not real well."

"Did you know a man named Bobby?"

McDaniel frowned. "No, that doesn't ring a bell."

"Mr. McDaniel, we are going to Houston to continue our investigation. We would appreciate it if you'd go with us. Maybe you can help us find 'Bobby' with the help of people you know. Will you go with us for, say, five hundred a day plus expenses?"

McDaniel rubbed his chin. Finally, he nodded. "Yeah, I'm not doing anything. I might as well help you boys."

"All right, get together some clothes, and let's go. We're in a hurry," Craig said.

After McDaniel quickly got his things together, Craig said, "We've got a couple more of our people outside. I'll introduce you when we get in the car." McDaniel nodded.

Craig opened the door when they returned to the car and said, "Mr. McDaniel has agreed to go with us to Houston, where he says Preston Lubricants is located. Mr.McDaniel, this is Agent Angie Reynolds and Agent Mark Grant."

"Pleased to meet you," said McDaniel. He looked closely at Grant. "Don't I know you?"

"Yes, but we haven't met. I was on the jury that acquitted you in that case over in Natchez," Grant said.

"Well, I guess I owe you one." He hesitated and added, "But I didn't know they let FBI agents serve on juries."

"I wasn't an agent then."

McDaniel gave him a quizzical look but didn't say anything. He got in the back seat with Grant and Alex.

A few minutes later, Karen called, and while he drove, Craig explained to her that they were heading to Houston with Leroy McDaniel.

"Why are you doing that? Just because some guy had a shirt

with a company logo in Houston doesn't sound compelling," she said.

"It's the only lead we've got. Do you have a better idea? We've got no idea where these guys are. And with one of their men in the hospital with a suspicious illness, they probably aren't going to stick around here. And one more thing. You can tell DNI Nelson and the head of DHS that if they put out a general alarm to law enforcement, these guys will just hide out until things cool down. They have a better chance to catch them before an attack by following our lead. They have no idea we have this clue."

"Yeah, I guess you're right. I'll let Tony know, and he can deal with the DNI and the DHS Director."

"Okay, we'll keep you up to date."

"Please do that," she said.

Craig told the others about his conversation. But before he could even finish, he got a phone call from Agent Khattak.

"Javad is dead," he said.

"Dead?"

"Yes, his liver and kidneys shut down. He went quick."

"Okay, thanks for letting us know."

Grant had lost his opportunity to learn anything more from Javad. He couldn't get information from a dead person. It was a literal dead end.

CHAPTER 87

WHEN BASS HAD told them that Javad was admitted to the hospital and wasn't doing well, Navid immediately thought Javad had been somehow exposed to radiation while working on the RDDs. He thought, *If Javad didn't open the lead container, how could that happen?*

Bass told them that they couldn't stay there any longer. They needed to move on in case the police were looking for them.

He said to Babak, "You drive the truck, take the others with you, and go straight to the old Preston warehouse. I'll drive the SUV to Galveston, pick up a boat, and meet you." Babak agreed.

They hurriedly packed, loaded the vehicles, and left for Houston.

After about an hour on the road, taking a route that bypassed New Orleans, Bass called the hospital to ask about Javad. He was convinced that Javad was suffering from radiation poisoning and hoped that Javad was so ill that he couldn't communicate.

His call was transferred to the receptionist in the Emergency Room.

"I brought in an employee today for treatment. His name is Javad. Can you tell me how he's doing?"

The receptionist paused, then said, "Hold on just a minute, and I'll get someone who can tell you."

"Hello, this is Dr. Bedinghaus, the emergency room doctor who's treating Javad. Who am I speaking to?"

"My name is Charlie Bass. I brought him in today when he was taken ill."

"He's resting. Why don't you stop by to see him? He can have visitors now."

Bass's eyes narrowed, but he kept his voice pleasant. "Can I speak to him on the phone? He knows a few words of English, and he'll be glad to hear my voice."

"I can have him call you if you give me your number. But I think it'll be better if you come here to see him. It'll cheer him up to see a familiar face."

"Okay, I'll come over right away," Bass said and hung up, his thoughts whirling. He figured Javad must be dead, otherwise they would've let him speak to the man. Plus, they'd done their best to get him to the hospital. *Probably so they could hold me for questioning or arrest me, but I won't play that game.*

A little farther down the road, he stopped at the local Walmart in New Iberia, Louisiana, and bought a pre-paid phone. He called Babak and gave him the new phone number. He smashed his old phone on the pavement in the parking lot and tossed it in a dumpster.

Then he decided to spend the night in New Iberia. If he kept driving, he would arrive too late tonight in Galveston to pick up the boat, anyway.

CHAPTER 88

THE HOUSTON SHIP Channel was arguably the country's most important stretch of water, except for the Mississippi River.

It connected the Port of Houston to Galveston Bay, which connected to the Gulf of Mexico. Both banks of the ship channel were lined with petrochemical plants producing nearly half the chemicals, plastics, lubricants, and other refined petroleum products in the United States. It was the second largest petrochemical complex in the world. The total investment in plant and equipment was in the hundreds of billions of dollars.

The Port of Houston was also a large import and export hub for grains, cotton, autos, and machinery. And it sat next to the fourth largest city in the United States — Houston, Texas.

A terrorist attack with enough radioactive material would shut all that down, potentially for decades.

It was the perfect target for the Warthog. He wanted to wreak havoc, and this would do it.

Warthog cruised along in the *Ocean Dream*, heading toward Houston at 15 knots. He had picked up the old party boat in Galveston today after negotiating the purchase by phone earlier this week. The weather was clear. There was a continuous flow of cargo ships and oil tankers in both directions. Eventually, Galveston Bay transitioned into the Houston Ship Channel at Morgan's Point.

He passed the Barbours Cut Terminal and later passed under the busy Fred Hartman Bridge. He noted that the wind speed was reported at SSE 5mph on his electronics gear. That meant when the RDDs were detonated, the radioactive cloud would drift up the ship channel toward Houston, covering all the primary petrochemical operations and ship terminals. It was a perfect setup.

Just after he passed Alexander Island, he entered Mitchell Bay. He began to pass by the huge Exxon-Mobil Baytown Refinery. Then he came upon the much smaller Lone Star Petroleum Distillates operation. And next door to Lone Star was the dock for the old Preston Lubricants warehouse, which he had recently purchased.

He decided he would set off the RDDs on the open top deck of the old party boat. Barak would set the timers to give them plenty of time to leave the area and be a safe distance away when the radioactive cloud erupted.

All was going according to plan, but even so, he was worried. Two things were bothering him.

First, there were the untested detonators. He had no backup plan if they didn't work. He hoped Babak had learned well from Javad and that Javad knew what he was doing.

Second, there was the fact that Javad died in the hospital. Surely that would bring the police into the equation. But he couldn't imagine how the police would have any clue regarding who Javad was or where he came from. They might not even know he died of radiation poisoning, though that was probably wishful thinking. He doubted they could track him down using his alias of Charlie Bass. There must be thousands of Charlie Basses in the country. That's why he'd used the name.

After he docked, he lowered the dinghy that came with the boat and climbed into it. He started the outboard motor to ensure he could do it himself without any problem if he needed it for his getaway. Then he climbed back up onto the party boat and then onto the dock, making his way to the warehouse.

All the doors were closed. He went to the personnel door, peered through the window, and, seeing lights, knocked loudly. He waited for what seemed a long time. He was about to call Babak on his mobile phone when the door opened.

Babak said, "We're uncrating the RDDs."

"Good, I want to get this done," said the Warthog.

He walked over to where the RDDs were sitting on the floor. Navid and Baraz were unloading the bag of batteries.

"I think we should top off these batteries just to make sure the detonators are strong," said Baraz.

"Okay, an hour, no more," said the Warthog. He was anxious to finish this and began snapping the batteries onto the chargers, which he plugged into the outlets along the wall.

"Here's what we're going to do. We'll detonate the RDDs from the boat's top deck right here at the dock. No one has any business in this warehouse or dock, so I don't worry about being discovered. We'll set the timers to detonate after exactly 4:00:00 hours. That should give us plenty of time to load them onto the boat and get far away and out of danger before they detonate," said the Warthog. "We're going to head to San Antonio. After we get there, we can figure out the next move. From San Antonio, there are a lot of alternatives for border crossings into Mexico."

Once the batteries were ready, Babak set the timers on

the RDDs. The Warthog noticed the countdown timers read 5:00:00 hours rather than 4:00:00 hours, as he had instructed.

"Why are the timers showing five hours to detonation?" he asked Babak.

"They are — but they're not. Javad explained there were multiple timers, but only one display, and his intention was to show the countdown display only for the timer with an hour more time than the earliest detonator setting. That was to make anyone trying to disarm the detonator think that they had an hour more time than they had," Babak said. "Actually, I think it's pretty clever. While they think they still have plenty of time to disarm it, it blows up in their face."

"Okay," Warthog said. He didn't really see the need to be so clever.

They began to take the RDDs to the upper observation deck of the boat. The RDDs were pretty stable, but they tied the legs of the RDDs to the bases of the passenger benches to secure them, just to make sure they didn't fall over. Once they moved the RDDs and secured them, the countdown timers showed about 4:15:00.

"Okay, let's get out of here," said the Warthog.

Navid, Baraz, Babak, and Ebi entered the warehouse and picked up their duffel bags to take to the truck.

The Warthog pulled a Glock 19 from his waistband, walked up behind them, and fired four shots. Bam! Bam! Bam! Bam! He shot all of them in the head, then, to make sure, fired another round into each man's skull at even closer range. Pools of blood began to form where their bodies had fallen.

CHAPTER 89

WHEN THEY ARRIVED in Baytown on State Highway 99, Alex was ready with directions to Lone Star Petroleum Distillates, 570 Bayway Drive, Baytown, Texas. He gave Craig turn-by-turn directions.

They pulled into the parking lot of a multi-story buff brick building surrounded by distillation towers, tanks, pumps, and pressure vessels. An old warehouse building was next door with a sign that read, "Preston Lubricants." The complex was right alongside the bay.

Craig said, "Angie, Grant, and I will check here at the office for the former Preston employee, 'Bobby.' Alex and Leroy, go over to the warehouse and nose around."

They all got out of the car and went their separate ways.

Alex and Leroy approached the warehouse.

"Stay outside but look inside through these windows to find out if anyone's here. I'm going around to the dock," said Alex.

Leroy looked in through the windows next to the door. He saw some movement but couldn't really see anything. He moved over to the next set of windows to see more clearly.

He saw men walking in from the door in the back facing the dock. They were talking, but he couldn't hear anything. Then he saw the man who had done most of the talking pull out a gun and shoot the others while their backs were turned. They fell on the floor, and he reshot them.

Leroy was in shock. He stood there shaking, trying to process what he just saw.

He heard Alex knock over a stack of empty barrels to get back to him.

The man with the gun heard the barrels fall, so he quickly exited with a duffel bag slung over his shoulder through the door out to the dock.

Leroy was still looking through the window when Alex ran back around the corner.

"What happened?" Alex asked, his eyes taking in the area.

"One guy shot the others," Leroy said, eyes wide. "Shot them point blank. He heard you knock over those barrels and ran out the back door."

Alex had already pulled out his weapon.

"I heard the shots before I could get around to the dock, and I ran back here as fast as I could to check on you. Let's see where he went. Follow me."

Leroy hesitated. He didn't know if the guy would shoot at him and Alex or what he might do. Leroy was brave but smart enough to know you don't bring a knife to a gunfight. And his switchblade was the only weapon he had.

But he figured he had to do something, so he followed Alex.

Alex kicked in the door, and they entered the warehouse. They quickly went out to the dock, where they saw the boat but didn't see the gunman. They had barely looked at the bodies on their way to the dock.

They ran down the dock to the stern of the party boat, Alex leading the way, where they had a better view of the bay. Then they heard an outboard motor start up and what sounded like a small watercraft pulling away. It was a small dinghy speeding across the water. And it was already merging with boat traffic, so Alex decided he couldn't start shooting now. All they could do was watch.

"Did you get a good look at him?" Alex asked Leroy.

"I'd know him if I saw him again," Leroy said.

"Maybe there's something on the boat," Alex said. Leroy shrugged. He'd already witnessed four murders and chased a murderer. He may as well check out the murder's lair too.

They climbed aboard and checked out the main deck but didn't see much.

Alex and Leroy climbed up to the observation deck. As soon as Alex got up there, he said, "The RDDs!"

Leroy said, "What?"

"Bombs!"

But then, what Alex saw as he looked closer caused him to catch his breath. Five bombs in stainless steel cases with timers — tied securely to the benches. He could see the timers showing 4:02:34 and counting down.

"Oh, crap," Alex said, as Leroy looked over his shoulder.

"You got any other surprises for me today?" asked Leroy.

"No, I think this is enough for one day," replied Alex.

Craig, Angie, and Grant ran out onto the dock at that moment. "What happened?"

"Craig, get up here," said Alex.

Craig quickly climbed up top. Leroy pointed to the bombs.

"How much time do we have?"

"The timers say about four hours. But look at the setup. We

don't have any idea how these things are wired. They might be booby-trapped. There might be multiple booby traps. None of us is an electronics or demolition expert! And it would probably take us at least an hour to get anyone down here who is. And this is radioactive material. We can't waste any time."

The timers now showed 3:58:12 and counting.

"Do you need me here on the boat? I don't know a thing about bombs," said Leroy, "and I'm the only witness who saw the shooter."

Alex said, "You can go back inside with Angie and Grant."

And so he did, to tell them what was happening.

CHAPTER 90

Leroy hurriedly entered the warehouse where Angie and I were looking around for evidence. He said, "Those bombs you're looking for are on the boat."

I told Angie, "Stay here." I wanted to keep her away from danger, which made no sense. We were already in danger.

I went out to the boat immediately.

"What's happening?" I asked.

"There's only one thing to do now. We've got to get these things out of here. We've got time. We can't just dump them in the bay and hope they don't explode. They'll contaminate the entire ship channel with radioactive material. I know how to drive a boat like this. My uncle had a fishing charter boat sort of like this. I'll take it out into the Gulf and dump them there," Alex said.

"Can't we get the Coast Guard out here and let them do it?" I asked.

"We don't have time to waste. I know how to drive the boat, and I have time to spare if I leave now," said Alex.

"But if something goes wrong?"

"And it won't go wrong by waiting around here?" asked Alex.

"But you're too valuable and not a government employee," I said with a shake of my head.

"I'm here to protect you, Grant, and it's safer for you if I take these devices away. End of story."

"I guess you're right," I said. "Then get out of here and quit wasting time!"

"See if you can get it started," said Craig.

Alex went down to the cockpit. He looked over the controls and started the engines. They fired right up. The fuel gauges showed the tanks were almost full. He quickly figured out how to operate everything, then fiddled with the radio and the navigation system.

"Okay, you guys get off the boat, untie the lines, and let me get out of here. I'll call you on my mobile phone when I reach the Gulf. I should have a signal if my battery's not dead."

"Good luck, Alex," I said, patting him on the shoulder.

"Thanks, see you later. I figure it'll take a couple hours to get to the Gulf, then I'll go further out and dump them with about an hour left on the timers. Then I'll put some distance between the RDDs and the boat before they detonate. Maybe we'll get lucky and the salt water will short out the detonators."

Craig nodded, jumped onto the dock, and I followed. We untied the lines and threw them onto the boat. Alex revved the engines and pulled away from the pier.

CHAPTER 91

ALEX CAREFULLY BUT swiftly merged the boat into the ship traffic passing Alexander Island. He figured he could significantly increase his speed once he got out of the ship channel into Galveston Bay. He could see on the map that it was about 3.5 miles to Morgan's Point, where the ship channel entered the bay. His watch said 3:20 p.m.

The RDDs were set to go off at 7:03 p.m. Alex knew from the weather information on the navigation system that sunset was at 6:31 p.m. He wanted to dump the RDDs before 6:03 p.m. That would give him about a half hour before sunset and even more time before it was completely dark.

The *Ocean Dream* cleared Morgan's Point at 3:35 p.m. and was now into Galveston Bay. Alex opened the throttle and increased his speed to 20 knots. He was now passing slower boats and ships. He moved out of the marked ship channel and over to the barge lane, marked by beacons. He passed the slower barge traffic, which only moved at about 6 knots. He kept his VHF radio on channel 16 to catch emergency calls from other ships and the Coast Guard.

He figured to reach Bolivar Roads, where Galveston Bay

meets the Gulf of Mexico, at about 4:45 p.m. — if he could keep up his speed.

He had clear sailing until he reached Bolivar Roads. Once he reached that point, there was more traffic, and he had to slow to 15 knots. He finally cleared the congestion and was in the Gulf at 4:50 p.m. Then he increased his speed to 22 knots, which was all the *Ocean Dream* would do.

He called Craig on his phone.

"I just passed out of the bay into the Gulf. I'm going to turn to the south and go as far as I can until about 5:45 p.m. Then I'll dump the RDDs overboard and head down the coast toward Rockport. Everything is going according to plan."

"We'll be waiting to hear from you. Call us when you can — and good luck!" Craig said.

"I will." Alex hung up and shut down his phone to save the battery.

He was now in open water, but it was calm, so he could run wide open. He still had plenty of fuel.

He had been thinking about precisely what he would do when he stopped to dump the RDDs. There were five RDDs. Each RDD was tied to the legs of the bench seats by two ropes. He looked around the cockpit earlier and had found a knife. He figured it would take him a minute to get up on the observation deck and then another minute to cut the ropes and drag or carry each RDD over to the railing. Then another thirty seconds to lift the RDD, throw it over the side into the water, and return to get the next one. So it should take him about ten minutes to throw them overboard and head off toward Rockport.

If he wanted an hour of clear sailing after the disposal, he should stop the boat no later than 5:53 p.m. He was satisfied with his plan.

Alex kept going as fast as the *Ocean Dream* would go — about 22 knots. The water was still calm.

Finally, he stopped the boat at 5:53 p.m. But before going up top, he had to use the bathroom urgently. He figured he had enough time for that. It took him a couple of minutes, then he grabbed the knife and went up to the observation deck.

He cut the ropes on the RDD closest to the starboard rail and tried to carry the RDD but found it easier to drag it to the railing. Once there, he heaved it into the water. The RDD/drone assembly was not only awkward to handle but also weighed more than seventy-five pounds. It wasn't easy work.

He returned and got the second, third, and fourth. There was now only one more to go. The display read 01:00:15. He thought, "Right on schedule. I'll have an hour to get away — at least twenty miles from here."

But Alex couldn't see the second timer display in the background, which actually controlled the detonators. The display only showed the fake timer that Javad had set up to fool anyone trying to disarm the RDDs. It showed an hour more time left to detonation than the real timer.

As he reached for the fifth RDD, there was a tremendous flash. Alex's last thought — in a fraction of a millisecond — was, "What the —"

The explosion was the last sound Alex ever heard.

National Reconnaissance Office satellites sensed the blast at exactly 6:03:00 p.m. The sensor data was immediately fed into National Geospatial-Intelligence Agency computers. The spectral data indicated the primary blast was C-4 military-grade explosive. The secondary explosion was from diesel fuel. The location of the blast was 28°58'23"N, 94°16'12"W, about twenty-five miles off Galveston. The Coast Guard, DHS, the DNI, the CIA Director, and the FBI Director were immediately notified.

DNI Kurt Nelson set up an emergency conference call with Tony, FBI Director Lambert, and DHS Director Pat Putnam.

"Well, I guess we should be celebrating. It could have been a lot worse. I'm assuming the blast was from the RDDs your people were tracking, right, Tony?" said DNI Nelson.

"Yes, the last update I heard was that one of our people had control of the boat and was trying to get it out to the Gulf before it exploded. At least that was successful, but we've lost a good man," said Tony.

"We don't know how much radiation was released. You'll need to decide how to explain it. The Coast Guard needs to cordon off the area for at least five miles in all directions. We don't want to create a panic, so there can't be any mention of radioactivity," said DNI Nelson.

DHS Director Putnam said, "I'll instruct the Coast Guard. And we'll get equipment out there that can measure radioactivity in the air and water."

"The President wants us to continue our investigation. He wants to know who's behind this. The Iranians apparently lost control of the radioactive material. Still, they weren't the ones who attacked us," said Tony.

"We all want to know, Tony. Let us know what we can do to help," said DNI Nelson.

"I will," said Tony.

CHAPTER 92

I WAS VERY concerned. We hadn't heard from Alex. He should have dumped the RDDs by now.

Craig's phone rang. He put the call on speaker.

"I just talked with Tony. I've got some bad news. The boat exploded in the Gulf. It sank, and we lost Alex," Karen said.

I cried out, "No!" I gasped and put my head in my hands. Angie tried to console me.

"But he had it all timed out!" said Craig.

"Well, maybe they were booby-trapped. There's no way to know," she said.

We were all stunned. Even Leroy, who barely knew Alex.

"He was a hero," said Angie, with tears in her eyes.

"Yeah, and we're going to find the person responsible," I said. Anger was beginning to replace my shock.

"I'm sorry about your friend. He was really, really brave," said Leroy.

I thought long and hard about how I could find out who the guy was that escaped in the dinghy. But I came up empty.

I said, "Alex was really a good man. He risked everything

for us, and he barely even knew us. It's not right. And we need to make it right."

"We're going to do all we can," said Craig.

"This can't be the end of the story," I said. But I really didn't know what to do next.

CHAPTER 93

IT HAD BEEN a month since General Ghorbani defected to the Russian Federation. The Russians had extracted a trove of information from the General, especially about their intelligence operations in Russia and the surrounding countries. The General had given them a list of Iran's operatives. The SVR and GRU were already busy tracking them down.

But now, Director Belyaev had decided General Ghorbani was at the end of his usefulness. That is, except as trade bait. He was tired of hearing Ghorbani's incessant questions about where his permanent residence would be in Russia and demands about the various perks he wanted.

The Iranians wanted Ghorbani back. They wanted to punish him but also to understand what happened, who was involved, and who to blame.

The Russians were willing to give him up, but they had nothing and no one they wanted to receive in return from Iran — but Israel did. And they knew that Israel was anxious to get their imprisoned Mossad agents back. So it seemed to Belyaev that a three-way swap could be worked out.

He suggested to Iran Foreign Minister Salar Mazanderani that the Russians might be willing to turn over General Ghorbani — if the Israelis would release the SVR spy Igor Arsenyev. He left it to the Iranians to bargain with Israel.

❧

The Iranians contacted Israeli Prime Minister David Baruch. He designated Mossad Director Weiss to negotiate on behalf of Israel. Weiss spoke with Iran Foreign Minister Mazanderani, who called him.

"Yes, we know that General Ghorbani defected, and you want him back," said Weiss.

"The General has a lot to answer for," said Mazanderani.

"And what is that?" asked Weiss.

"That's none of your business."

"Yes, of course. We are willing to help you if you help us," said Weiss.

"And what do you want for your help?"

"We are very reluctant to let Igor Arsenyev go back to Russia. He stole quite a few of our most sensitive secrets. And he knows some of our methods, so the price will be very high."

"We understand. What do you want?"

"We want Lior Kovitz and Yoav Tilman," said Weiss.

"Perhaps we can agree to Tilman, but Kovitz is impossible!" exclaimed Mazanderani.

"Then we will have no deal, and you will not get your General," said Weiss.

"I'll see what I can do."

"Call me when you have the answer. Goodbye," replied Weiss.

❧

Two days later, there was a conference call between Belyaev, Weiss, and Mazanderani.

"We will be ready to exchange the General in a week, say December 16. We suggest making the exchange at a neutral location, like the Zurich airport," said Director Belyaev.

"Yes, we can agree on Zurich," said Director Weiss.

"And we agree with Zurich," replied Mazanderani.

"We have one more request," said Director Belyaev. "We would like to make the exchange before 7:00 a.m. We have our reasons."

"We have no objection. It will get everyone home during the day," said Mazanderani.

"I assume the General will object to returning to Iran?" asked Weiss.

"We have ways to handle that," laughed Director Belyaev.

"All right, our staff can work out the details. If nothing else, it's a pleasure doing business with you," said Weiss. He leaned back in his leather chair and stared out the window at the sea in the distance. He felt he had done a good day's work for Israel.

CHAPTER 94

DECEMBER 16
ZURICH, SWITZERLAND

THE FLIGHT IN the Falcon 2000EX private jet from Moscow was smooth. General Ghorbani looked forward to seeing his new home in Novosibirsk, 1750 miles east of Moscow on the Ob River.

Director Belyaev had told him it was a comfortable city in which to live, except for the winter. He had even given him several travel books that showed photos of the sights, such as the multiple museums and the first-rate zoo. And there were diverse cultural activities such as the opera, the art festival, and the science fiction festival.

The General was looking forward to learning Russian so he could assimilate into society. He doubted the Iranians could find him in the hinterlands of Russia. He would be forgotten after a while, he hoped.

The General thought it was strange that he would be taken to Novosibirsk at night. General Galkin told him that it was so he could arrive first thing in the morning and have the whole day to get acclimated. He looked out the jet's window but couldn't see a thing except for the twinkle of lights here and there. He was getting used to the late sunrises now that winter was almost here. Sunrise in Moscow was now not until 8:35 a.m.

At about 6:00 a.m., the attendant brought the General a glass of orange juice and a muffin. The General thought it was very considerate as he drank the juice and ate the snack.

It took the gamma-hydroxybutyric acid/flunitrazepam mixed into the juice about thirty minutes to take full effect. The General got very drowsy, then lapsed into a deep sleep.

The plane landed in Zurich at 6:30 a.m. It taxied to the building near the southeast end of the terminal, which housed the Jet Aviation FBO operation. The aircraft from Tel Aviv and Tehran were already sitting on the apron near the Jet Aviation building.

At precisely 6:45 a.m., representatives from Russia, Israel, and Iran, all armed with weapons in plain sight below the ribbed waistband of their bomber jackets, descended the stairs. They met on the tarmac between the planes. It was only 33F, but the wind was calm. They discussed the exchange procedure. The men being exchanged would be brought to within fifteen feet of the spot where they were standing.

Iran would first release Yoav Tilman to Israel. Then Israel would release Igor Arsenyev to Russia, and Iran would release Lior Kovitz. Finally, Russia would release General Ghorbani to Iran. They went back to their planes to fetch their hostages. Tilman, Arsenyev, and Kovitz deplaned and walked to the rendezvous spot. General Ghorbani was brought down from the plane unconscious, strapped to a gurney.

The representative in charge of the group from Iran motioned one of their entourage to come over. He was apparently a medical professional who examined the General and nodded his approval.

At precisely 7:00 a.m., the exchanges began. By 7:10 a.m., the exchanges were done, and everyone was back on their plane.

The exodus was controlled by the Zurich tower. The Russian plane left first, followed by the Israelis, and Iran was the last to leave.

General Ghorbani was still sleeping like a rock.

CHAPTER 95

AS DIRECTED BY the NSC, the Coast Guard announced the Gulf of Mexico exclusion zone was reduced to three miles in diameter. They said the toxic chemicals were dissipating but were not yet to a safe level. They announced previously that a boat carrying toxic materials, with EPA approval, was transporting barrels for disposal when it exploded for unknown reasons. They declined to provide more information to the press. The press was suspicious they were not being told anything close to the truth. Still, they had not been able to unearth any information to disprove the Coast Guard announcement.

It was unclear to the US authorities how many RDDs had exploded — or if any of them had just sunk harmlessly to the bottom. They only knew for sure that one had exploded. But the radioactivity was surprisingly less than expected, so maybe the others just sank.

Meanwhile, Director Russell was busy. The CIA had working agreements with many industry trade associations to finance the use of private contractors, like Russell & Associates, to do specialized work that US government employees were forbidden to do. If the CIA thwarted a threat to a particular industry with the help of a private contractor, the trade association would pay the contractor plus a very hefty bonus or, more accurately, a reward or bounty. In return, the CIA would focus resources on identifying and squelching threats to those particular industries.

Tony contacted the head of the US Petrochemical Manufacturing Association. He presented a request for payment for stopping the threat to the multi-billion dollar petrochemical operations along the Houston Ship Channel. But because of national security concerns and the desire to avoid panic if it was known that dirty bombs were involved, Tony declined to provide any details. The President of the Association, Theodore Brasfield, didn't want to pay without any evidence that he could share with his board. He stonewalled Tony.

Tony asked President Cameron to intervene, as it would be a bad precedent for an industry association not to pay when requested. He knew the President was a long-time friend and supporter of the Association and likely had some influence over them.

A handwritten note was sent to the US Petrochemical Manufacturing Association as follows:

The White House
Washington, D.C.

Dear Ted,

Pay up. They saved your ass.

And a man lost his life.

Be grateful — and generous!

William Cameron

Within a day, the money was wired to Russell & Associates.

CHAPTER 96

DECEMBER 20
NATCHEZ, MISSISSIPPI

KAREN ASKED TO schedule a meeting in Natchez with the team to review the operation and distribute bonuses. I requested that we meet at Iyyakchush Plantation, where Angie and I were still getting settled. We initially decided to live primarily at Wexford House and use Iyyakchush on the weekends — and maybe more during the summer. But now, feeling more secure at Iyyakchush, we decided this would be our primary residence. With help from Miss Pearl and Miss Doris, Angie decorated the house for Christmas.

And after the attack at the gas station, with the revelation that Maaike van Leersum and her husband might be connected to the Chinese, Tony agreed to fund some major security improvements at Iyyakchush.

Before leaving New Orleans, Angie and I invited Leroy McDaniel to work for us as our property manager and live at Iyyakchush Plantation. He agreed to come, but only temporarily. Whether he stayed permanently depended on whether he could transition away from working on the river, which he said was in his blood.

We planned to renovate the upstairs of the carriage house for Leroy and the downstairs for the security team. Meanwhile, Leroy could stay in Natchez. And we gave him the old Ford pickup that Mister John had stored in his carriage house. It didn't take Leroy long to get it running.

We also decided that Miss Doris could help Pearl as needed at Iyyakchush until we were settled and decided on the permanent arrangements.

Karen invited Ross Taylor to attend the afternoon meeting and meet the team. He arrived in Natchez the morning of the meeting, flying from Dallas to Jackson on his private jet.

When Ross arrived, I said, "Ross, we're very sorry about your friend, Alex. He was a good person, a friend, and a brave man. And we're still working to find the people responsible."

Ross said, "Yes, he always did his duty without worrying about his safety. It's a shame we lost him. He was a good friend of mine for a long time."

We all went into the parlor and took our seats. Miss Pearl brought plates of refreshments and sat them on the coffee table.

I said, "Miss Pearl, when Leroy returns from town, please ask him to join us."

"Yes, sir, Mister Grant," she said as she left the room.

Karen took out a large envelope. "As you know, if we fend off a national security threat or a direct terrorist attack, we can receive awards from industry associations. In this case, we saved the petrochemical industry along the Houston Ship Channel, which avoided a national panic and the severe economic consequences if the attack had been successful," she said. "Therefore, we have been given some extra funds to be shared by the team, and Tony sends his congratulations.

"Grant will receive three million dollars. Without his discovery of the link to Preston Lubricants, there would have been no way to prevent contamination of the ship channel and maybe even the City of Houston.

I had mixed feelings about an award this large. It was a lot of money, but I realized my skill was unique, should be used in extreme circumstances, and amply rewarded. But my life was constantly at risk. I still felt like a bird in a gilded cage.

"Craig and Angie will receive three hundred thousand dollars each. They put their lives on the line protecting Grant.

"And we will award Sharon Honderich a total of two hundred thousand dollars. She protected the team's identities with her ingenious disguises.

"Leroy McDaniel will be awarded a sum of one hundred thousand dollars. Though he's not a team member, without his knowledge of the oil industry along the Gulf Coast, the RDDs would not have been found in time."

Ross added, "We are very proud of the team. You prevented a national disaster. Let's raise our glasses in a toast to Russell & Associates." He raised his glass, as did the rest of us. Karen had cleverly explained my role in this episode in such an ambiguous way that Ross would not understand, except as extraordinary intelligence analysis. Still, I thought the comments by Ross were very sincere considering he had no idea how we operated.

Ross walked around the room and shook hands with each of us.

"We can tell Leroy about his award when he returns from town," I said.

"And I'll call Sharon later today and tell her," said Karen.

"Would any of you like to see the view from the widow's walk?" Angie asked. I loved how excited she was about the new house. She had been busy redecorating and giving the place a touch of her personality.

Craig and Karen nodded, and Angie said, "Okay, I'll take you up. How about you, Ross?"

"No, I don't like heights — I get vertigo. I'll stay down here with Grant," he said.

Angie nodded and led the way upstairs to the belvedere.

I said to Ross as the others left, "Let's go out to the front porch. We can still enjoy the view without going to the roof."

Ross agreed, and we walked out to the long porch. Even though it was early December, the temperature was mild, in the low 60s, and we were wearing light jackets.

Ross asked, "Is there much traffic along the river?"

I replied, "Several barges and other ships pass every hour, even at night."

At that moment, the front door opened, and Leroy walked out.

"Leroy, this is Ross. He's the owner of the company," Grant said.

"Pleased to meet you, Leroy," Ross said as he extended his hand.

But Leroy stopped cold and made no move to shake hands. He looked hard at Ross.

"I know you," Leroy said.

I thought, "*What?*"

"I don't think so," said Ross.

With a frown, Leroy said, "I saw you shoot those four men in the Preston warehouse. It was you, all right. Killed them execution-style, shot them in the head, point blank.»

I couldn't believe what I was hearing. Leroy sounded like he was so sure.

"You're mistaken. It must've been somebody who looked like me," Ross said.

"Nope, it was you, all right." Leroy's face was getting red.

"Then it's your word against mine," said Ross. I could see he was getting angry.

"I bet your fingerprints will match those found on the tools and equipment you left there."

I looked back and forth at the two of them, not sure what to think, though I wasn't getting a good feeling from this. I said, "Well, that'll settle it then. Both of you just calm down."

Without warning, Ross pulled a Glock 19 from his waistband.

"I bet that gun will match the bullets, too," Leroy said. His rough-and-tumble life working on the river had taught him not to take any crap or back down from anybody.

"Shut up, or I'll shoot you right here. Put your hands up, both of you."

"Don't push it, Leroy, do what he says," I said.

We both raised our hands. We were standing in the middle of the porch, our backs to the front door. Ross Taylor had positioned himself to face us, the porch stairs behind him.

"Keep your hands up while I search you for weapons," said Ross.

"Okay, okay," I said.

"Shut up!"

He stepped toward me, waving the gun back and forth in his right hand. I tried to remember exactly what I had learned from Alex. I watched Ross's eyes closely.

When Ross moved close enough, preparing to search me — and as soon as he glanced again at Leroy — I leaned slightly to my left and quickly grabbed Ross's right wrist with my right hand, then reached over with my left hand and grabbed the top of the gun and twisted — hard! The gun clattered to the porch floor and skidded out of reach.

Ross and I lunged for the gun, but Leroy kicked it further away, almost off the porch. At the same time, Leroy reached into his pocket for his switchblade. He brought it out and snapped open the blade. Just as Leroy swung at him, Ross saw the glint of the knife blade and jumped back. Leroy missed, but Ross lost his balance and fell backward down the steep steps, landing on his head and neck. He didn't move.

Leroy stood in the middle of the top step and peered down at Ross lying there. I looked over Leroy's shoulder.

I said, "Damn, Leroy. You missed him with the knife, right?"

"Yeah, he jumped out of the way."

We scrambled quickly down the steps.

I checked him over. Ross's head was bleeding, and his neck was twisted at an unnatural angle. I couldn't feel a pulse, but I wasn't a medic.

We couldn't tell if he was breathing or not.

"We've got to call a doctor. He looks in bad shape," I said.

I pulled out my phone and called Angie.

"Get down here right away. Ross is badly hurt."

It took them only a few minutes to get to the front porch, where they saw Ross lying on the ground. In the meantime, I called 911 and asked for an ambulance.

We told the others what had happened. They were shocked to hear that Ross was the man Leroy had seen at the warehouse.

Karen finally said, "Nobody pushed or struck him, right?"

"No, he jumped out of the way and lost his balance," I said.

"Then we need to leave it at that for national security reasons. If he survives, then he can stand trial for murder. But if he's dead, it was just an unfortunate accident, right?"

We all nodded. Karen called Tony and told him what had happened. He agreed with the plan.

Meanwhile, all we could do was wait. Miss Pearl brought damp towels to put on Ross's face and more for the head wound.

I turned and said, "Leroy, you saved me."

Leroy ran his hand over his head and through his hair. "Well, I guess that makes us about even."

CHAPTER 97

AFTER ABOUT TWENTY-FIVE minutes, we heard a siren in the distance. Then, finally, an ambulance and the sheriff's car pulled into the driveway.

The paramedics examined Ross. They felt for a pulse, checked his pupils, and listened for any sign of breathing. Finally, one of them said, "This man is dead. He died either from a broken neck or a concussion."

Adams County Sheriff Charles Bowen stood watching the paramedics. As soon as they pronounced Ross dead, the sheriff took over.

"All right, I want to talk to anyone who saw what happened."

I stepped forward and said, "Leroy and I were talking with Ross on the front porch. He was standing in front of the steps telling us a story, and he took a half step backward and lost his balance. He fell straight back and landed near the bottom of the stairs on his head and neck.

Sheriff Bowen said, "There wasn't a fight?"

"No, sir," I said.

"Nobody pushed him?"

"No, sir," said Leroy.

"Well, we'll see what the coroner says. He may have more questions for you two."

The paramedics left, and the sheriff waited for the coroner.

In about an hour, the coroner arrived. He looked at the body and investigated the scene. He asked Leroy and me the same questions and seemed satisfied with our answers.

"I want to examine the body closely, then I'll make a judgment. But my preliminary conclusion is that it's just an unfortunate accident."

Sheriff Bowen said, "I think it would be a good idea if y'all stayed in town until the coroner makes his official ruling on the cause of death."

We all nodded.

Sheriff Bowen tipped his hat and left.

After he was gone, I said, "We need to find a way to get Ross's fingerprints to confirm he was the man at the warehouse. Then we'll know for sure if we got the mastermind of this attack. It's just hard to imagine why he would do it."

"I'm sure the FBI lifted prints off everything found at the warehouse," said Craig.

Karen said, "Tony will have a way to check against his fingerprints, I'm sure."

She called Tony. He said, "Ross was in the Marines, right?"

"Yes, I think so. Just a minute. Craig, was Ross in the Marines with Alex?"

Craig said, "Yes, Alex said they joined in 1999."

Tony heard him and said, "We can get his prints from the Marines. They have them on file but didn't start putting fingerprints of new soldiers into the IAFIS system (the FBI's Integrated Automated Fingerprint Identification System) until after May 2000."

⤶

Three days later, the FBI matched Ross's fingerprints with those found on the battery charging equipment in the Preston Lubricants warehouse. And the bullets that killed the four men were from Ross's gun.

Karen, Craig, Angie, and I were all together in the office when the news came in, and there were smiles. We'd found our guy. But it was so ironic that Alex had saved us, and that Ross's actions had killed Alex — and that Ross was his best friend and our boss. But obviously, Ross didn't know we were working on this case, and Alex hadn't told him.

Angie hugged me and said, "Let's take a long vacation. This case is closed."

But it wasn't closed — not yet!

CHAPTER 98

SIX MONTHS LATER
NATCHEZ, MISSISSIPPI

I WASN'T COMPLETELY satisfied with the story I had written. Something was off. I couldn't accept the FBI's explanation for Ross Taylor's motivation for the terrorist attack — money.

The FBI said that he planned the terrorist attack because of his anger at the US for their treatment of the countries and people of the Middle East. I believed that. But they also said he had made bets in the stock market that would have profited him by over one billion dollars if the attack had been successful — and that the money must have been his prime motivation. I didn't believe it.

Plus, I wanted to know why he killed Navid, Baraz, Babak, and Ebi in cold blood. That made even less sense, or did it?

I went to work to find out. I found a loose thread and started pulling.

Before I tell you about that, I want to remind you that I found during our last major case involving a rogue Chinese Politburo official, that I could establish a connection indirectly.

That is, if I had a direct connection with a person, and they were in direct contact with someone else, I could hijack that connection myself.

In this situation regarding Ross Taylor, I had two possibilities. I had met him myself at Iyyakchush, and so I was part of the larger narrative that led to Navid.

In addition, Leroy had a connection with Ross and with Navid at the Preston Warehouse when he killed all of his accomplices. So I could also attach myself to the same narrative through Leroy. The narrative never goes away when someone dies. It's always there, you just need a way to get to it. I know that's a little hard to understand, but that is the best explanation I can give.

And I found the answer to my question about the Ross's motive in the first meeting between the Warthog and Navid.

I realized I had initially looked at the meeting through Navid's eyes through my indirect connection, but needed the Warthog's perspective.

I replayed the conversation in Warthog's mind until I reached the following exchange:

"Well then, quit stalling and tell me what you have."

"I have enough Cesium-137 to contaminate an area of ten square miles and the means to transport and disperse it. Let me show you," said Navid as he fired up the iPad.

If true, I know the perfect target — the Houston Ship Channel.

Navid showed Warthog the drawings and videos. But the material was in Farsi.

I need to show this to my men who speak Farsi.

"Can I take photos for my associates to review?"

"Yes, but only a few pages."

He clicked photos of a few pages on the iPad and recorded one of the training videos.

These weapons seem perfect. I need to think through the details of a plan first to see if it's feasible, though.

"I want to buy these RDDs, but I don't know how much money I can raise. How much time can you give me before you go to another buyer?"

"I want twenty-five million dollars, and you have two weeks."

There's an opportunity here to make a lot of money from the sudden panic and economic disruption. I can use that money to fund other attacks worldwide.

"'That's a lot of money."

"There are terrorists in Chechnya who would love to explode these devices in Moscow," said Navid.

"Yes, but they can't raise the money that I can."

"Okay, you have two weeks!"

So now I had the answer to my first question — Ross did try to make money from the attack, but his purpose was to expand his terrorist activities. Now I wanted to discover why he killed four men in cold blood. So I decided to look into his memory after Javad had died in the hospital, using my connection with him to get to the narrative that I already had accessed.

What I found was…

Javad can't provide any information now, but the authorities are aware that radioactive material is in the area and will be trying to find it. They'll be looking for suspicious-looking people, especially Middle Eastern. Once the devices explode, they'll lock down the area around Houston.

But nothing was definite there except he was thinking about the possibility of capture. So I moved on to the time right before he shot them. And what I saw was…

Ross jumped off the boat onto the dock and walked toward the warehouse, where the others were packing up. He thought, *If we crowd into the truck, spotting us will be easy. I'll have a much better chance escaping by myself. And I don't want to leave any loose ends, so unfortunately, they've got to die.*

And after Warthog shot them, he heard Alex knock over the barrels outside, trying to get back to Leroy. He decided to take off in the dinghy instead of the truck.

So now I knew Ross was a terrorist at heart but put self-preservation first. Like so many people, he was complex and flawed.

We have now reached the end of the story, except to say that Angie and I will devote our time to getting settled at Iyyakchush Plantation in safety and happiness until the next US national security threat, when we will be called once again into action.

EPILOGUE

GENERAL FARZAD GHORBANI was court-martialed by the Iranian military, found guilty, and executed by hanging. He was convicted not only of negligence in allowing radioactive material to escape the control of Iran but for divulging state secrets to the Russian Federation.

Dr. Hossein Yazdani finally awakened from his coma. The conclusion of the interrogations by Mossad was that he prevented the radioactive disaster from being worse. He reduced the amount of Cesium-137 in each RDD by fifty percent. It was the lowest amount he could use without potentially raising suspicion. He was concerned that the material would wind up in the hands of terrorists and did what he could to minimize the impact. He accepted a position at CERN on the Hadron Collider in Switzerland under a new identity.

Admiral Ahmad Mousavi was relieved of his duties as Secretary of the Supreme National Security Council, reduced in rank to Captain, and force to retire. The religious leaders had decided there must be accountability for the SNSC's approval of the ill-fated plan. The rivalry of the General and Admiral, therefore, had no winner, only losers.

Farzin Sadeghi and his mother, Roya Deghani Sadeghi, assumed that Navid and Baraz were dead, though they never had definite confirmation. With the help of her cousin, Zubin Deghani, the hawaladar, they gained access to the money stashed by Navid in various cities, primarily in the Middle East and Europe. They fled Iran and resettled in Paris, living happily with Farzin's new wife and baby.

Alex King was posthumously awarded the National Intelligence Medal for Valor. Ross had sent him to protect Grant before his opportunity to buy the RDDs arose. Alex never told Ross that Grant and the team were working on stopping the RDD threat. He kept his mouth shut, just as Grant had asked.

The FBI continued investigating Ross Taylor to determine his connections with terrorists. They found he held a complex assortment of stock market short positions and various call-and-put options on the S&P 500. These investments would have netted him over a billion dollars if the attack had been successful. The ironic thing was that Ross never knew Grant was working on thwarting his RDD threat until it was all over and he had failed. But actually, his priority was to damage the US economy as an act of terrorism.

The Department of Defense, working with the Department of Energy, eventually recovered the four undetonated RDDs from the bottom of the Gulf. The exclusion zone was ultimately canceled after the radiation was sufficiently diluted by the deep waters of the Gulf of Mexico.

CIA Director, Tony Russell, told Israel that the Iran RDD situation had been resolved within the borders of the US. He promised to give Mossad Director Levi Weiss more details the next time he saw him in person.

Russia was told by one of their spies working in the United States DHS that the Iran RDDs had been found and secured by the CIA. That was all the detail he could provide. Russia's surveillance of Grant Markey yielded nothing significant. The only unusual occurrence reported was a visit to a hospital patient outside of New Orleans, a visit to a resident living near the hospital, and, on the same trip, a visit to a chemical company outside Houston. Director Belyaev decided to stop regular surveillance of Grant.

Iran never learned the whereabouts of the RDDs. They assumed that, most likely, Israel had found them and had eliminated the threat.

Maaike van Leersum served twenty-one months in federal prison for impersonating a US Customs & Border Protection agent. Grant found through his indirect methods that the Chinese MSS pressured her husband to hire the gas station kidnappers by threatening Wu Ming's parents living in China if he didn't cooperate. And Maaike's involvement was to protect them, too. The FBI continued to watch Wu Ming for suspicious activity.

Farzad Ghorbani, Navid Sadeghi, Baraz Sadeghi, Ross Taylor, Javad Azimi, Babak Farrokhzad, and Ebi Rahimi were all dead.

Justice, though always imperfect, had been served.

9 781734 852936